STAY
WHERE I
CAN SEE
YOU

KATRINA ONSTAD

STAY WHERE I CAN SEE YOU

HarperCollinsPublishersLtd

Published by HarperCollins Publishers Ltd

First Edition

HarperCollins Publishers Ltd
Bay Adelaide Centre, East Tower
22 Adelaide Street West, 41st Floor
Toronto, Ontario, Canada
M5H 4E3

www.harpercollins.ca

Library and Archives Canada Cataloguing in Publication

Title: Stay where I can see you / Katrina Onstad.
Names: Onstad, Katrina, author.
Identifiers: Canadiana (print) 20190168848X | Canadiana (ebook) 201901684898
ISBN 9781443457231 (softcover) | ISBN 9781443457248 (ebook)
Classification: LCC PS8629.N77 S73 2020 | DDC C813/.6—dc23

Printed and bound in the United States of America
LSC/H 9 8 7 6 5 4 3 2 1

FOR MIMI, WHEN WE'RE OLDER

NOTHING WOULD GIVE UP LIFE:
EVEN THE DIRT KEPT BREATHING A SMALL BREATH.

—THEODORE ROETHKE, "ROOT CELLAR"

Gwen,

I heard your news. Remember Gus from the bar? He sent me a link. I didn't believe it at first but it was definitely you in the picture. Just with a new name. Older but you. That's a lot of money. It's not quite right to say congratulations when it's only luck that you won and someone else didn't.

It looks like we both left the city. I went north for a few years and then I tried to find you. Did you ever try to find me?

Hard to imagine you as a mother and a wife. I wonder if your husband knows what you were like before.

I'm back in the city now. Come meet me. We should talk. I wouldn't want anyone to get hurt. I never wanted that.

I wanted to say also that I did love you. Sometimes over the years I wondered if you knew, and if you ever loved me back.

SUMMER

1

GWEN

In black marker, the cheque read: $9,961,176.80. Gwen cradled the left side, and Seth the right. The cheque was the size of a twin bedsheet and as light. Gwen imagined walking toward Seth and folding it in half, then quarters, until they met in the middle. But part of the deal, she'd been told, was that she couldn't let go until the photos were done. So she stood far away from him, across the landscape of the cheque, trying to catch her husband's gaze. He was grim-faced and mildly squinting beneath his glasses, staring straight ahead. She recognized the expression from terrible moments in the car, swerving in ice and snow with the kids in the back seat, preserving all of their futures with only his reflexes.

In the centre of the crowd, Eli jumped up and down and waved. Next to him, Maddie nodded, frowning.

Phones flashed. Gwen smiled too late.

"Would you like to keep it?" asked a purposeful young

woman in a blazer, and Gwen said: "The money?" The woman laughed and said: "No, the novelty cheque."

"Oh. I don't think so."

Seth excused himself to use the restroom.

"Are you a lucky person?" a reporter asked Gwen.

Gwen looked at him. She had never considered herself lucky or unlucky. She was ambivalent about magic shows, and believed psychics were hucksters. But she had helped her daughter craft a dreamcatcher one afternoon when Maddie was small. She'd strung it by the kitchen window where it twirled calmly for years, its web and feathers gathering dust and light, hinting at something fantastic and unknowable. Then Maddie became a teenager and declared that white people with dreamcatchers were committing cultural genocide. Gwen took it down.

"Of course I'm lucky," said Gwen, and the reporter snapped a picture of her with his phone.

"Very lucky," added Seth, who was at her side again, his hairline damp.

Gwen could picture him in the bathroom, looking in the mirror, splashing water on his face, holding on.

"Put your arm around her," directed the reporter.

Gwen thought about all the different winners who had been in this banquet room. The same lottery officials and photographers would show up for someone else next week, but this week, they were celebrating the Kaplans for the achievement of random good fortune. Still, Gwen knew that someone in the room—maybe many people, maybe most people—sensed that what the family deserved and what had happened were out of alignment. The lottery stories that people loved were both simpler and darker: parents of an ill child in need of experimental medical treatment; the widower with the foreclosure notice nailed to his door. A waitress who picked the numbers based on her dead daughter's birthday—that was something to get behind. That deserved a lump in the throat. Theirs wasn't even a very dramatic amount, by certain standards, curtailed as it was just below the magic $10 million. It was enough money to attract only the one reporter from a community paper in their suburb, seventy minutes northwest of the city through traffic.

A young man in a soiled dress shirt began collecting empty water bottles and half-eaten pieces of cake. Gwen searched his face for judgment. But he rattled the sticky grey plastic bin and left the room without looking back, and Gwen was relieved.

The woman had asked her the wrong question. It's not: *Do you believe in luck?* But: *Have you ever been poor?* Gwen doubted that she would have answered honestly, because over there stood Maddie and Eli. She had shared the contours of her past with Seth, but he met Gwen later, when she had a low-paying job as a receptionist at a dentist's office—regular poor, not street poor.

But if Gwen were moved to truth, she would tell the reporter: *Once I sat on a street corner not far from here, holding out an empty coffee cup, next to a sign handwritten in ballpoint pen: PREGNANT AND HUNGRY (and only the latter part of that was true).*

That was a long time ago. Gwen had arrived at the lottery offices in a minivan that she cleaned last week at a gas station, vacuuming up crumbs and scrubbing at the mysterious stain on the back seat. *Look what I've pieced together.*

Gwen imagined staring the reporter in the eye and saying it loudly: *Look at this life of accidents and tell me how to feel about luck.*

× × ×

It took several minutes before the waiter appeared. He ran through the specials, gazing at a point in the distance, and poured the water so quickly that it sloshed over the rim of Gwen's glass.

"We should've brought the big cheque," said Seth. "Then we'd get the big service."

"Can I order the lobster?" asked Eli.

"I don't think Dad wants you to get lobster," said Gwen.

"Since when?" Seth said.

Gwen looked through Seth's streaky glasses and said: "Never have I seen you want lobster, or consider lobster, or regret not getting it."

"It's always too expensive. But not tonight."

"Okay, I'm going to get it, and eat its little claws!" announced Eli. Gwen saw Seth's eyelids flutter.

"Don't get it," she said. "It makes Dad uncomfortable. Get the steak."

"Why no lobster again? I forget."

"Because of God and the scuttling creatures at the bottom of the ocean," said Maddie. "I just want a salad."

"I'll get the steak," said Eli. "Probably shouldn't eat what scuttles."

Seth ordered a bottle of wine from the bottom half of the wine list, though not the very bottom. When he and Gwen clinked their glasses, she saw again that flash of terror in his eyes, but by the second bottle, her husband was slippery with glee.

"So what are your dreams for yourself?" Seth asked, poking at his grapefruit givré. Eli and Maddie looked up from their gelato.

"Seth, that's an impossible question," said Gwen, but she liked that he had asked it. Someone who knew him less well might measure Seth's slow nods and long pauses and conclude that he was meek, but Gwen knew there was boldness in him where it mattered. At a party, Seth would glance around a room to see who was alone and make a beeline to provide comfort. Kindness moved him to action.

"This isn't really that much money—" Seth continued.

Eli guffawed. "Yeah, right!"

"And Mom and I are going to discuss what to do with it in a responsible way, but there's a little room for dreaming. Don't think too hard, just answer the question, first thing that comes into your head: What's the dream you have that you can't make real without money?"

Eli answered quickly: "I want to see the Habs play the Leafs, and I want you to fix the game so the Habs slaughter them and I get to sit in a box with a Slurpee and laugh."

"Done," said Gwen.

Maddie was quiet. Gwen noticed that she hadn't finished her ice cream.

"Mads? Any illicit fantasies?" asked Seth.

"Not really. I guess this will make university tuition a bit . . . easier."

"Come on, don't be so practical!" Seth reached across the table as if he was going to muss her hair, then thought better of it, and pulled his hand back.

Don't stop touching her, Gwen thought. *Don't be afraid of her growing up.* Maddie's body took up so much more space than it had even a year ago, but she was always trying to fold it up, hanging her head into her chest, standing with her legs crossed tightly. Her hands, large and strong, were often half hidden under the cuffs of her shirtsleeves. She remained determined, a kid who always did her homework on Friday night as if leaving it until Sunday was reckless—what if she needed more time and there wasn't any? But Maddie's doggedness, which Gwen usually admired, lately seemed depressingly adult in nature—a drive to get things done solely for the grim satisfaction of completion. Gone was the impatient, buzzing little girl, face tilted high. At least once a week, the whiplash speed of her daughter's transformation took Gwen's breath away.

"I need to think about the impractical thing," said Maddie.

"You'll get back to us," said Seth, turning his body to his wife. "My dear, rich wife?"

Gwen spoke quietly: "The city." She watched Seth's face, blank for a moment, then a slow smile. Gwen smiled back, relieved. Now they were conspirators, united against the life they had claimed was chosen. So Seth had wanted it, too, thought Gwen, and pictured the two of them side by side brushing their teeth at night and in the morning, and again at night, and never saying out loud that they secretly wished to be elsewhere. She was touched. He had loved her enough to pretend.

"We're moving?" said Maddie.

"I don't want to leave my friends," said Eli. "I made select."

"They have soccer in the city, too," said Gwen.

Seth pushed his empty plate away and dropped his fork with an emphatic clang. "Let's go for a ride."

MADDIE

Outside the restaurant, the evening stretched on under a blushing summer sky. People pushed past on naked thighs and calves. Joggers. Strollers. Gwen and Seth stood still on the sidewalk. Maddie thought they looked like brother and sister: pale and the same middle height—not short, not tall. The grooves around their mouths and eyes were amplified by the sun. Her father's mess of brown curls swung in all directions. Her mother's long hair was already streaked with grey, but she wasn't even forty; she was always the youngest mom among the moms.

There was a movie theatre across the street, and Maddie moved closer to a couple looking at the marquee, then back to their phones, reading reviews to each other: "It only gets seventy-four on Rotten Tomatoes," said the woman. "This guy posted: 'Elegant, almost obscene filmmaking.' I don't even know what that means."

They were only a few years older than Maddie, but had passed through to the other side. They had graduated university, maybe. They had jobs, and were on a date. They had made a plan, decided what to wear, and would sit in the dark theatre together, knees touching. It was all so close, Maddie thought. Coming at her. Careening.

Grade 11 had been the year she became alert to flesh. She would walk through the halls of school and feel the boys walking by as if they were passing through her, their skin and bone soldered with her skin and bone for a brief moment, and then they would pull apart, leaving traces. She had to close her eyes to bear it, breathe steady. This wasn't just one boy, either, but all of them: the loners, the flat-eyed jocks, the boys in the sweatpants trying to hide their erections. All of them brought Maddie to a throb; then that feeling blurred with disgust, serrated at the edges and brown at the centre. She was zipped inside a suit of longing. She couldn't get out of it. She had the terrible feeling that one day she would step out of her skin and scream: *See?* This *is what I am!* But then, she was sure, she would crumble, just soft pieces falling down, down, and her mother would be there, frantically trying to put her back together. *What's wrong with you?* Maddie asked herself. *What's wrong with your head?*

Her friend Emma had gone out with Liam R. for four months. Maddie had watched closely, mourning Emma's absence, scanning her phone to make sense of it. Emma wasn't sure but she decided to sleep with him anyway in the fourth month. It wasn't her first time: Emma had shrewdly arranged a one-off at camp the summer before to take the heat off. "The first time's going to be terrible anyway," she'd told Maddie. "So why not do it with someone you don't really care about?"

Emma's waiting with Liam R. wasn't just a prude thing, but a suspicion that Liam, with his fast-blinking eyes, was stupid, and possibly cruel. Emma eventually succumbed, and they had sex she described as weird and porn-y (he didn't want her to look at him; he left a handprint on her bum, etc.). A week later, he invited someone else to prom—a grade 10! Emma returned quietly to the group of kids who had been her friends for years. Maddie couldn't comfort her because she had never had sex, and so she couldn't recognize the place her friend had been wandering, only that she returned from there changed. All her friends who had had sex seemed this way after: relieved and tired, mildly victorious. Maddie ached with curiosity. She wanted to get it done.

"Dad says we're leaving the van in the lot." Eli popped up next to her. He was born with wheels instead of feet. He was everywhere. "He said he 'accidentally tied one on.' One what? What did they tie, Mads? What accident?"

Maddie expressed her irritation with her brother's bouncy chatter by ignoring him.

Seth waved his arm and a taxi stopped. Maddie was surprised how easy this looked: every third car was a taxi. She had only been in a taxi four times in her life.

"Take us to the nicest houses in the city," said Seth to the driver.

"We might buy one!" said Eli.

"You got cash?"

Seth passed the driver a credit card.

The taxi smelled like candy. A small ceramic elephant swung from the rear-view mirror.

"Tell me where to go. I'm no real estate agent," said the driver.

Maddie watched the elephant and wondered if all taxi drivers were as angry as this one.

"Let's start with Forest Hill," said Seth.

"Really?" said Gwen. "Isn't that a bit posh?"

The taxi hacked a path through traffic, rushing them down an alley, then darting back into the stream of traffic on Yonge Street. Maddie rolled down the window. Electronics shops, Shoppers Drug Marts, McDonald's—so in the city you get all the same chains as in the suburbs, but just more of them, thought Maddie. The stores repeated themselves every few blocks, with lines of bodies marching in one door, out the other. You get so many people.

A cyclist wearing a little cap and a courier bag across his chest smacked the taxi's back door with his fist. Jarred, Maddie leaned back from the open window. "Goddamn you! Share the road, fuckwit!" screamed the cyclist, his thick, hairy leg at the window, pumping.

"FUCK YOU!" screamed the cabbie, speeding up, leaving the cyclist behind. "Fucking bicycles!"

Eli was delighted, and Gwen gave him a disapproving shake of her head.

Ascending out of downtown, Maddie watched tail lights curving ahead, a car moving up the hill as if it might achieve lift-off toward the sky. They turned. The houses came into view and the neighbourhood streets were empty. Red brick and gable. Twin lions crouched on a porch like giant salt and pepper shakers.

"See that driveway? It's probably heated. In the winter, they don't have to shovel. The electricity just melts the ice away," said Seth.

"Let's go south," said Gwen.

"Look at that brass roof," said Seth. "It needs to be polished. That's the problem with brass roofs. Lot of upkeep."

This made her parents giggle, for some reason. Maddie watched her mother reach out and stroke the back of her father's neck.

Soon there were no more sidewalks. The houses were so big that an entire block held only three or four of them. Maddie leaned out the window. Trees reached taller than the houses, still in the night heat that hit her face. It was quieter than she knew the city could be. Maddie breathed deep.

"Stop the car," said Gwen.

"You pay—" the driver snapped.

"Keep the motor running."

The taxi pulled up in front of a stone house set far back, with vines spilling over the roof, curtaining the windows, making Maddie think of hidden princesses. The house was empty. Electricity buzzed around them. Maddie could feel it shooting out of overhead wires and closed-circuit cameras, and red security eyes blinking in doorways. There was no human sound besides theirs.

Maddie's parents spilled out, followed by Eli. Maddie hesitated in the back seat, watching them. In the centre of the driveway was a large lawn with a fountain. A shot of water exploded, then ceased. The three of them stood looking at the water spiking and retreating.

Maddie opened the door and went to join them.

"Penis fountain," said Eli.

"Gross," said Maddie.

Gwen approached the pool at the bottom of the fountain.

"You'll get wet!" Seth called. Maddie thought that her mother looked ghostly in the dark. Gwen turned to them, then back to the fountain, and stepped inside.

"What if someone comes . . ." said Maddie, glancing around. This was not like her mother, to split off from the family, to put her feet in a fountain that might not have been cleaned in a long time, to basically break and enter. From March to November, she made Maddie and Eli wear sunscreen every single day. She had had Maddie's phone set to "tracking" until just last summer, years after other moms turned it off. She was not a woman who stepped into strangers' fountains. She was a woman who made you wear a helmet on a sled.

But Maddie knew, too, that there was something unknown at the centre of her mother, some heavy curtain drawn there. Maybe behind it, her mother was wild—a fountain jumper, or a woman who dared to walk around on a June day without sunscreen. Maddie bit her lip.

"Eww, Mom!" said Eli.

Gwen raised her hands and they all waited for the water to explode. The heat hung heavily. Then—fast—a stream of water, and Gwen's hands were on top of it, pushing it down. She laughed as water sprayed sideways, soaking her dress, splattering the driveway. Seth laughed, then he went to Gwen, said something Maddie couldn't hear, and held his hand out. Gwen looked up at the rush of water, then took Seth's hand and stepped out of the pool, leaning on him, laughing, all the way back to the taxi.

Oh, thought Maddie, *my mom is really drunk*. She was relieved to make sense of her mother's behaviour.

Seth directed the taxi driver home, toward the freeway that would take them through the valley and out of the city. Maddie rolled up the window, regretting that she, too, hadn't climbed in the fountain. She leaned her forehead against the window as malls and towers streaked past. Eli fell asleep, leaning on Maddie's shoulder, his mouth hanging open. She let him lie on her, resting a hand on his leg. Then her mother put her hand next to Maddie's, the edges of their palms touching.

Maddie remembered the couple outside the movie theatre. She would never know which film they had chosen. She would never find out if they were in love, or just friends. She would never see them again. Why did this sit on her like a loss? So many people passed by in a day. That's just how it was. *Get a grip*, she told herself.

The taxi entered the gates of Shadow Pines, passing house after house, one barely distinguishable from the next. Maddie knew the layout of each house, and the people inside. The Donnes. The Yorks. The Sandus. Grace Cho's family, where she babysat every third Saturday for Grace's parents' "date night." The flicker of TVs through curtains. A tricycle forgotten on the sidewalk. For the first time, Maddie realized that these houses were trying to look like the ones in the city. "Neo-colonial," her dad called it. It sounded fancy but it looked disposable: every house was the same, tightly packed, one next to the other. Thin low fences easy to peek over made the backyards feel like a long shared park. The brick siding was an unnatural shiny silver, and the trees were shorter than the ones in the city. Maddie knew that all of Shadow Pines had been cornfields forty years ago. Below that there was probably an Indigenous cemetery, Maddie thought, imagining layers of concrete, corn husks, bones, all stacked atop one another like stripes on a flag.

They pulled into the driveway. The bill was $354. Maddie saw that Seth entered a generous tip into the credit card machine. She liked that, and thought, *Suck it, cabbie. My dad's the boss.*

GWEN

That night in bed, Gwen asked her husband about his own dream. It turned out that Seth's dream was to use the money to make more money—on his own terms, for once. He worked as a financial manager at an app incubator, and every time he said it, Gwen pictured a hospital ward of tiny cribs, rows of smartphones tucked under baby blankets. He told Gwen that he longed to move out from under the shadow of the CFO he worked for. He had been watching closely, and he saw opportunities, but when he pointed them out, it didn't matter; he was respected enough, but powerless. He couldn't make things happen; he helped things happen. Now he wanted to make decisions he owned, and watch them spiral out into the world, useful and lucrative. The decent, steady salary he'd brought in for years was a burden, he confessed, not an achievement. Since he moved over to tech from government a decade ago, Seth had been forced to witness many above him cashing in and cashing out, had watched them waving goodbye while he remained in amber, crunching numbers. He felt like a janitor, he said, pushing paper instead of a broom.

Gwen was surprised. She had not known he was unhappy. She had no brothers and a grim, explosive father she hadn't seen in years. Male anger was recognizable to her, but not male sadness (though maybe they were the same, she thought). Seth was so upright, so infallible. Theirs was a happy marriage, and she was almost certain that he was happy in it. Before Seth, Gwen had assumed that everyone was mostly suffering. While people could get through their days with pleasantries and work, they were, in private, broken. But then she met Seth, who slept soundly, and sometimes even laughed in that deep sleep, a burst of contented sound. So she was surprised that he wanted more, even if it was just a little more. With his shirt off, the pull of gravity on his soft chest, he told her that his boss—young, always wearing wool runners that looked like slippers—was a moron, and now he was free, he was finally almost practically free. She had bought a lottery ticket, something she had never done before. And she had made him free.

"I've got crazy heart," said Seth.

Gwen, still a little drunk, put her hand on his chest and felt her husband's rhythm racing, a change from its usual calm volley.

"Don't have a heart attack, okay?"

Seth squeezed her hand, then dropped it, moving fast down her torso, through the waistband of her underwear. This was a surprise. They had just had sex on the weekend, which meant they were at least a week away from the next time, according to the tacit marital agreement of middle age. But Gwen felt the pull, too, and kissed his neck, and they began to wind into one another. Seth was unusually frantic, his breath shallow and panting.

"Slower," said Gwen, guiding him inside her, letting the familiarity give way to something foreign, deeper. Gwen wondered if every experience she had now would be different because she had money. Seth seemed more vivid to her, but angrier and distant, too. He was loud when he came, and he offered to finish her with his hand, but she declined. It had been a decadent day already; there was too much pleasure bearing down. She should deny herself something and fall to sleep restless and uncertain. This, above all things, seemed right.

At 3:26 a.m., faintly, faintly, in a room far away, an alarm beeped.

Gwen bolted upright. Seth slept, snoring lightly, on his back. He never heard anything at night. She found her nightgown in a ball at the foot of the bed, let it fall over her body.

Gwen moved down the hall, to Eli's open door. The square mat on the floor next to his bed continued to bleat, announcing his absence. She had found it online, and waited for it to go on sale, because it was German and expensive: a mat that would set off an alarm with the pressure of the sleepwalker's feet.

The bed was in disarray. Gwen turned off the alarm and listened hard, but there was only silence. She walked quickly down the hall, looking for other open doors. Down the stairs. The stairs scared her most. She leaned over the bannister, checking for a body.

She saw Eli in his statue state, standing at the closed refrigerator, as if waiting for it to open itself. In sleep, unlike in the day, he was so patient. His eyes were open, his arms dangling next to his little boy underwear.

Gwen got close and whispered: "Let's go upstairs, Eli. Time to go." He never responded, but this phrase was the key, and it ignited him. He turned, taking small, old man steps. Gwen walked behind him as he scaled the stairs slowly, one at a time, in the deep darkness.

He lay down on the bed gingerly, as if he were sick, protecting his own body. She pulled up the quilt and gave him a light kiss on the forehead. In the morning, he wouldn't remember the details of what had happened, but he would know that something had. When he was younger, Eli, his heavy Pull-Ups dragging down the waistband of his pyjamas, would pad into Gwen and Seth's room the morning after sleepwalking, announcing, "I had the fuzzies last night." He was proud to name the shadowy experience, those nights that were distinct and differently formed but unknowable to him.

On the back of his door was a calendar and a dangling pen stuck on it with tape. Gwen squinted to find the date. She made a mark. It had been over a month since the last episode, which was good. Perhaps he really was growing out of it, as the doctor had promised. The calendar was a small sadness for Gwen. Gwen knew that Eli wasn't lacking, and every other surface in his room was covered with evidence of a cheerful boyhood. She took comfort in the baseball cards, trophies, graphic novels, the jockstrap atop a pile of schoolbooks. Still, this little calendar bothered her. She wanted her children to know only lightness, to be drifting along toward adulthood as if on a steady conveyer belt. His suffering was small, but it was something she couldn't protect him from, which made it much worse.

The worn carpet of the hall; the holes on the door from the various posters and pictures that had been pinned there over the years—all of it seemed dipped in strangeness. Something profound had changed, and for a brief moment, Gwen forgot what it was. And then she remembered: *We have money.* It was simple. *We have money.*

In the hallway, Gwen stood outside Maddie's door with its puffy cloth-covered "M." She pushed the door open slightly and stood for a long moment, until her eyes adjusted and she could locate the rising and falling of her daughter's body. She felt, as always, relieved.

Yet darkness pushed at Gwen's edges. It had done so for years, but this was different. What had happened to them was the muscle that popped the lid off the jar. They were public now. They were in a newspaper, and online. They were known. Her photo could be seen. This meant the past could come crawling out, limb by limb, slick with age and rot.

Gwen shook her head, pushing those thoughts back down. She was just a mother, and a wife, and she deserved a change of fortune, didn't she? The city was indifferent to her back then when she was young, and it would be indifferent now. And she wanted the city, too, had missed it desperately, in fact. The chaos and crush. The lit buildings, subways, sidewalks, park benches—all spaces blanketed with people. It would be lovely to be invisible in a crowd.

Gwen moved to the window, and pulled back the blind. A patch of darkness by the hedge rippled. She squinted at the shape. A person? A thing? She'd lived with those questions for years, waiting for the crisis, knowing it was inevitable. It was only in the last few years, really, when Maddie was closing in on adulthood, no longer a child that could be snatched away—it was only then that Gwen had begun to relax. Idling, unfamiliar cars lost their dark intentions. She was, at last, beginning to feel safe. Lulled, maybe.

But looking out the window at the black shadow, the fear came, pushing down on her chest, as it had for eighteen years. Ah, yes—this again! Even though the feeling portended disaster, its return was almost a relief, because it was so familiar.

But then the shadow outside was gone. It was just a hedge, a lawn in need of a trim.

Gwen dropped the blind and looked at Maddie, curled and breathing deeply. The move would be good for the kids, she thought. An opportunity. *We are so grateful.* That was the right way to feel about luck.

Gwen climbed in bed next to her daughter. Seth had told her, gently, that she should stop this ritual. But Maddie never said anything. They had been sleeping in beds together since Maddie was born, when it was just the two of them. There had been no money for a crib. Gwen would wake up in the morning to Maddie's soft face, already awake, gazing at her own, each hypnotized by the other. She wouldn't dare now to put her arm over her daughter, but instead faced the back of her head, comforted by the smell of her lemony hair in the little distance between them.

What Gwen had suggested—moving back to the city—was a risk. It could be dangerous for her, for all of them, but especially for Maddie.

And yet—oh, she wanted it. It had been so long since she'd been unsafe. Gwen rolled onto her back, looking up at a shelf of Maddie's stuffies on the wall. The matted paws of the bunny Maddie named Sleeping Beauty dangled down. *Maybe once you've been bad, you never lose that longing for it*, thought Gwen. *No matter how much you tamp it down, a part of you always wants to bleed.*

FALL

2

MADDIE

They stood in the foyer, shoulder to shoulder. Then Eli split off, bouncing. Their boxes had preceded them, and their furniture, too, which was suddenly miniature, the wrong scale for the vast living room. Maddie watched her mother moving through the rooms, sniffing deeply.

"It's toxic," Gwen announced.

"It's just paint. It's nice," Eli said.

Gwen turned to Seth. "The kids need to go outside while we air it out."

Seth nodded. He struggled with the latches on the tall windows.

This was how it was with her parents: Gwen steering, and Seth acquiescing. Maddie had never seen them fight.

"The pool is filled!" yelled Eli from the kitchen.

Maddie looked at Gwen. "There's a pool?" Gwen frowned, nodded.

"Surprise!" called Seth.

Maddie followed, into the yard. Tall shrubs and a high fence on all sides blocked the neighbours, like they were at the bottom of a hole. The pool's water belly was pocked with leaves. A long white tube snaked from its edge into a hole on the pebbled concrete. Eli ran circles around the perimeter, barefoot.

"We got it cleaned," said Gwen. "Eli, don't run. You can't go in without an adult. Kids drown in pools all the time."

"Kids drown in bathtubs, too. You told me that," said Eli, poking at the surface with his bare foot.

Maddie knew that Gwen would make her supervise Eli in the pool. A half hour later, she was lying on her stomach on a towel by the edge while Eli did cannonballs.

"Don't splash me!" Maddie wore her mother's black bikini, the only one she could find in the boxes. It was too small, she decided immediately, her breasts and thighs spread across the towel. She could feel her body all the time these days, like a separate thing she carried around, like a mean Siamese twin harassing her.

"Watch me!" cried Eli.

Maddie didn't, but peeled herself from the towel, and dove in. She was a good swimmer, but no one she knew swam anymore. When she went to the local pool with her friends, they worked on their tans and then moved in a group to the shallow end, standing and talking loudly. Then they all moved out of the pool in the same group formation. In. Out. In. Out. Until supper.

What were her friends doing right now, in the last days of August? May would be finishing coding summer school. Raj would be working at his parents' restaurant. Emma would have just returned from camp in Algonquin Park. When Maddie had gone to say goodbye, Emma's bed was covered in stacks of folded clothes. She showed Maddie her new whistle (there had been a lynx attack one year). Maddie had never been to camp. She feared bears, and lake bottoms, and it was expensive. In summer, her parents took her and her brother to a motel in upstate New York with a pool and nearby outlet mall, then on to Montreal to visit Seth's parents. But her grandparents had moved to Florida, and then they won the money, so this summer, they hadn't gone anywhere at all. Maddie felt a pang of missing out.

She turned on her back and looked up at the sky, thick with white strands—pollution or clouds? Maddie tried to remember if the city had issued a smog alert. Two airplanes went by each other, wings almost skimming. Eli swam closer.

"Jayden told me that fifty percent of people who win the lottery end up divorced," said Eli.

"Don't worry about that."

"I'm not. Just saying."

But Maddie had watched divorces in Shadow Pines. She'd seen her friends carrying two backpacks—one clothes, one schoolwork—because they switched houses every three nights. She wondered about her parents' marriage sometimes. She considered the age difference, and the way they had met: in a dentist's office where her mom was a young receptionist. It wasn't creepy to her, but it might be, if they were someone else's parents. Her parents were so in love that they had Maddie right away, without even bothering to get married until Maddie was two. Happy accident, said her mom. In two years, Maddie would be the same age as Gwen when she became a mother. This was unfathomable to Maddie, as likely as becoming an astronaut in two years, or speaking perfect Japanese. She wouldn't be all that different in twenty-four months, would she?

"Do you want to go to that boys school with the uniforms?" Maddie asked, splashing Eli.

"I don't know," said Eli, splashing back. "Why wouldn't I?"

Maddie could tell that it had never occurred to her brother that all of this was anything but excellent. He'd bought their parents' line perfectly, and saw his new private school (the potential new school—"God willing," she'd heard Gwen say into her phone) as a place of non-stop sports, field trips to Paris, video games at lunch.

"There won't be any girls there. And you won't be rich compared to everyone else," she said. "People will probably think you're the poor kid. The poor kid from the suburbs. They'll make fun of you."

"So what? Who needs girls?" Eli looked wounded, then popped under the water and swam away.

Maddie considered her meanness. She would never be so crappy with anyone but Eli. And then, other times, he triggered a love in her that she felt for no one else, the soft, familiar love she'd felt for him as a baby. He was a stuffy come to life that only she could protect and understand, and he was hers alone. But maybe she was thinking only of photos: Maddie at six, surprised face, holding the baby they said was Eli. She used to study those photos because there were so few of her as a baby. A long time ago, when they had been moving to Shadow Pines, several boxes were lost. People didn't keep everything on the computer then. There was just one picture of her mom holding a little baby they claimed was Maddie. Her mom looks like a teenager; her arms covered in black rubber bracelets, her hair chopped short. In the picture history of Maddie's life, she started at Eli's birth.

"What about you?" Eli popped back up, having forgiven her,

and fluttered in the water. "Do you want to go to that fancy school for gifties?"

Being labelled gifted meant Maddie had always been in classrooms down the hall from everyone else. "It's a private school education in the public system," she'd heard her mother say. But what was so good about being set apart? She remembered a tiny boy—he had some kind of disease, they said. He'd come to the gifted program for a month only, in Grade 6. See-through skin, eyes scooped. He was difficult to look at, and so, after the initial teacher-sanctioned niceties, no one had looked. When the boys played chess, he sat by the window silently, watching, feet not touching the ground. He murmured the occasional answer, but when they had tests, he didn't lift a pencil. He seemed like an artefact of an earlier kind of human, something found, encased in ice.

Maddie wondered what had happened in the washroom that day. She was at the end of the hall, playing Speed with Emma, fast flipping playing cards. The boy came out of the bathroom door with his hair wet, his face slack, his skinny body twisted. He stopped. There was a rip in his thin T-shirt, at the neck. Maddie stopped flipping cards and he looked at her, maybe for the first time. His expression was wild, helpless. Maddie froze under his gaze, and he zigzagged, retreating down the back stairs fast, dripping. Three boys came out after him: a boy she knew, Matt, and two seventh graders. Matt glanced at Maddie with a look of defiance, and disappeared down the stairwell. Maddie went to the hall window and watched the boy walk across the parking lot and onto the boulevard, and down the sidewalk, until he was gone. Gone forever. Never came back. He didn't even pick up his backpack.

Maddie wondered if there had been an investigation into the incident. Maybe people had been punished, but she never heard about it, if that was the case. You never really knew how bad the thing was. She had never said anything. They were little. She was only eleven. What could she have done?

"I don't want to be special," said Maddie. "I just want to be normal."

"I don't think you're special," announced Eli.

She laughed, and dunked her brother under the water, holding him lightly, one, two, three—just enough to feel him struggle, the way sisters do.

GWEN

Dear Mr. Kaplan,

I am not used to writing these kinds of letters, but I hope you can understand that I must. I write not for me, but for my daughter, who is fifteen years old ("before" photo enclosed) and was once very beautiful. Unfortunately, due to a terrible car accident last year (drunk driver) her face is horribly disfigured (after careful consideration, I have decided to spare you the "after"). My benefits have run out as I was laid off last winter, and because the plastic surgery my daughter requires in our society is not life threatening, we are faced with the difficult scenario of being unable to help her rebuild her face.

"What? No 'after' picture? Rip-off!" yelled Eli.

"Oh, this one is unbearable." Gwen winced.

"I smell a scam. Put it in the scam pile," said Eli.

"What if we'd won the eight-hundred-and-thirty-five-million-dollar jackpot? Imagine all the people who would have surfaced then."

"We got off easy," agreed Eli, and they both pondered the bigger win.

The first request had come at the old house, a call on the landline from Very Old Man Benwether. Gwen added a "very" because his nickname had been Old Man Benwether back on Gwen's family street in Procter, Ontario, two decades ago. He needed just $1,500, he said, to pay for the final stage of some dentistry work. Where his teeth had been were now only raw, exposed nerves. He had lost the house, he told Gwen, and lived alone in a bachelor apartment, with no benefits since the downsizing, and barely any government pension. Gwen took his address, and his name—not "Mr. Benwether," as he'd been for decades, but "Jonathan Benwether." She wrote him a cheque, and on her way to the Goodwill with another load of clothes and dishes, she dropped it in the mailbox.

Gwen didn't know why he was the first, or why she had thought he'd be the last, but soon after came the flood. Alumni associations. A great-uncle twice removed of Seth's. Cousins and clerks. A woman who worked at the pharmacy in the strip mall with whom Gwen had been friendly (but not a friend) over the years. Gwen was shocked by the distance of these relationships; these were not people who occupied the corridors of their lives. They were shameless.

She changed her email, but Eli scoffed, "Don't you know they'll just scrape your address? There's literally actually no email that can't be found. I have Ronaldo's address."

Paper letters followed them, forwarded from their old house. Just the existence of these letters, the effort to lift pen to paper, to procure a stamp—that effort was the strongest signal of their need, the saddest part.

At night, Gwen asked Eli to sit at the dining room table

with her and sift through the pleas. The six stacks of letters and printed emails were divided into piles: (1) personal appeals from people we know; (2) appeals from strangers; (3) charitable appeals from organizations we already support; (4) those we might support; (5) those we've never heard of; and (6) Eli's favourite pile, marked with a yellow sticky: CRAZIES.

Dear Mr. Kaplan.

(They almost never approached her, Gwen noticed, going straight for the patriarch. But it was Gwen who handled the household finances, who knew where every penny was allocated and always kept to the budget.)

Have you ever heard of the Raelians? Well, let me tell you about the Elohim—very cool extraterrestrials!—who founded this planet and have sent us many prophets over the years, including Jesus and Buddha (ever heard of those guys?? I think so!). Google it! Anyway, we Raelians believe firmly that it is through the transmission of sexual energy that we can achieve radical self-reconstruction. They (we!) have awesome seminars in France every summer, where people get together and experiment with lots of ~~stuff~~ things, including each other. I would love to go but unfortunately, my current job (if you can call it that) doesn't earn me the money to make the trip. All I need for my self-reconstruction in Nice, South of France, is $3,654.75.

"This guy wants us to pay for him to go have sex with a bunch of alien people in France," said Eli admiringly.

Gwen noted that Eli was completely comfortable with their

new financial circumstances. "When's our cash coming?" he would ask happily. "We better think about parking our money in a savings account with high interest rates!"

Then, in a thin airmail envelope, a translucent sheet of paper in a cramped scrawl: *Hello, Please please please please please I beg you please help me! I need just one million dollars and they will release me from this cellar!*

"I'm calling the police about this one," said Gwen.

"Mom, just toss it," said Maddie, who had wandered in wearing a bikini, her bare feet padding across the hardwood floor. "If someone was really held hostage in a cellar, how would they write this letter?"

"With their Raelian MIND!" yelled Eli, who was now doing wobbly cartwheels around the empty dining room.

Seth wasn't surprised. He told Gwen that there are Orthodox Jews who make a career of begging, and it's not without holiness to live this way. He'd read about a man who travels from Jerusalem to New Jersey annually, hiring a driver to take him to the homes of the local *ashirim*, all the rich men, knocking on the doors and offering jokes in exchange for cash. The Talmud says to give a 10 percent tithe. Isn't it better to just ask, Seth said, than suffer in silence or envy? Gwen listened and frowned. Seth was deft at pulling snippets of Jewish identity from the air when a life lesson was required, but Gwen wasn't entirely sure where they came from. Isaac, Seth's father, was a self-proclaimed "holiday Jew," and his mother, Enid, was a Methodist, from Wales. Seth hadn't gone to Hebrew school or even had a bar mitzvah. Early on, Gwen and Seth visited a synagogue in Montreal on day one of Rosh Hashana. Seth wore a keepah over his curls, looking handsome. The woman rabbi delivered a long sermon on interfaith peace. Afterwards, Seth spoke wistfully of the intimidating old rabbi at his grandparents' synagogue, with the beard so long that Seth was always hopeful he'd pull a rabbit out of it. That was the end of synagogue. But Gwen liked this link, however faint, to a substantial past.

None of Gwen's relatives came forward. She hadn't had contact with them in years, and anyway, her married name was a shield. She had wondered if her father would surface, but he had ranted often about those people taking handouts, and prided himself on needing next to nothing. Gwen's contact with her sister had dwindled to a Christmas card, and Nancy was rich enough already. Seth's family, on the other hand, seemed to have a "It doesn't hurt to ask!" policy, and many of his more distant relatives popped up with requests. The big ones were easy to turn down: *No, third-cousin Elphie, we can't buy you a new car.* But the small ones were more of a nuisance: $150 here, $50 there. If Seth remembered the person at the asking end of the note, Gwen would send the money. There was so much need in the world, and so close by, and Gwen had tried not to feel its pull for many years. The B'nai Brith called. Planned Parenthood. Alzheimer's Society. The Centre for Missing and Exploited Children. The Kaplans had left some footprint of their inclinations by their donation patterns over the years. Their soft, guilty places (which Seth accessed so well at tax time) were ripe for kneading and exploitation.

Gwen was overwhelmed. She flipped through the letters, unable to open another. *What can we possibly do for so many?*

Seth walked through the room, on his phone. Gwen could tell by his low pitch that he was talking to Tom, the young software developer he was courting. Gwen had met him last year at a Christmas party in Seth's office. She hated Seth's office, with its atmosphere of forced fun, stacks of Nerf guns and giant faux farm-tables where everyone sat shoulder to shoulder. Most demeaning was a wall where employees were encouraged to write slogans in chalk: "LET WHAT YOU LOVE BE WHAT YOU DO!" "DON'T SAY I WISH—SAY I WILL!" When visiting, Gwen was tempted to rub her body against the wall and erase every word.

At the Christmas party, Tom first looked at her with earnest intent, like a Mormon at the door, but when she explained that she was just a wife and mother, his concentration disintegrated and his eyes drifted to a point over her shoulder. Tom had a software idea that Seth wanted to turn into a business, a pitch that Seth's company had passed on, quashing Seth's recommendation for investment, yet again. Even though he was no longer just a corporate accountant but a financial manager, he joked that he did the books for people who didn't read books, and anyway, they weren't even books, they were spreadsheets. He'd been passed over for the CFO job twice.

But as he hovered in the doorway, murmuring, "Mmm-hmmm . . ." and "Exactly!" into this phone, Seth sounded happy and boyish. It was a voice Gwen associated with stories of Seth's childhood, when he'd been a very good magician, hosting magic shows in his apartment building and tracking down older magicians from the phone book, showing up on their doorsteps to take in their wisdom. Gwen loved this detail of Seth's life before her. Little Seth in a cape sewn by his mother. The image spoke to her husband's inborn hopefulness; he was a bringer of joy, a kid who saved his money for a dove named Frederico when other kids were buying cigarettes.

In imitation of Seth, Gwen announced cheerfully that she would send money to three of the letter writers. She wanted to show Eli generosity. She wanted to model for her kids the person she wasn't sure she was. That's why she'd agreed to a house with a swimming pool. It was such a little, modest pool, Seth argued, and summers were so hot now. Gwen thought it was decadent and dangerous, its black mouth waiting in the yard to gobble her sleepwalking son. But Gwen wanted to be a person who wasn't afraid, a person who had a pool. So she had agreed, and Seth had squeezed her shoulder. She would swim in it tomorrow to show herself it was okay.

"Mom," said Eli, tossing a letter aside, exhaling with sudden boredom. "Can I play video games?"

MADDIE

The school spread over an entire city block, a squat Edwardian red-brick box, cut vertically by windows skinny and blank. Maddie stood at the crosswalk across the street and stared at the steady push of teenagers making their way up the small staircase to the arched entrance. It was ugly, she decided. An old-fashioned lunatic asylum. Maddie knew about Frances Farmer and how women got locked up and lobotomized; she'd had a Kurt Cobain phase a few years ago.

Kids called it the U—the University School—because it backed onto the campus of the city's biggest university; a prestigious holding pen before the next one. At the interview, Gwen and Seth had pointed out the display cabinets holding trophies, and the alumni wall with the impressive accomplishments of a hundred years of students—CEOs, a prime minister, "industry leaders." Victorious sports pennants dangled from the ceiling of the gym. Still, the whole building smelled of bananas, just like every school.

The school was a compromise: it was private, and affiliated

with the university, but with many kids on scholarship. No uniforms. Co-ed. Yet it fulfilled her parents' criteria, though Maddie had not known until they moved that any criteria existed. Apparently, her education up until this point had been just barely acceptable. The school was, Maddie overheard Gwen say on the phone, "exclusive" and "rigorous" with a "social justice component." *A private school in the private system!* thought Maddie.

Maddie had heard of the U in Shadow Pines. She'd even come up against its students once at a debating tournament, and been crushed (topic: *Does every citizen have a right to die at a time of choice? Commence!*). To get in at this late stage, in the final year of high school when her marks mattered most, was very difficult, the dean had told her at the interview, shaking Maddie's hand with her onion-skinned one. The U's attrition rate was extremely low; most of the kids had been enrolled since sixth grade. You come, you never leave. Maddie was lucky, so lucky, she was told, the onion-hand now in her mother's clutch. This made Maddie think: *So who am I replacing? What happened to that student who left?*

They were stupid, really, to let her in. They didn't know her, and had only granted admission to the paper version of her, which had been curated over many years to impress. Maddie was a very good student, but she did not see herself as brilliant, the way so many kids were, the way her friend Raj was. Raj would sit quietly in the back row and listen to the history teacher ramble on and on (while glancing nervously at Raj, waiting for it) and then raise his hand, open his mouth and in one perfect paragraph—no "uh," no "like"—explain that she had missed the single most crucial point, and that point was usually the cornerstone of some theory that no one had ever thought of before until Raj.

Maddie made sure she put up her hand just enough to get points for being called on, but really, she was wary of confrontation. She had joined the debate team because she should, and it seemed appealingly like fake conversation; every angle could be prepared for in advance (she was, subsequently, only a reserve in tournaments). Maddie liked facts, numbers, dates. She liked poetry, not novels. Poetry was bound by a little box, but novels were impossibly wide, like weather. Maddie could, after reading whatever else had already been written about a poem, construct a tidy analysis. But she couldn't see through to the other side of the facts, or even the poem, which she examined for rhyme and structure, not feeling. Fighting with information made her stomach flutter. "Think critically!" the teachers would always say, but they didn't mean it, really. They meant: Work harder. Do well. Get into a good university. Get going on the business of being old.

Because of this tingling certainty of her own fraudulence, Maddie had decided that her place was somewhere near the back of the pack, even if she got top-of-the-pack grades. Once a teacher had said, "Everyone believes they're the main character," but Maddie had never felt that. Maddie felt she was outside the story, moving sideways next to her genius friends, crablike.

Maddie adjusted her backpack, and pressed the button for the light at the crosswalk.

She knew that if she turned quickly, she would see Gwen skulking somewhere behind her.

"How do you feel, honey?" Gwen had asked her as they came out of the subway together.

"Excited," Maddie murmured.

"Not scared?"

"I should go."

Gwen had leaned in for a hug, which Maddie accepted. Her

mom was meant to walk east, to the subway that would take her back to the new house. But Maddie knew that if she looked back, Gwen would still be standing and watching. As long as she could remember, Gwen was in the hallways of her school, or if she was not present, Maddie would catch a glimpse of her through the classroom window, in the distance, walking across the field or sitting on a bench at the edge of the parking lot. It was weird, probably, and she never told her friends because sometimes it felt sweet to be craved like that. But last year it had bugged her so much that they'd had a family meeting, and Gwen had promised to back off.

Maddie didn't know how she felt about the stalking today because she didn't want to think about Gwen. She had no room for Gwen. Not today.

Maddie had been telling the truth: she wasn't scared. There was curiosity, which she reported as excitement to appease her parents. She was ready to be done with all of it, these last months of her childhood. That ending was the only thing that felt real to her, looming and tangible. She crossed the street without looking back.

× × ×

In the hallway, before the last period of the day, Maddie stood with her schedule in her hand, like a tourist checking a map. She had made it through her first four subjects, and lunch (a quiet corner of the cafeteria; a few pleasant enquiries from student council types—no trauma), and now she had to locate Advanced History: The West and the World. The room, once discovered, was underlit. Except for a few posters—Nelson Mandela and a world map—the walls were mostly empty. Students were already seated around a large oblong table. As Maddie walked in, they raised their heads, scanning her.

"Please, latecomer, join us at the Harkness table, won't you?" said the teacher, crooking his finger. He was young. His beard was the only feature that set him apart from the students at the table, and his blazer covered the words on his T-shirt so that only a red "E" could be seen.

Maddie took the one empty seat.

"What, you may ask, oh new student, is a Harkness table. Anyone?"

There were a few indulgent giggles.

A boy said, "Big tables that cost the school thousands of dollars, so we can now put on the website: 'Look, our school has Harkness tables.'"

"Exactly," said the teacher. "They're also meant to facilitate debate and discussion, which are my two favourite D-words. You must be Madeline Kaplan."

Maddie nodded.

"I know these clowns from yesteryear, but to you, a warm welcome, Ms. Madeline. I am Brian Goldberg, but convention dictates use of the honorific, which in my case is doctor, as in PhD, not MD. I can't help you with your physical deficiencies, only your intellectual ones." Maddie had met this kind of adult before. His neediness made her nervous.

"Hi," she said.

"And let's also extend a 'hi' to the curriculum." He leaned back, hands behind his head. "What, oh children, is economic interdependence?"

They took off immediately, each angling to be heard. Maddie listened, assessing. They spoke like news pundits. It was all familiar, really, even the binders and logos on the sweatshirts.

The brands were better, more expensive: more Apple computers than Dells, more iPhones than Samsungs.

"Are all economic decisions rational?" asked Dr. Goldberg.

A boy answered slowly, in a quiet voice that Maddie couldn't make out. The room dropped to the boy's quiet, too, so there was just him murmuring and the rustle of traffic and trees through the open window, the soft clicking of laptops. Maddie turned her head to try to see him, but he was two bodies down, and difficult to find. She saw only long hands, and thought: *He talks like music sounds.*

Across the Harkness table, a girl sat extremely still, her head bowed, hair draping her face, as if staring at her computer. It was a posture of great concentration, but Maddie recognized the delicate inflation and deflation of her chest: she was sleeping. Suddenly, she reared, hair falling back to reveal a long, pointed chin, narrow eyes snapped open.

"Don't kick me," Maddie heard her hiss to the girl on her left, who was suppressing giggles. The boy cleared his throat, continued, but the spell was broken.

"Very good, Joshua. You spent your summer reading," said Dr. Goldberg. "Clara, try to keep awake. It's only day one."

Maddie wanted to catch the boy's eye, thinking she might offer a reassuring glance, but she still couldn't see him clearly from her seat. When he leaned forward, she saw a shock of black hair, then he pulled back again and was gone.

After class, Maddie found the two girls waiting in the hall.

"How's it going, newbie?" asked the sleepy girl. "I'm Clara. This is Sophie." Sophie was smaller, with a soft, expansive face to contrast her friend's knife-like expression.

"We're your unofficial ambassadors."

"Yes, unofficial. Officially, we represent nothing."

"Zero."

"But unofficially, we wanted to welcome you."

Maddie read the conversation, parsing the ratio of mockery to sincerity. She knew about Darwin, and adaptation, and that she'd need to learn the correct codes to survive.

"Which way are you going?" Sophie asked.

Maddie zipped her backpack, closed her locker. "Home, I guess. Subway."

"What are you signing up for?"

"I do debate, UN, chess club and Free the Children," said Sophie. "She does less because she's all dance all the time."

Clara did a quick pirouette. "Royal Academy. Also, I don't want to free the children. I want them caged, for profit. What's your thing?"

"Good afternoon, girls," said a teacher walking by.

"Good afternoon, Ms. Frick," they chimed, in perfect synchrony, voices softer and younger. Then they turned back to Maddie, heads tilted expectantly.

"I did UN at my old school," said Maddie. "We didn't have a chess club. I like photography." She didn't, particularly.

"Oh, you should sign up for the photography club. Last year James Chen got into Columbia based on his portfolio," said Clara.

"I still don't get that," said Sophie, rolling her eyes.

"Remember those pictures of the old people in the nursing home? They were really beautiful," said Clara.

"Oh, true."

"God, I was kidding. They were so cliché!"

Sophie laughed tightly.

The three walked through the hall, Sophie and Clara pouring information about where to eat at lunch, which teachers were the best, which bathrooms to be avoided. There wasn't talk of boys. They were beyond boys, Maddie guessed. For these two, it would be men.

"Get us on Snapchat," said Clara.

They left her at the front door of the school, scattering to their various activities. They were almost running, like they were being chased. Maddie was relieved. Now she knew what was required of her. It would be her usual balancing act, then: She would be likeable, and a little to the side. A hard worker. A good student. A decent friend. That should be enough to get through until June.

Outside, in the warm September air, Maddie walked down the steps, and then exhaled, looking back at the building.

A small woman rushed by, pulling a girl by the hand. She was calling rapidly in a language Maddie didn't recognize. A boy rose from the steps. Maddie recognized him as the melodic boy from History class. He came toward the woman, speaking the same language. His pants were unusual, neither sweats nor jeans, and with a crease in the front. He didn't look at Maddie, or at the other kids clouding the sidewalk. The woman kept talking in a steady current, loud and high pitched, fluttering as if something terrible and unjust had passed. The boy stood, and the girl leaned into him; she looked to be about Eli's age. Maddie guessed that the woman was his mother, but because he was taller, and so anchored while she flapped around him, he seemed older than her. He nodded sympathetically, looking her in the eye steadily until she had drained herself of words. Then, when her shoulders sagged and she was smaller still, silent at last, he laid a hand on her back.

Maddie could see his face fully now, and it was beautiful. No one had lips as red. She felt a catch in her breath.

She watched him guide his mother up the street, into the crowd. The girl, presumably his sister, took his other hand. His mother leaned into him, and Maddie saw that his pants were too short, so there was a small gap between the cuff and the shoe, like the gap at the joints of a marionette.

Joshua. She remembered his name, and knew immediately that he would matter to her. Maddie kept close that certainty as she walked to the subway.

Crossing the street, she felt eyes on her, the way she did when her mother was at school. She turned back slowly, but Joshua was gone. There was a man standing by the trees that flanked the school's entrance. He might have been looking at her, or just at the sky. Still, a current rippled through her. He was too still, too directly in her line of vision, as if wanting to be seen. She sped up slightly, to the entrance of the subway, glancing behind her one last time before descending the stairs underground. The man was gone.

GWEN

After Maddie had entered the building that morning, Gwen settled on a public bench on the sidewalk next to the U and waited. She had Maddie's schedule on her phone: Calculus. Ten minutes before Gym. Gwen let the waning sun—the last hot sun of the autumn, surely—settle on her skin.

The bell rang. The doors flew open, and from her vantage point on the sidewalk, Gwen could see the kids in their gym clothes filing through the doors onto the field. A whistle blew and they began to run around the track. Clusters of girls with ponytails ran together, loud voices overlapping. The boys wore baggy shorts that moved like skirts in the breeze. Gwen craned for Maddie—oh, there she was! Another ponytail, running alone. Her legs looked strong in her shorts. Maddie had always been effortlessly athletic even though she had stopped playing sports.

Gwen hung her head in hiding. She was embarrassed by this habit, which had proven unbreakable. She felt no need to do it with Eli. He was safe.

What would she do with her day now, in the city? Gwen wondered. What would she do without the women of Shadow Pines? They had been on the Parent Council with her. Their children had slept on her sheets, wiped their hands on her towels, eaten her dinners. She and the women had come together in the aisles of supermarkets and the hallways of schools, scattering in the twilight with the arrival of the commuter trains.

A month ago, Gwen had staged a ritual to formally end it. She put out a tray of fruit and a coffee cake, which she'd baked along with the offering of a dozen cranberry loaves. She wrapped each cranberry loaf in cellophane and pink twine, and stacked them in a pyramid on the console by the door, ready for when the women streamed in.

They seemed to all arrive together, with kisses and hugs at the door, purses deposited next to the loaves. Because the house was littered with the chaos of moving, they gathered in Gwen's kitchen, which was the same as their kitchens, and stood eating off the china that Seth's parents had given them at their wedding.

One by one, they leaned in.

"I'll miss our coffees," said Liza, laying a hand on Gwen's bicep.

"Who will run the art table at the Fall Fair?" moaned Jimin. "No one mans the sponge painting station like you, Gwen."

True. Gwen remembered that at Liza's craft table, the scissors were too dull to cut the egg cartons, and the kindergarteners wept over their failed spiders.

"One good thing about you leaving is that I won't feel so bad about my own crappy birthday present wrapping," said Rachel.

Josie laughed. Zoe raised her eyebrows: Rachel's voice always slithered. When Gwen had a party to celebrate week-old Eli's arrival from the hospital, Rachel—mother of three girls—said: "Boys are never born cute, isn't that what they say? Give him time."

Gwen was going to miss Zoe most of all. They had been friends since Eli was a baby rolling on a blanket next to Evelyn, Zoe's daughter. Zoe, her husband, John, and Evelyn lived several blocks over in a house that was nearly identical to Gwen and Seth's. But their block was one of the last to be built in Shadow Pines, and gave the impression of an afterthought, as if the developer had run out of time and materials. If seen from above, one block would appear photoshopped to perfection; the other a warped mirror image, details slightly askew. The latches on the windows of Zoe's house were plastic instead of metal. The cement in Zoe's driveway lacked Gwen's groomed edges. Gwen's street was lit at night by retro copper gas lamps. Bulbous green onion-like lamps scarred Zoe's boulevard—wobbly, easily cracked.

Zoe joked about it: "Look at our trees. They're skinnier and less leafy. Even the kids on our block are lousy students." This was a joke, but it was true that Evelyn struggled with reading and had an explosive temper.

When Gwen sent Zoe photos of the new house (tentatively: *Was this bragging?*), Zoe emailed back: "So now do I get the same house on a shittier block? :)"

This bluntness was the attribute that separated Zoe from the other mothers—Shadow Pines mothers tended toward tidy and contained, irony-free—and drew Gwen to her. Zoe distinguished herself also by running a bookkeeping company out of her garage (where the remote control door opener never worked) and loudly proclaiming her need for copious doses of antidepressants. Gwen loved to visit Zoe among the papers and spin in her office chair, offering comfort as Zoe paced, complaining about her clients and her fears for her difficult daughter.

One muddy spring, Zoe discovered that John was having an affair with a woman he'd met online. It turned out that the chest-thumping certainty that had drawn her to him and was now an irritant still had currency away from Shadow Pines. In that garage, over many weeks, Gwen watched as her friend survived this earthquake in her home, raging and weeping and settling, finally, on the dark truth of male entitlement. Zoe came out exhausted but accepting; this was the price of a husband who required a steady stream of victory. She couldn't change it, she had said, no longer crying, and Gwen nodded, while clinging to a secret smugness, knowing she'd chosen a different kind of man, rare and loyal.

For eleven years, this had been the shape of her life. Gwen was a good listener among the women. She said little of her own past. At first, this was because of the deliberate tight buttoning required to hold it in. But over time, in the course of many long afternoons listening and nodding, she came to wonder why no one seemed to want to know her. Lately, she had resented them for not asking, even though this wasn't fair. So she let go of the rope she was tugging, the one that held at its distant end the possibility that these women were awful. It was easier not to hate them, and what choice did she have? She would stay in Shadow Pines. There was nothing waiting for her anywhere.

Instead, she provided comfort when heartbreak happened behind doors in Shadow Pines. And there *was* suffering: parents with dementia, and kids with learning disabilities. The recession took jobs. Todd Branson, Else Branson's husband, used to amuse the kids by swinging his briefcase in full circles like his arm was a propeller. He got laid off, and the Bransons sold their house and moved away.

But those heightened moments were spikes in the long flat line of Gwen's life; most days were quiet. Gwen volunteered at the kids' schools because she read that kids whose parents were involved got better grades and had "better outcomes." And it turned out that somehow her own mother had rubbed off on her: Gwen was good with crafts and baking. She kept an eye on grocery store sales, and the fridge was stocked with healthy snacks. But since the kids had become older, and she often didn't need to be anywhere at 3:30 p.m., Gwen had been growing restless. There was weightlessness to her time, thin as the air in an airplane cabin. The days were so long now. She had started watching *Coronation Street* at noon, something she had never done before. When she cleaved away her fear, she saw, clear and shining as a desert watering-hole, her desire for the city. She never said it out loud, not to herself, not to Seth. And certainly not to the women.

The mugs were emptied, and eyes turned to the kitchen clock above the door. A few of the moms had younger children, and needed to be home to make lunch. The fluttering of excuses drifted around the room: there were errands, always errands, and playdates approaching, and homes to tend.

At the doorway, the hugs came with promises to keep in touch, which they would, though it might not be the same, everyone agreed (could never be the same, thought Gwen). Zoe was the last to leave, plucking her cranberry loaf from the table in the foyer. She turned to her friend: "John keeps talking about moving back to the city," she said. "Wouldn't that be nice? We'd be neighbours again." Gwen nodded.

Zoe clutched the loaf and sniffed: "Who's going to take care of us?"

Gwen reached for her friend. She hugged her and felt tears welling up.

When they had gone, Gwen set the dishwasher and swept the floor. She looked out the window. Two o'clock. She didn't have to pick up Eli at the pool for three hours, and Maddie was babysitting Grace Cho.

She looked down at a lone cranberry loaf in its plastic sheath; someone had forgotten to take hers, perhaps pointedly. Gwen considered the loaf. She took an armful of items from the craft cupboard, dumped them on the table. Then she stuck googly eyes on the top of the plastic-wrapped cake. She glue-gunned yarn along its sides. She sprinkled sticky pink glitter all over the body. She looked at it, picked up a kitchen knife and stuck it in its back. Then she shook her head, looking at the sparkling, murdered thing: What was *that*?

The stereo was still hooked up, waiting to be packed. Seth had wondered if they even needed to take it, now that every-thing was digital. He had always been indifferent to music. But Gwen had loved music once, been rescued by it, had been the girl in the bar listening too closely to bother dancing. The CDs at the bottom of the buffet that held their china were coming with them, even if CDs were obsolete.

In the bathroom, Gwen rifled through the medicine cabinet. Between medicines and Band-Aids, she found Maddie's black eyeliner. She smudged it around her eyes until they were black sockets, a death mask.

She drew the blinds. Gwen had chosen a CD of girls whom she'd seen live twenty years ago, girls with guitars and SLUT written across their bellies. She hit Play. The clamour filled the house; drums forward, bass drowning out the lyrics. Young, young girls, Gwen thought, and their wailing filled every corner of the house, past the framed pictures of the family at the beach, and gathered around the Christmas tree and the menorah, past bags of linens and boxes of cutlery.

Gwen felt herself peering over an edge, down into darkness, leaning and curious. For so long, she had felt unfinished; she was a box with the flaps open. The smallness of her life surprised her. It's not that she had expected greatness. When she was the age at which children form their expectations for themselves (Maddie's age; Eli's age), she had expected exactly nothing. And in adulthood, she had worked only toward stability, striving each and every day to simply hold it together, to provide, to be substantial enough that her children could dream and wonder and be happy on the stage of her bowed, strong back.

But now—now there was this money.

The money meant that she and Seth wouldn't have to work as hard to ensure the kids' safe passage into adulthood. The kids were getting so old, anyway. Maddie was done, really, and Gwen had given her a good childhood, she was certain. There had been no major bumps—no rehab, no academic implosions, like the children of other mothers. Maddie had always been a good kid, with good grades and polite friends. Even her crop tops weren't all that cropped, her choices mature. If she often seemed contained and furtive about her inner life, that was just adolescence running down the clock. Maddie had not been in trouble, and this gave Gwen a surge of pride, and made it bearable that she would be leaving soon.

Gwen wondered if she had summoned the money from some other world, a place of ghosts and gods or exploding black holes. It arrived just as Gwen was waking at night with the strangest thoughts: *We could move into the city.* And then, defiantly: *If Seth won't go, I could go alone.* She had, just this spring, before the money, found herself on the computer one night, perusing apartment rental listings. Apartments high in the sky, with one bedroom, and views of twinkling glass columns. Her family was nowhere in this scenario. She had climbed back into bed shaking.

In raising the kids and running the home, there had been no time for unhappiness, and she'd rarely felt it, really, or not in the way of women who were overlooked by their husbands, or tethered to unhappy children. For Gwen, the stirring was a need for completion; the possibility to revisit a life that was just beginning when it had been interrupted by motherhood. Her hometown was landlocked. The river had dried up when she was a baby and most of the stores on the main street were empty. Procter, Ontario, was for leaving, and Gwen's truncated youth, just a couple of years long, belonged entirely to the city.

And now the opportunity was upon her again. It was upon all of them, and that was even better. They could go together, back to Toronto, and plug themselves into the great socket and come to life. She didn't have to choose between her family's safety and the city.

She told herself that the money made the threat recede. They would have a good security system installed in the house. So much time had passed anyway. For years, when she'd driven in for a museum trip or an appointment, she'd kept her eyes wide, and her kids tightly in hand. But surely the danger wasn't real anymore. They could live in a nice neighbourhood, far from where she'd lived before, surrounded by people she'd yet to meet, people who were softened and cocooned by money. Together, in this imagined Toronto, the darker elements of the city would be kept at bay.

The music wrapped itself around the detritus of the house they were leaving, and settled on Gwen, lying on her back, looking up at the ceiling, smudged eyes closed.

So they moved.

The bell rang in Maddie's school.

Gwen strained to spot her daughter through the crowd of kids moving past the windows of the school. This was Gwen's last September with Maddie in the role of a child, and she wanted to see her for just a few more minutes, to take her in, to revel in her.

Gwen checked her watch. Eleven thirty. Surely, time to go— back to the house, the unpacking, the purchasing. A man and a woman walked by quickly, blocking Gwen's view. The man was talking angrily, his hand gripping the woman's upper arm, tightly. The woman looked straight ahead, unresponsive, as if she were pretending she was walking alone, somewhere else. Gwen's body seized sharply.

The couple disappeared, and the hallways of the school emptied out. Gwen's breathing settled, but the familiar distress remained. It was time to go but she couldn't bring herself to move from the bench. It wasn't only that she wanted the rush and comfort of seeing Maddie. There was something else keeping her in place: Gwen felt that she was standing sentry over her daughter. She was her protector. There was duty in it. She would stay for just another hour.

3

GWEN: BEFORE

At seventeen, Gwen left home. She didn't exactly "run away," breathless and chased. She took a bus to the city and no one stopped her.

Gwen's mother had a thin, tapering voice and unfocused eyes. She had been a Home Economics major at community college when she met Gwen's father, who worked at the cement plant. She didn't finish school, but she was industrious. She could sew, and bake, and made curtains for the living room out of fabric scraps she found in a department store basement. It was a tremendous performance of domesticity for a very small audience—Gwen, her sister, Nancy, and Gwen's father—but the truth was that she was severed from her kids, as from the world. She left the house only for errands. On the first of each month, she sat at the kitchen table with a stack of twenty-dollar bills handed over by Gwen's father. Gwen watched as she put them in smaller stacks, each bundled with an elastic and marked by a strip of white paper with her perfect, musical handwriting: *mortgage, groceries, bills, gas.*

After school, as she fed Gwen and her sister toast and orange slices, she would lean on the counter and stare at them, her eyes dialling in and out. She looked at her children like she couldn't believe they were hers. Then when the plates were empty, she'd wash them in the sink, and retire to bed at 4:30 p.m. The alarm rang just before 6:00, when Gwen's mother rose again and returned to the kitchen to cook dinner, so she would be in process when the front door opened at 6:15.

Her father had violence in him, though it never landed directly on their bodies. He kicked at walls, and raged at injustices meted out by his bosses. He drank beer out of the can, one after the other, standing in the kitchen until he couldn't stand anymore. Mostly this happened late at night, and Gwen could shut her door, put on her headphones and wait it out. Her mother never engaged, and her father's rants were lengthy and for no one. The hum of them was like listening to the same song every night. Sometimes doors would bang. Something might smash. Then, the next morning, Gwen's mother would be standing in the kitchen blankly, and eggs would be waiting for Gwen and Nancy.

In adolescence, Gwen transitioned into Dorothy, locked in a dream, always inside the tornado. She walked through the school halls inside the tornado, sat at the back of class inside the tornado, ate dinner in the tornado while her mother and father ate in silence. Music helped; it cut through, as did the drinking. Her best friend, Laura, was the source of vodka and albums, and they would take the bus two hours into the city and wander the mall downtown, shoplifting eyeliner and white foundation. Gwen remembered the comforting touch of Laura's hands on her head, dying Gwen's triangular haircut black in the bathroom at the mall, the dirty sink streaked with dye and the girls running out, laughing, faster than the security guards.

Their favourite bar was Palmer's, at the edge of Chinatown where the smell of restaurant fish steamed up from the grate out front. It had a neon palm tree sign and the best bands. Gwen could see herself from above, with the other girls in their leather jackets and tank tops, saying *Yes, yes, yes* to whatever was offered—to the weed, the fingers, the alleyways.

The proposition of adulthood was marbled with danger. A billboard appeared at the mall: a man with a scabbed face and Jesus-cheeks. A counsellor had come to her class in Grade 7, rolling in a TV on wheels to show a video about condoms: "Don't get AIDS—like ME," warned the dying drug user, a line Gwen and her friends repeated to each other in the cafeteria, holding up hot dogs, giggling. Still, they snatched handfuls of free condoms from the walk-in clinic, filling their purses.

So Gwen had never expected pleasure, exactly. The stories of the first time, traded at sleepovers and next to lockers on Monday mornings, never included pleasure. More often, the details involved boredom. They usually included the humiliation of boys who were stupid and finished fast and said comical things when they did. (Laura had lost her virginity on a summer trip to Europe with her parents, in a barn with an Austrian boy who right after shouted "America!" and offered her a handful of hay to clean off.) Boys were unearthly and difficult to make sense of. Yet Gwen had hoped—at the very least—for kindness.

"Let's not go back to Procter," shouted Gwen to Laura, bouncing up and down in the mosh pit. And they didn't.

× × ×

Daniel was the sound guy on the nights when he made it in. Gwen stood far away, watching him set up the stage, then retreat behind the mixing board, fingers working the mysterious knobs. His lean face seemed to be melting, slipping between boy and girl. When he first looked up and smiled at her, she gasped.

Laura asked if he was Métis.

"He's from Sudbury," said Gwen, even though she wasn't entirely sure what that ruled out. (Everyone she met was from somewhere else, small towns that Gwen looked up in the atlas at the reference library where she went to keep warm, poring over art books and napping between the stacks. She liked to locate her new friends' hometowns on maps: Gull Lake, Smithers, Sault Ste. Marie.)

So that would be her first time: with Daniel, on a piece of foam he used as a bed, in a tiny room in an apartment he shared with two other guys. She wondered if he could tell she was the only girl in the world who hadn't had sex. To her relief, lying completely still seemed to suffice. Through the whole thing, Daniel kept shaking his long hair out of his eyes and asking her if she was all right. "You okay?" and on and on, for exactly eight minutes, marked by a blinking digital clock in the shape of a beer can. And afterwards, he held her close so she could barely breathe. Only when he fell asleep could she finally relax, her head against his skinny chest.

The second time, he said, "Wait—your turn," and each time they had sex after, she came, and with each shudder, she tilted toward love, and her loneliness receded a little.

She called home and her father yelled, said she should never come back. Then her mother took the phone. Gwen could hear her walking away from her father, a door shutting.

"Gwyneth—be safe," she said, quietly. "And if you need to come home, I'll make sure you can."

Gwen hung up immediately, her heart racing. Some part of her, the part of her that felt like crying, was thrilled and covetous of this surprising and beautiful pronouncement.

She wouldn't need to call on that kindness for a year.

× × ×

Laura met a guy and left for Vancouver, and so it was just Gwen and Daniel. Gwen adored Daniel's apartment, with the itchy Mexican blankets, and the thin sliver of translucent orange soap in its dish. There was the potential for squalor, with three nineteen-year-old men living together, but Daniel kept the place military clean. He lined his shoes up against the wall, and Gwen's, too. He would climb out of bed in the dark if he sensed something was amiss somewhere in the apartment, leaving her while he scrubbed a lone plate in the sink. He hung his four T-shirts on hangers that were evenly spaced in the little closet. Gwen curled up on the foam, under the blanket, watching these gestures repeat, sometimes several times a day. "I'll take care of you," he said, or that's what she felt he was saying, pulling up the blanket, kissing her on the forehead before he left, off to unknown places. "Stay here," he said from the doorway. "Don't go anywhere."

Gwen didn't take him literally until the day she did leave the apartment while he was out, walking to investigate a Help

Wanted sign, then over to the library to pass the time. When she returned a few hours later, Daniel was cross-legged on the mattress, knees bouncing, eyes wide. "I got worried," he told her. Gwen apologized, surprised to have had this effect, any effect, on another person. She liked weighing on someone, even if his outsized response tugged at her insides, a warning. Still, she comforted him.

From then on, Gwen had to check in with Daniel's roommates if she was leaving the apartment. This was the pact. Daniel needed to know where she was at all times, he said, because he loved her. She revelled in the word "love."

With his permission, Gwen took a job in a donut shop. At sunset, after wiping clean the racks and hanging up her hairnet, Gwen walked south to Palmer's. She would nod to Gus, the twisted grey manager. He never spoke to her, just grunted in passing, if that.

The boys revered him, but Gwen felt queasy watching his big belly testing the buttons on his plaid shirts. After the customers had gone, Gus would pull a wad of cash out of his pocket, and the boys would gather around. Very slowly, Gus distributed the bills, always making someone do just a little extra before getting theirs. "Daniel, how about you bring me a beer?" He would watch Daniel carefully, eyeing him as he walked. Beer delivered, Gus would hand Daniel his cash, holding up his empty palms. "You'll get paid the rest tomorrow, dickheads," he'd say. But Gwen knew there was always something left. She saw the bulge of the cash roll in the drooping back pocket of Gus's jeans.

Daniel got a kick out of him, though, forever a foster kid, looking to be taken in. Gus did very little but it was enough

for Daniel. He slapped Daniel on the back after he'd success-
fully fixed the mixing board, and Daniel beamed. He invited
Daniel into the tiny room he used as an office, a stinking box
with a mop leaning in the corner and paper strewn across the
desk. Daniel told Gwen that Gus liked to show the boys his
gun, stored right in the desk drawer, maybe loaded. Gus would
wave it around, especially when someone screwed up. Daniel
said he thought this was stupid, but Gwen could tell that he was
impressed, too, recounting Gus's manly madness.

On Daniel's birthday, Gus gave him as much beer as he could
drink. Daniel drank until he puked into an empty box backstage. It was Gwen who had to lead Daniel by the hand out of
the bar. Gus leaned in the doorway, watching.

Often, her job was to get Daniel home, his boneless legs dragging, his tall body resting on her aching shoulder. She was small
but strong, and he didn't weigh much, despite his height. Up the
street they went, leaning into one another like two cigarettes in
a pack. He raged lightly or hard, depending on the night, thrash-
ing and spitting. She dropped him on the mattress. She knew
to take off his shoes and line them up carefully by the wall for
morning because that was how he liked it.

At the bar, with the music, Gwen was happier than she was
in the little apartment. When the bands set up, Gwen sat on her
stool, beer bottle in her lap, Discman on, watching Daniel flip
switches that turned the lights from red to green to blue. The
crowds were men and boys, mostly. Gwen loved the girl bands,
but they were few and far between, and the girl singers looked
at her with suspicion. The boys were a little nicer, swaying their
long hair and talking to her shyly as they set up, then springing
to life with a violent thrash once the music started. They didn't

hit on her much. She was baby-faced, and she was Daniel's, which seemed to matter.

On the rare occasions when she was moved to dance, Gwen would slip out from behind the stage, and into the centre of the crowd. She would be lifted right atop the heads, lying on her back, carried from body to body. She would see above her the criss-crossing beams and lights, water-stained ceiling panels. One night the singer was making sounds, not words, like doors slamming, over and over, and the bassist was standing on top of the speaker, twelve feet in the air, looking down at Gwen. A hand tried to grab between her legs, and Gwen flung herself off the carpet of the crowd. Or maybe she didn't escape; maybe she was just expelled. Either way, Gwen landed by an amp, her head hitting the stage. A chunk of her scalp scraped clear away, hanging like a tissue from the stage's lip. She lay, dazed on her side, until a bouncer scooped her up and carried her backstage.

"Oh, Gwennie," said Daniel, wiping her blood-streaked forehead with a rag. He was sober that night, because he was broke. "I'll take you to the hospital."

Gus blocked the door. "If you leave now, you won't get paid for tonight." Daniel pushed past him.

The ER nurse took one look at them and immediately found a bed, pulling the curtain shut. Daniel fell asleep in a chair, and Gwen felt a surge of relief. She used a remote control to crank herself to sitting, then crank herself back down.

Finally, a different nurse appeared, breathing through her mouth, letting Gwen know she was giving off a sour smell of bar and donuts. Self-conscious now, Gwen noticed that her jeans were ripped at the knees, her dyed black hair unwashed. Blood had poured over her right eye, crusting it shut.

"Are you using?" asked the nurse.

"Using what?" Gwen was genuinely puzzled.

"Heroin."

"What? Oh—no," said Gwen.

"What about him?" Gwen looked over, and saw Daniel as the nurse might see him, sitting slumped over, chin to chest.

Gwen shrugged. The nurse cleaned her eye. She sighed. Then she gently lifted Gwen's arm and examined her wrist. She touched the purple bracelet of a bruise. Gwen flinched.

"That didn't happen tonight."

"I fell at work." Gwen pulled her sleeve down to her fingers. The nurse looked at her, and Gwen turned away. The nurse left the room.

Gwen wanted to tell the nurse that she shared her concern, but that all of this was temporary.

The nurse returned with a flyer: *Women's Crisis Line*. They both looked at Daniel, passed out, and Gwen put the paper in her pocket. She wanted to explain to the nurse that there was comfort with him. She required the simplicity of their life together. She wasn't willing to let it go, not yet. Before waking him to leave, she threw the paper in a wastebasket.

After that, whenever she was at the bar, Daniel told her to stay where he could see her. "I just like to know where you are," he said. "In case something happens."

This is where Gwen would like to stop, where she does stop in her head, settling on that one request: "Stay where I can see you." That could be the climax of a love story about a sweet boy from a northern town who looked out for a girl. But there were all the things she didn't tell Seth, didn't tell Maddie, as if by keeping the story untold, she would create a world where such things never happened at all.

Still, go back to those first months. They were kids listening to music and holding hands, walking back to the boy's apartment as the sun rose. That was the city she held close. That was the youth she wanted to remember. In love, and away from her parents. She could stop the whole story there. If only.

4

MADDIE

On Friday night, Gwen sat at the new dining room table, pulling felt. Maddie watched her from the doorway. The table had arrived yesterday. Her mother had showed her how the centre popped out, repeating what some sales guy had said, "Butterfly leaf. Internal cable and ball bearings for a smooth transformation. Solid walnut. Designed by a Danish firm called Fordin, which is a combination of 'Odin' and 'forward.' Handcrafted in the UK." Maddie couldn't tell if Gwen was joking or not.

"Come sit with me," said Gwen. "This poor owl needs wings."

Maddie checked her phone: she had time. As a little kid, she had loved the cupboard in the living room with its clear plastic bins of buttons and string, loose balls of wool unravelling. She had spent hours digging around in that cupboard.

But when she got to high school, Maddie learned that despite her mother making a gallery of her stick people and sunsets, she wasn't artistic. She basically sucked. Back home, her friend May had a sketchbook, and she would sit in the lunchroom, tossing off portraits of her friends, one after the other, that were beautiful and true, saying, "Oh God, it's nothing." Maddie knew that her own pictures were stiff, with wonky perspective. Heads too small always. A lack of necks. She had no feeling for it. She couldn't solve art.

But at home, her mom would still pull out the clay and the paint from time to time. Maddie liked that crafts made her mother happy. Maddie thought of her mom as a shaking bird in a pocket, but her nervousness stilled a little when she sat at a table, fingers working, hunched over a creation.

So far, Gwen had made a fox, a snake and a bird, each the size of a golf ball. Maddie wondered if she had been crafting all day.

Maddie sat beside her mother. She picked at the piece of brown felt with a needle, pulling the wings out. Doing this childish activity, she felt content, but then, next to that little-girl feeling was that other thing you get, like you've lost something.

Gwen was looking at her too hard. "Oh, what am I going to do without you when you go away?" The spell was broken.

"You'll be fine, Mom."

But Maddie couldn't picture it either—her in one place, Gwen in another. Maddie's earliest memories were of her mother crawling into her bed, placing her hand on Maddie's heart. Her dad would come eventually and extract Gwen. When he'd ushered her out of the room, he would return to Maddie and give her a kiss on the forehead. "Mommy's tired," he'd say. "Sleep now."

Maddie stood up and handed Gwen the tiny wings. "Yours. I need to get ready."

As she walked away she glanced back at her mother, bent

over the table. The curve of her back reminded Maddie of Gwen leaning over Eli's crib. "Can you believe it?" she'd say with astonishment, looking down at Eli's chubby body, his feet in tiny socks. Maddie would come to see, too, standing on tiptoes next to her mother, who exclaimed: "Look what we have!"

× × ×

After a long time in front of the mirror, Maddie decided to go to the party underdressed and makeup free. It was better not to try, probably. She wore jeans and a tank top. Her one concession to fashion was the chunky black sandals with the high heel, bought with money her dad left on her dresser: three hundred-dollar bills. She had never held money like that, and he had just put it there with a wink.

Seth sat in the living room with his laptop open, frowning at the numbers spinning on-screen. He had a new company, Maddie knew. Something involving software for small businesses, totally boring. Seth looked up. "I smelled you before I saw you," he said. She halted.

"Too much perfume?"

"Just right. Come here."

Maddie did, and leaned down to give her dad a kiss on his forehead. He gave her hand a quick squeeze.

"Did you talk curfew with Mom?"

"Midnight."

"How will you get back?"

"Subway."

"Money?"

"Yes."

"Phone charged?"

"Yes."

Gwen appeared, with the owl in her hand, hovering next to Seth. She didn't comment on the sandals, but she raised an eyebrow. Suddenly, Maddie felt the strap above her right heel rubbing into her skin, as if to articulate Gwen's unspoken thought: the sandals were an impractical choice. She would have a blister, or worse, by morning.

"Who is this girl again?" Gwen asked.

"Clara."

"What do you know about her?"

"She's in a lot of clubs. She dances."

"Keep your phone on," said Gwen.

"Please don't text me."

"I won't! Just keep it on."

"Seriously. I might not even check in. It doesn't mean I'm dead."

Gwen went in for a hug, and Maddie ducked suddenly, as if she needed to adjust the buckle on her sandal. She recognized her own cruelty, but so what? *You can't just touch me whenever you need to*, she wanted to say. *You don't always get to pull me in.*

Seth stood up and put his arm around Gwen, whose eyes were downcast. "She'll be fine," he said, and it was unclear who he was referring to.

× × ×

They were waiting outside Clara's house, on a grassy hill. "House" wasn't the right word: mansion. Castle. Three cars sat in the long driveway.

Clara's upper body was collapsed over her long legs like a rag doll, her feet bare. Sophie sat cross-legged, clicking at her phone. They both had their hair down, and it was long and straight, like matching sheets on a clothesline. They have so much hair, thought Maddie. More hair, perhaps, than necessary.

"You look delightful," said Clara, drawing out the word "delightful" just enough to unnerve Maddie. "Sophie said my feet are too gross for these shoes."

She gestured toward a pair of high-heeled sandals, just different enough from Maddie's that Maddie knew she had bought the wrong ones. Maddie reflexively complimented Clara's feet. But then she looked closer, and saw that Sophie had a point. Clara's feet were sausage raw. Bones jutted out from the side like extra toes. Each smaller toe had a rough circular callus at the knuckle.

"Disgusting. Am I right?" said Sophie. Maddie made a non-committal sound, somewhere between supportive and a shrug.

"Not disgusting when I'm the Sugar Plum Fairy, coming this holiday season." Clara said it in an old-movie voice. The kids at the U used voices more often than her old friends did. They put on accents, throwing in the catchphrases and jargon of commercials and movies, always winking and nodding at texts that Maddie half recognized.

The three girls walked along Yonge, past the flower shops and clothing stores.

"The likelihood of this party sucking is about seventy percent," said Sophie.

"That seems generous," added Clara.

"Leo used to go to the U, but he got kicked out," explained Sophie.

"What did he do?"

The girls exchanged a look. "Stole a test," said Clara.

"Hideous," said Sophie, stopping in front of a window display of frilly dresses.

"Not if you're a prom queen," trilled Clara.

"Or a Disney princess," said Maddie, surprising herself. She thought, guiltily, of her friend Emma, who had gone on a Disney cruise two years ago, when she was already too old: "It was so tacky—and so fun!" She bought Maddie a *Little Mermaid* key-chain. Maddie had only facetimed her once since moving, and her heart ached suddenly for someone who knew her.

"Let's go in," said Sophie.

Clara was buoyant. The salesclerk, a middle-aged woman whose paperback novel sat open and facedown nearby, looked at the three girls and said, "We're closing soon."

Clara pointed at watches and rings behind the glass counter, which were obediently pulled forth, laid out on a silk cloth. Sophie twirled between the low tables, fingering the envelope-thin stacks of folded sweaters and shirts.

Clara held out her hand, which now, on her left wedding finger, held a gold ring with a thick green stone in the centre. "What do you think, guys? Will Tony get it for me?"

Sophie twirled over. "Oh, definitely. Let me take a picture."

She snapped a photo of Clara looking pouty, the ring by her face. "Tony's in the military," Clara explained to the clerk. "So I only see him at holidays. But he's coming home soon, and he wrote me that we're getting engaged. At least, I think that's what it said. His emails arrive very redacted. He's high up, you see." The clerk's lips tightened. Maddie wanted to back out of the store.

"I don't even really know what he does. Just that he loves me." Clara sighed.

"It's eleven hundred dollars, miss," the clerk said.

Clara looked at the ring more closely. "A nice setting," she said. "I'll be sure to send him your way. Once the ship docks."

Maddie left last, with a quick backwards glance that she hoped would pass for an apology.

They walked past vans, giant concrete mixers, plastic over windows—a neighbourhood under renovation, everything improvable. A man in work boots at the top of a ladder hooted as they passed. Sophie curtsied.

"Ever heard of feminism, asshole?" yelled Clara.

Maddie laughed, but she could not get oriented. She did not know how upset to be.

The sun was dropping fast. Days were getting shorter, thought Maddie. She could feel the fall coming, and wished she'd brought a jacket.

The music identified the house. A faint, pulsing drumbeat that grew louder as they approached and turned up the long path toward the front door. They stood next to tall marble pillars. A word she'd read in school popped into Maddie's mind: "portico."

"Speaking of Disneyland," said Maddie mockingly.

"Bit much, right?" said Clara. "He's okay, really. A little . . ." She paused. "Privileged."

Maddie pictured Clara's three cars. Kids at the U were always talking about privilege, Maddie had noticed. She hadn't heard it much before, this slippery word. Sometimes privilege seemed to be measureable by stuff, and sometimes it seemed to be an internal state, to be gauged by others. Maddie suspected it might be meaningless when tossed around by people she knew, but deathly important to people on the wrong side of it. But what were the sides, again?

"Hey, Jared," said Clara to a boy who appeared behind them, trailing vape.

"Hey," he replied.

Maddie recognized him from the fields—a soccer player. Cute.

"Did you bring anything to drink?" he asked. "It'd be cooler if you did."

They laughed, and Maddie recognized it as a line from a movie, but couldn't identify which one.

Sophie pushed open the heavy door without using its brass ring knocker, and went first into the crowd. It was like a concert: hot and moist, deep with people moving in all directions, calling for one another, scanning for the lost and missing.

The girls were carried along by the crowd, past a fireplace, toward a vast kitchen. There were empty chip bowls on the island, and fast-food boxes stuffed with empty pieces of greasy wrapping. Clara found a fridge, concealed in the cabinetry.

"Check it," she said, opening the door to reveal row upon row of beer bottles. "Here."

Maddie took the beer. She hadn't seen this label before: a cartoon fox and the word "microbrew." She had only drunk beer featured in beer ads, and never loved it anyway, wishing always for something sweeter. But tonight she would drink fast, because she was thirsty, and it dulled the noise that knocked on both sides of her skull.

She finished one beer in the kitchen, squished between two texting girls. She drank a second while following Sophie and Clara through the mansion. They stopped frequently and traded one-liners with boys and girls, always laughing and touching, arms slung around shoulders. Clara introduced her differently each time: "This is Maddie. She's our genius friend from Slovenia." "Meet Maddie. She's actually an android." "Andrew, this is Maddie. She came to the U when her father took a job in counter-intelligence."

"Everyone's named Andrew," said Maddie.

Clara could drape herself anywhere. "You're the best, most favourite Andrew," she said, now nestled in the lap of a blushing boy.

Sophie led Maddie through the bodies to the basement. Two girls stood behind the bar in a vaping cloud. Maddie went past them toward another fridge, knocking against the soft backside of one boy, maybe deliberately. This fridge was full of beer, too, as if the refrigerators were replenishing themselves.

Kids were lying on the floor, lining couches and chairs in front of a large-screen TV. Maddie could barely make out an image of a man in a straitjacket, his eyelids pinned open with metal claws. Then flashes of a different man being kicked and beaten, blood streaking across his face. The boys closest to the screen leaned closer.

"So gross!" said Sophie.

"Shut up, Soph. The man is genius," said a boy, not turning his head.

"I love this movie," said Clara, who had left behind the boy upstairs—probably stiff and pissed off, thought Maddie. "Have you read the book?" Clara dropped down on the couch, squeezing between bodies.

Maddie shook her head, making a note to google later: "Eyeballs. Genius."

"You should join the film club," Clara said.

"Jesus, Clara, she doesn't have to join everything." Sophie sat on a couch next to a girl with a longboard under one foot. Sophie and the girl kissed—hard, Maddie noted. The longboard moved back and forth under the girl's foot, and Sophie ran her hand through the girl's hair. When the kiss was over, Sophie rested her head on the girl's shoulder and turned her attention back to the movie.

The man on the screen was now wailing and begging to be released, and Maddie needed air. She split off from the girls. In a corridor, she tripped on a litter box that had been shoved there, maybe on purpose. Cat litter sprayed into the hall, and a single, dark turd landed at her feet. Maddie looked around to see if anyone had seen. Then she headed upstairs and through French doors into a backyard.

At the edge of the pool, Maddie imagined diving into the water—down, down, down to the wobbly bottom. A circle of kids sat cross-legged on a patch of lawn nearby. Maddie went closer, to see what they were looking at so intently. She tripped over a wicker chair as she approached; her footing was off. Her heel throbbed from the sandal. She was drunk, she thought, and caught a whiff of floral. There it was, something beautiful on a vine, tendrils climbing and choking a trellis, pink poking through the dark.

"We're playing spin the bottle," said one of the boys. "Wanna play?"

"Mmmmm," said Maddie, falling to her knees.

"Is that a yes or a no?" Fuzzily, Maddie recognized some of their faces from school.

"I'll just watch," she murmured. She put her beer down, and then observed without moving as it tipped over and the liquid poured out into the grass.

One boy was obsessed with rules. The kisses were accompanied by shrieks and handclaps, but were also brief and chaste. A boy kissed a boy. More shrieks. A girl kissed a girl. Things she'd done with dolls. There was nothing to be turned on about.

Maddie lay back on the grass and looked up at the stars, trying to find that pink smell.

When she looked around again, the group of kids was gone. The music had stopped.

She stood uncertainly and made her way into the house.

Maddie felt wrapped in black, her eyes dry, the room pulsing. She needed to find Clara and Sophie. She needed to get home. But where was the front door? She stumbled into one of the fireplace rooms. A girl played guitar. She had a craggy singing voice, buried beneath the mumbles of the crowd.

"You okay?" asked a boy, and Maddie nodded.

She kept walking through the house, looking for her friends, and then reversed and reconsidered the word: Were they friends? she wondered. Up the staircase, over the bottles (at a knocked-over beer bottle on a Persian rug, Maddie thought: *That will stain*, and then sighed with recognition because she was, for a moment, just like her mother), Maddie felt her stomach fold in on itself, but held her sickness in. A closed door might reveal a bathroom, she thought, turning the knob.

By opening the door, she let in a beam of light from the hallway, illuminating shapes in space: an animal perched on a bed, and behind, the chalk outline of a person. Then the outline moved—repetitive, slamming. Now Maddie saw that it wasn't an animal. It was a girl, because she collapsed from her knees onto her stomach, as if the air had been let out of her. *Is this sex?* thought Maddie, who had never seen sex before, not live, just sometimes online, where the hairless women made fake noises and the men looked angry.

This, though, real life—this was truly shocking. The flattened girl's neck bucked, and her long hair flew from her eyes, which were bleached in the shadows. Maddie thought: *Not sex. Not good.* Maddie froze, letting the scene slide, waiting for the pieces to land and take a shape, something recognizable, with mean-ing—but then she stepped back. She removed herself from the picture and pulled the door shut, her heart racing.

Immediately, she felt a hand behind her and thought: *Oh God no—don't push me in there.* She turned quickly, panicked, and the hand dropped from her back. Joshua, in the dim hallway. They were alone.

"I know you," he said.

"What is it?" she asked, frantic.

"What's what?"

But he couldn't explain what was going on in there either, she realized. Even if he had seen it, too, he couldn't explain it. The only one who knew what happened was that girl, that unrecog-nizable girl.

"I have to get home."

"Are you okay?" he said. Maddie had to shove him slightly to get by. He was light, wiry, and she felt that she could lift him up and place him anywhere, like an empty suitcase.

There, at the bottom of the stairs, was the door to the out-side. In the living room, she could hear the girl with the guitar still singing quietly, a song Maddie didn't recognize. She was so tired of knowing nothing, of all the scattered dots that she couldn't join. She pushed open the door, running sideways onto the walkway, the strap of her sandal cutting into her tendon like a dull butter knife.

With minutes to go before her curfew, Maddie reached the back gate at home. Her presence set off a floodlight, catching both her and the black pool in its beam. She stood on the porch, peering in the doors to the kitchen. Lights shone in the living room still. Her mother would be up, maybe her dad, too. The worst. She was officially wasted.

Maddie opened the door and stepped quietly, aiming toward the back stairs. But her sandals clicked on the hardwood, setting off a human rustling in the living room.

"Maddie?" called Gwen. Maddie sped up, leaning on the bannister as she ascended the stairs, calling backwards over her shoulder, "I'm home." Gwen's steps quickened, too, but Maddie outran her mother and slid into her bedroom. She shut the door and stood in the dark. She could hear Gwen outside, and see the shadow of her feet in the crack of light beneath the door. Gwen paced, and Maddie knew she was deciding whether or not to come in.

Maddie realized—and this was weird—that she wanted her to. She was hungry to tell anyone, maybe even her mother, about the evening: the girl on the bed, the litter box, the pool kisses. But she was too drunk, and Gwen would be too careful in her response, too greedy for details. Maddie's desire to spill her stories could never ever match Gwen's desire to swallow her whole.

This small, beer-soaked revelation made Maddie even sadder. She wanted to love her mother like she had when she was little, when Gwen was almost a playmate, the two of them similarly locked in child tasks and conversations. She didn't want to see Gwen as clearly as she did now, this floating, tremulous woman, so much younger than the other mothers, almost, in some way, younger than Maddie. She missed her other mother. She missed her other self.

Maddie watched Gwen's shadow pull away from the crease

of light. She took off her sandals and saw a blurry line of blood encircling her right ankle, as if someone had grabbed her there and dragged her across cement. Maddie threw herself on the bed, the ceiling undulating, until she finally fell asleep in a dark, fast thrum.

5

The first time Daniel hit her was the same night Gwen watched the band fronted by a singer who would soon become famous, and then overdose in a hotel room a few years later.

The night they performed, the band was furious, glorious. The lead singer's long knotted hair concealed his face. His low guitar swung by his hips. They would end up on *Saturday Night Live* and in arenas, and that night, everyone could feel their success coming, the first drops before a hurricane. People couldn't get tickets, and the crowd outside stayed in the cold to hear them through the walls. The woman from the Chinese restaurant came out and shooed them away from her windows.

When the musician sang, Gwen was moved almost to tears. His voice was speaking for her, through her, holding her. She went deeper into the crowd, pushed and pulled back and forth by the bodies, eyes closed, encore after encore.

Afterwards, Gwen moved backstage to find the singer. She wanted to tell him something. Past the stacks of beer bottles in boxes, she saw him sitting alone in the closet that passed for a green room, its walls graffitied and smashed with holes. He had a notebook on his lap, head bowed as he wrote. He looked up at her, his hair falling away, and the not-yet-famous face was curious. Gwen opened her mouth to speak, but there were two hands on her shoulders, wrenching her backwards into the hall. The door slammed shut on the singer. Gwen was dropped back in the shadows against a stack of chairs, her right side stinging. Daniel's height increased; his hands grew bigger. He expanded.

"What are you doing in there?" he said.

Gwen shook her head, and his open hand moved flat across her face. For all her father's volcanic rumblings, she had never been hit, and she almost laughed that it was Daniel who did it— Daniel, of all people! She reeled backwards, chairs clattering, her cheek inflamed, her eye loose in its socket.

After a pause, he came to her, gathered her in his arms. A rescue. "Oh no," he said, as if he'd walked in on the aftermath of an accident. Was he crying? His upset added to Gwen's confusion. "I'm so sorry, I'm so sorry."

Gwen stepped back, out of his arms. Daniel looked at her almost fearfully, unsure of what she would do.

She walked out, through the back door, into the rain. A group of fans craned their necks, disappointed it was just her.

She was stunned into calmness, walking and smoking, considering her options, the welt on her face beating. Gwen counted her money—twenty-seven dollars. Her vision was foggy in her right eye. She remembered the feeling of her head on Daniel's chest at night. She remembered her father's fury, and the sound of the TV always on in the house, and how no one from her family had come to find her when she left.

She did a little math: Stay at the donut shop for another ten weeks. Get enough cash together. But for now—Daniel. She made a list. *His sad eyes. A one-off. He'd only hurt her that one time, accidentally, when she'd been talking so close to that bartender and he pulled her by the wrist. He was sweet in bed. He was a good person. Everyone makes mistakes. He didn't know what she was doing with that singer. He didn't know about trust.*

Soaking wet, shivering, she walked to Daniel's apartment.

When he came back to find her lying on the foam in the dark, he kissed her shoulder and wept and promised. She lay still, wishing she found it harder to make the choice, but in fact, it was easy. She turned to hold him.

× × ×

For a time afterwards, Daniel was only gentle. His hand hovered near Gwen's waist, not on her, as if he were asking permission. When he went anywhere without her, when she wasn't in his line of vision in Palmer's, he asked people to keep an eye on her, and she took that for caring. "Phil's around if you need anything," he'd say, nodding at a squat boy with a rabbit-twitching nose who passed for a friend. "Phil's looking out for you." The best thing about Phil was his lean, blond dog, whom everyone called Dog.

On her eighteenth birthday, Gwen walked the beach boardwalk with Dog while Daniel slept on his foam. Dog hated the leash, a piece of yellow rope, and pulled at Gwen's shoulder violently, sometimes glancing back at her with surprise, seeming to say: *Oh, it's you—are you still there?*

× × ×

Daniel vanished for days. "Bender," Phil said, and the word felt right to Gwen: Daniel's behaviour would bend this way and that, and so would her life. Days were calm, then twisting. When he did reappear, his pretty face was a little different each time, puffed or bruised or skinnier.

Gus grabbed Gwen by the arm, while she sat at the bar watching a band. "Where's your boyfriend?"

"He's sick."

"He's fired. Look what he did to my fucking dishwasher," he said.

She glanced behind the bar at the dishwasher, open to reveal a rack of unwashed glasses.

"It looks fine," Gwen said.

Gus sneered. "*That* dishwasher," he said. One of the Sri Lankan guys from the kitchen was tying a garbage bag behind the bar. Harsha was his name. A slow smiler. Younger, even, than her. They had spoken a few times, or as much as was possible with his broken English. Sometimes she brought the dishwashers cans of Coke from the donut shop, smuggled out in her pack on a hot night.

Gwen waved at Harsha, and he turned, revealing a dark welt over his eye. Half his face was lumpy and grooved with bruises. He ducked, avoiding looking at Gwen.

"That's your boyfriend's work," said Gus. "He's a fucking maniac." Gwen stared and tried to rise to go to him, but Gus's hand was on her arm. Harsha picked up the garbage bag and walked in the opposite direction, quickly, out of the bar.

"Tell Daniel to stay away," said Gus, squeezing hard before releasing his grip.

Gwen never asked Daniel about Harsha. She tried to imagine a scenario in which the boy deserved a beating, but there wasn't one. She held it close, this knowledge of what Daniel was capable of, let it needle her chest. But she said nothing, turning it over and over until she couldn't bear it anymore. She stopped thinking of Harsha. She kept moving forward as if nothing had happened.

Soon after, the little scaffolding around their life together tumbled down. His roommates locked Daniel out. Gwen didn't know why.

For a few weeks, they stayed in the living room of a high school friend of Daniel's, until the guy's girlfriend said, "No more." Gwen had her donut shop money, but all the landlords wanted first and last month's rent, and she could never get it to add up.

At first, they crashed in the corners of people's apartments. Daniel had Gwen pack and repack her backpack until he deemed it correct: largest items on the bottom, lightest on the top. Then Daniel said he didn't like how Phil looked at her, so they moved out of the apartment where Phil sometimes stayed, and slept on the street. Gwen asked about the shelter by the mall, but Daniel told her that was for the really bad off. Anyway, there were bedbugs, and addicts who would steal your stuff. Worst of all, couples were separated at night.

It wasn't so bad sleeping outside. It was temporary, just this one summer. They lay in sleeping bags in the doorways of print shops and bookstores—anywhere people didn't stay late or come early. Daniel kept them apart from the squeegee kids who slept on cardboard and old mattresses; they wouldn't be dirty like that, he promised. He arranged their belongings carefully, away from view, and blocked Gwen in, protecting her from passersby with his body. Still the streetlight came in, and Gwen's sleep was staccato, broken by rattling trucks, unidentifiable snaps and smashes in the distance. The birds came before the light, loudly chirping, triggering the heat.

In the morning, Daniel walked her to the door of the donut shop. She could clean herself there in the bathroom with paper towel. She hid a little of the money she earned in the lining of her bra, a pink one that chafed under her arms, but was pretty— a castoff from Laura. With the rest, she bought fast food and apples in Kensington Market—apples because she had the sense that they should eat better, that better food might help Daniel.

At the mission in Moss Park, Gwen waited in the churchyard while he went inside to shower. She rested her back against a tree, shaded from the sun, sleepily watching the men go through the door for the free dinner, one man after the next. Daniel would emerge with wet hair, offering her half a sandwich, or pasta in a paper cup. She would lean against him under the tree, eating and watching the men file back out.

Slowly, she decided that maybe what she had seen at the bar wasn't that bad after all. In the bar light, Harsha's face might have looked worse, and probably he was okay. Daniel didn't get mad at her anymore, even when she had to stay late at work. He waited outside, shoulders raised, watching through the glass as Steve, the manager, closed up. When she saw Daniel eating an apple, Gwen felt pleased, as if she were taking care of him, and he was worth taking care of.

One night, they lay their sleeping bags next to the bathrooms in a dog park on the west side. It had been twenty-four days since the time he punched her in the stomach. Gwen marked the days in her notebook with check marks.

The bathrooms were locked for the night, the smell quelled. In the dark, on her back, using the sleeping bag as a mattress because it was too hot to get inside, Gwen could imagine that they were camping somewhere beautiful. "Is this what it's like up north?" she asked Daniel.

She rested beneath his arm. He told her about a bear who broke into his foster mom's house when no one was home. The bear had opened a window and crawled right in. It pulled all the food from the shelves in the kitchen and opened the refrigerator, crushing a milk carton and smashing a glass jar of peanut butter. His foster mom came home from work, and Daniel walked in to find her standing in front of the piano, puzzled, gazing at the peanut butter all over the keys. Daniel, who was ten, said, "Maybe the bear played the piano."

Gwen loved the story of the musical bear, and watching Daniel's face in the dark, falling asleep as he told it, nuzzling against him. There was a dark coda to it, though: he should have locked the window, said the foster mom. Soon after, he was sent away again.

At dawn, dogs came barking and rooting around Gwen's sleeping bag. She opened her eyes to a park worker opening the padlocks on the bathroom doors, releasing a waft of urine cake.

She turned to Daniel, but he was already gone.

At the donut shop, Steve didn't let her in. He told her she was dirty, and gestured behind the counter, where a new girl stood. "Now that's a good worker." The girl gave her a look like it wasn't true.

Gwen cradled her pack in her arms, and argued about money he owed her, but Steve kept shaking his head. She'd only ever been paid in cash. There was no record of her working here. She didn't even have a social insurance number.

"Sorry." He shrugged, eyeing her as she backed onto the sidewalk.

Where was Daniel? Gwen waited across the street from Palmer's on the sidewalk, her legs crossed, darting inside McDonald's to pee, then going back to her spot, her stomach churning. She had a UTI—she knew it from the sharp stab in her crotch. She'd need to get to a clinic.

A man tossed a dime at her. She picked it up, wishing it was a quarter because she needed coins to do laundry. Gwen didn't bum often: it was boring, and Daniel didn't approve (but she was the one who took their clothes to the laundromat). In her backpack she carried a sign in ballpoint pen: PREGNANT AND HUNGRY. Only the hungry part was true, but she didn't feel guilty about lying—either someone would give her money, or they wouldn't, regardless of her story—unless people were genuinely sad for her. Older women, mostly, crouched down and told her of services available, of God's love, and when that happened, Gwen was ashamed. But most people ignored her entirely. Young men hissed at her to get a job. A teenage boy called her a cunt as he threw down a dollar, which she kept. If she saw a cop, she would pack up and slip into the crowd before he got to her. That was the most tiring part: to always be scanning, anticipating, waiting to be told, in some way, that she was in the wrong place, as if there were somewhere else she could be.

× × ×

Days later, Daniel showed up at the reference library, on the second floor where Gwen liked to sit. He looked changed yet again—not just thinner, but faded. She stood up from the newspaper she was looking at and he pulled her close, his neck rusty and familiar. "I got us a place," Daniel said.

She followed him to the area next to the university. The houses there had skylights and stained-glass dormers. Daniel stopped in front of a small brick house that looked like a cottage.

"For you," he said.

"Me?" Gwen asked.

She stepped inside and saw sugar white couches. A bright blue painting of a triangle hung above the fireplace. It, too, was beautiful. There were people huddled in blankets and sleeping bags, and beer cans and cigarette butts scattered on the floor, but it still resembled a home. Daniel slapped a guy on the shoulder, and Gwen thought: *Oh no.* She cringed, waiting for a fight—but she had misinterpreted; the touch was affectionate. They hugged, and the guy smiled at her, explaining that this was the home of a professor. "A professor of what?" Gwen asked, but nobody answered. The professor had invited a student to stay there while she was on a semester-long sabbatical. But it turned out that the student was a junkie, and she'd brought over not just Daniel and Gwen, but several other stragglers from Palmer's and around. Together, they drew the blinds and broke the ice machine on the fridge door. They could all wait out the fall, then, among the professor's books and music (classical, mostly, and jazz that sucked. Someone stomped those CDs to pieces).

The bedroom sheets were dirty, but they were sheets. A room with a window, and a blind—a museum installation of how people lived. Gwen had almost forgotten. She dropped her backpack and took off her shoes, wiggling her toes in her mud grey socks. Daniel came to sit beside her. Gwen already had an art book open in her lap, glossy black and white photos of kids playing stickball, making mischief in New York City.

"You're smart," said Daniel. He kissed Gwen on the neck. "You'll go to university one day, and we'll be through."

Gwen stiffened. "No," she said. And to herself: *He's better. Look where he brought me.*

Daniel put his hand on her back, then moved it to her breast and stopped. "What—?"

She had forgotten the money, tucked in her bra. Daniel held up the wad of bills. A wave of panic rose in Gwen—

"It's for us . . ."

Daniel lunged. The photo book fell. Gwen dropped to the floor in a ball, a reaction learned in school to prevent a body from catching on fire: stop, drop and roll. But he was strong and uncurled her shrimp shape, put his hands around her neck and bore down. *He isn't like a girl after all*, thought Gwen, gasping. *He is a bear.* And then she blacked out.

×××

In her years with Seth, only some parts of this time of her life came out. Gwen did describe the painting over the fireplace, and the band that became famous. One day, walking through a park with Maddie in the stroller, Gwen said to him, "I slept here for a while, right over there, by the bathrooms." And when Seth stopped walking, she saw a look like pity move across his face. She immediately regretted saying anything. It would take too long, she would have to go too deep to make any sense of it. She picked up the pace and walked away.

Gwen sometimes wondered if something had happened to her brain in that time. Before every one of Eli's hockey seasons, parents were required to stand in the cold arena and listen to the coach lecture about concussions. She thought about a player's brain, slamming around in his skull like a puck in a net, and she thought about her own. Could that be a reason, then, for what she did? Such speculation was a search for an excuse, even though, Gwen knew, there was none.

When she awoke from the blackout, Daniel had held her, and wept his apology, and Gwen had been silent. She stiffened her body, fixed her gaze, said, "It's okay." This was the only thing to say; the words always soothed him, and as he shrank back down to a human size, broken and apologetic, she could use that extra space to get her bearings, to try to figure out what to do.

Daniel had a plan, he said, but there were actually many of them. A plan to get more vodka, a plan to get sober, to get an apartment, to go up north—the plan was always changing. He would go out in the day, but Gwen stayed in the house. Wrapped in the professor's quilt, she couldn't hold her thoughts in. They tipped and spilled. *I've got to get up from here*, she would think, and then she'd find herself in the bathroom, looking in the mirror at her face, ashen and unfamiliar. Back to bed.

The lights had gone out, and it was cold. Snow fell. Someone had begun burning the professor's books in the fireplace to keep warm.

That day, Daniel must have come back, and he must have said: "Let's go," but Gwen didn't remember that part. Gwen didn't remember the walk to the donut shop, but she remembered standing at the back door in the dark, grey chunks of alley snow around her feet. Light leaked through the cracks around the heavy door, which would be unlocked at this late hour for the garbage run, she knew. The front door would be locked, the Open sign turned off, and Steve, in his baseball hat, would be cleaning, preparing to go home.

So they walked in. The cart of trays was empty except for one filled with pink donuts, frosted, covered in rainbow sprinkles. Why were they still there at this hour? Gwen wondered. Maybe

Steve was taking them home. Maybe he had a party to go to, a daughter waiting.

Steve had his head inside the juice case, wiping the glass, his bum sticking out, and Gwen thought of Hansel and Gretel: maybe Daniel would just shove him right in. But Daniel plucked him out instead, and Gwen saw the look on Steve's face—eyes darting, uncomprehending—and then, on seeing Gwen against the wall, next to the tray of pink donuts—rage. Gwen closed her eyes. Then it was just the sound of thumping flesh and Steve's little moans.

"Get the money! Get it, Gwen!"

Gwen opened her eyes to Daniel on top of Steve, who was still flailing, bucking, a puddle of blood forming on the floor under his head.

Gwen did. She floated to the cash. She punched in the code and it sprang open. There wasn't much, really—a few twenties and some smaller bills. Gwen held them in her fist.

Daniel sprang, grabbed her, and pushed her to the back door. Gwen looked behind her at Steve, on the ground, still. She stopped: *Don't die, don't die . . .* Daniel pushed her again. *Don't die . . .* And then she saw Steve's body seize and undulate, like a wet red fish. He groaned and uttered a string of sounds. Gwen made a move to get closer. "What? What did you say?" But Daniel yelled her name. He was shoving past her to open the steel back door. While Daniel struggled with the handle, Steve looked up at Gwen through one puffy eye, pinning her with a look disgusted and furious. "Gwen!" Daniel called. She looked away from Steve, at Daniel bouncing up and down by the open door, his hand extended. Gwen stood still for a moment, refusing Steve's gaze, then extended her hand to Daniel, moving toward him. But at the door, Daniel didn't take her hand. Instead, he grabbed the bills she was carrying, and he sprang into a run through the doorway, onto patchy snow, toward the dumpster. Gwen stumbled out, her ears ringing, to see if it was true, if he was really running away, and she saw him sprinting down the alley. Behind her, the heavy door slammed shut.

Gwen didn't weigh her choices. She didn't measure the risk, or calculate her culpability. She didn't reject calling the police. She didn't decide not to open the door and return to the bleeding man, crouching and whispering into his ear, next to his gaping mouth: "Shh, now. It's okay. Help is on its way. I'm here."

She saw Daniel running, and it was as if she saw a human-shaped hole suddenly appearing in a concrete wall: this was her chance. Gwen fled in the opposite direction. She raced down the sludgy alley, past the graffiti walls and bags of garbage, and burst onto College Street. The crowds were thick, and she turned in each direction, scanning for Daniel. She picked a direction and ran, head down, panting.

Gwen envied serial killers, bank robbers, true villains—proud and defiant, agents of destruction. She hadn't enjoyed it, the havoc they'd wreaked. What she had to live with was something else: she had done nothing. That's what she would carry.

6

GWEN

The restaurant was funeral parlour chic. If there were windows, they were hidden behind sheets of blood-coloured brocade. The light was low. Men wore suits and ties, and sat across from younger women who locked them in place with their eyes. The older women dined with each other, without men, their skin painted and plumped and their ages unknown.

The steakhouse was solid and permanent. Tom's choice, of course. It outlasted all the hot restaurants, enduring in its brick box in the financial district. "So uncool, it's cool." Seth told Gwen that was how Tom had described it. Gwen strained in the darkness to make out the print on the heavy menu as they waited for Tom and his wife.

Gwen recalled that when Seth first met Tom, he had come home excited that night, raving about an incredible presentation for a mobile app for small businesses, a thing of mystical, industry-shattering potential. If he'd had a soundtrack to his enthusiasm, it would have been the trumpets and strings of *Thus Spoke Zarathustra.*

"Such a clean business plan. Growth potential," he had told Gwen, phrases that made her sleepy. But his company was still riding high on the success of the fruit-flying app, and they had passed on Tom's pitch.

Then Gwen bought a lottery ticket, and within forty-eight hours, Seth quit his job and called Tom.

Now, with Seth's investment in Tom's idea, he could be a partner. Now Seth was a boss in the field of "digital human capital management." She could see that Seth liked how it sounded: futuristic and aggressive, and a little sexier than what it actually was (payroll software). Tom had already named the company "BuzzSwitch," which Gwen thought sounded like a failed European dance band.

The problem, Gwen identified, was Tom. She had met him for the second time (though he clearly didn't remember her from their Christmas party introduction nearly a year ago) recently in the new office space, which was empty except for a long harvest table. Tom was thirty-four and had the kind of manly, angular jaw that was bequeathed, passed down from generation to generation in a velvet-lined box. Seth didn't know him that well, except that he had a solid reputation from an earlier start-up that sold for $35 million. His walk was spring-loaded, and at the party where Gwen first met him, she heard him make a cheering noise while on the phone—"Whoot-whoo!" he said to whoever was on the other end. He struck Gwen as a freshman jock, always on the verge of a high-five. But he was a grown-up with a wife and twin toddlers, it turned out, though Seth had only discovered that one day when the nanny came by the office, briefly.

90

Tom wanted to celebrate closing their first round of invest-ment. They were locked down or locked in, Gwen wasn't sure. She didn't ask for dollar figures. It seemed ridiculous, in fact, this odd mating ritual of sniffing and seduction. No one knows anything, Seth had always said before of the funding process, scornful of too much risk. But here he was, in his new suit, exhilarated, rising up out of his seat to greet Tom and his wife, Julia. They arrived in a cloud of spiky scents, lotions and sham-poos evoking forests, doling out handshakes and cheek kisses.

"If you can bear it, the porterhouse deserves to be eaten practically raw," said Julia, dropping to her chair, unfolding her napkin. Gwen was seated across from her, and Seth across from Tom. Paired off. Gwen thought of Thanksgiving dinners with Seth's relatives where the women did dishes while the men watched football. She had loved those nights for their predict-ability, their strain of noise and fellow feeling. Family was novel to her still.

Gwen held the menu at a distance. Then closer. She couldn't read the words very well, yet she could make out Julia's smooth-ness; she looked almost wet. The tips of her long hair rested on her chest, exposed beneath her low-cut, sleeveless blouse. When she lifted the water glass to her lips, a hard, long muscle popped in her bicep, then retreated when the water was set down. Gwen watched this puppetry several times: water, flex, water, flex. To be this beautiful in the world would be strange. A woman like that might have reason to be suspicious of anything that seemed like kindness.

They ordered (Gwen did not get the porterhouse), and the men performed the ritual of the wine. Tom smelled it first, then swirled it in the glass several times while Seth murmured about vintage. Tom declared the wine "amazing."

"We should toast the boys," said Julia, and Gwen was puzzled: What boys? Then she realized that Julia meant Seth and Tom. Tom did look like a boy, in his funny shoes. But Seth—she glanced at her husband. He had dark circles around his eyes, echoed by his glasses. He was not boyish in any way, except perhaps his curls, though they were ever so slightly shot through with grey.

"To BuzzSwitch," Seth said.

Gwen saw that his smile was strained as he tried to wrap his mouth around the terrible name "BuzzSwitch," and this brought forth a pang of love for him.

"To the deal," said Tom. "The first of many."

Gwen found the wine bitter, but said nothing.

As expected, she was quickly abandoned to talk to Julia, while Tom and Seth sequestered themselves, bantering about work.

"So, Gwen," said Julia, delicately sawing her meat. "What makes you happy?"

Gwen tilted her head. "Pardon me?"

"Do you think that's a terrible question?" Julia leaned in, a tiny piece of steak on her fork held aloft in the air. "I'm trying it out. One of our executives said it's a good alternative to the ice-breaker: 'So, what do you do?' That question can be so loaded for people, you know, especially women who—"

She stopped then, filling the rest of the sentence with her bright smile, and raised the nub of steak to her mouth and popped it in.

"Women who don't have jobs. Stay-at-home moms, I think you mean," said Gwen. She almost admired Julia for trying to circumvent the question: "What do you do?" Gwen had experienced often how her answer—*I'm at home with the kids*—led to a sag in the conversation, a glance around the room for a more intoxicating partner.

Julia leaned back and raised her chin, declaring: "I think being a stay-at-home mom is a completely legitimate life choice. Your children are lucky to have you. Our society is far too work obsessed." Gwen recognized this posture, too: the standing ovation, mistaking the accidental circumstances of her life, an emotional decision made so many years ago, for virtue.

She wanted to get away from the subject. "What makes *you* happy?" Gwen asked.

Julia touched her mouth and laughed. "Oh, it does sound insufferable, doesn't it? I don't think I'll use it anymore." She dabbed her chin. "I'm in marketing, with a boutique firm," she said. "I might offer my services to the boys once they're up and running."

"Aren't they up and running?"

"Up, absolutely," said Julia. She pushed her plate away from her. "But running? Not quite yet."

Gwen picked up her water glass, her mouth suddenly dry. How much money had Seth put into the company, then, the up-yet-un-running company?

The fall chill had slipped in from behind the dark curtains and wrapped itself around Gwen. She thought about Maddie, at home babysitting Eli. In the old house, their three bedrooms were so close together that she could hear Maddie through the walls. But the new house was sturdier, and Gwen was losing her bearings. Last Friday night, she had suspected that Maddie's footsteps were drunk. This had happened before, of course. The Shadow Pines moms weren't naive. They discussed and reported to one another incidents of drinking and smoking weed, though the perpetrators were mostly other people's kids, out-of-control kids. Their own kids, they agreed, were normal, experimenting on special occasions, but nothing to worry about. Gwen didn't discuss her own fears about alcoholism in her daughter's DNA. Instead, she tried to assuage her anxiety by sending Maddie links to articles about the dangers of teen binge-drinking to the growing brain. But her tentative grasp on the situation was looser now, in the city. Gwen knew nothing of the places where her daughter was, or the people around her, just as she knew nothing of her husband's days, stirring at the great pot of money out there, hoping to skim some for himself. For them.

Julia steered the conversation back to the kids. Gwen ran through their achievements. And then she surprised herself by saying: "It's not really a choice."

"What isn't?" asked Julia, who looked expectant, curious.

"Not working. It just happens. It feels temporary, and then one day . . . it's all you can picture. I'd try to see myself in an office, with my kids far from me, and it was—grotesque. I mean—for me, not for you—" Gwen fumbled. Julia tilted her head, concentrating. Julia was trying, Gwen thought, and so she continued, saying more than she had said in years. More than what was asked. "I couldn't make it work. It's a failure of imagination, I guess, more than anything else. I couldn't see any other way."

Julia took a sip of wine. "I couldn't imagine not working," she said. "Is it terrible to say that when they go to preschool in the morning, with the nanny, I'm relieved?"

Gwen nodded faintly, but the confession made her heart race.

"It's boring, don't you think? All day, every day?" Then Julia did an impression of the twins whining. "*I don't want to get dressed, I don't want to eat that . . .*"

Gwen resisted the urge to say, "But you'll miss so much." She might have said that once, when the kids were young and their hands were in her hands, but now she wasn't so sure she even believed it. The kids' absence loomed, and then what? There were so many ways to be, and she, Gwen, was locked into just the one—mother—forever.

Julia mistook her silence for discomfort. "I'm sorry. That was rude. I think what you do—all day—I think it's amazing." And then, again, "It's a legitimate life choice."

They held each other's gaze for a moment, but the men turned and snatched them back. The conversation landed on the excellent new violent TV series that had replaced another excellent cancelled violent TV series. The men vibrated from their professional triumph. The wine ushered the four toward laughter and familiarity.

"So where do you cottage?" Julia asked.

Gwen had never heard the word "cottage" used as a verb.

"We don't have a cottage."

"We're on Georgian Bay. I was hoping we could commiserate about the water levels."

Tom said, "It's a nightmare." Seth made murmuring sounds of consolation, even though Gwen knew his childhood summers had passed by inside an air-conditioned apartment in downtown Montreal, and he had a terrible reaction to mosquitoes.

"Climate crisis," said Julia.

"Well, that's one theory," said Tom, and Gwen couldn't tell if he was joking.

"We could barely get the boat through this summer, it's become so shallow. It's entirely possible that next year, we simply won't be able to pass through the channel."

Gwen pictured Julia, Tom and a set of whining boy twins on the deck of a yacht, stuck between rocks, Julia waving her thin arms in the air, waiting for a helicopter rescue. "What will happen to your cottage then?" asked Gwen.

"What do you mean?"

"If no one can get to it. Will you just . . . abandon it?" The house would go to rot, overtaken by weeds. Wild animals would nestle in the feather quilts and eat the French milled hand soap.

Julia considered this, and said, "I suppose we'd have to fly in."

Seth picked up the cheque, which Gwen tried to glance at, unsuccessfully. Outside the restaurant, Tom kissed Gwen on both cheeks and slapped Seth on the back.

"You'll have to come to the cottage this fall," said Julia, turning to Gwen. "I really mean it. The leaves change and, oh, it's been lovely speaking to you. I spend my days around marketers and you're . . ." Gwen waited a little eagerly: What was she? Julia studied her. "You're unusual."

Gwen appreciated this. She felt unusual all the time.

Julia's little purse hung over her thin shoulder like tissue caught on a branch. Gwen leaned in and they kissed, too. Gwen could see at that range that Julia's muscular arms were covered in goosebumps.

As Seth waved a cab, Gwen tried to identify this unshakable cold. She had felt it before, she knew. *Oh*, she thought, as Seth pulled out his credit card and asked the driver if he'd take it: *I'm worried about money.*

MADDIE

Maddie discovered that at 3:30 p.m., after the last bell, a new kind of school rumbled to life. Kids clustered in the halls in sports uniforms, heading toward the gym, zigzagging across the fields with sticks and balls. What came before—the books, the teaching, the workday—had been just preamble. Something rabid ribboned through them all. You stayed to show who you were by signing up for stuff, preferably stuff that would help you get into a good university. Maddie knew she had to do this, too—teachers had told her; Clara and Sophie had told her; her mother had told her—but she wasn't sure which door to enter as she walked the halls, peeking in the classrooms at various clubs gathered around the Harkness tables. Colourful handwritten signs dangled from doorways with masking tape: LGBTQ ALLIANCE. ROBOTICS CLUB. FUTURE PROGRAMMERS. PERCUSSIONISTS UNITE!

A figure in a chain-mail mask, body locked into a skintight white body stocking, approached the Model UN sign. Maddie started before realizing what this was: a fencer. A voice came out from the mask, muttering to itself: "Wednesdays at three thirty, room 207." Maddie watched the fencer wandering off down the halls in little white shoes as delicate as slippers.

"Maddie!" cried Sophie, popping out of a doorway. "You're lost. You need an awesome social justice credit, right? Behold: the Centre for Community Values and Action."

Maddie beheld the Civics room, and Dr. Goldberg perched lightly on a stool, bent forward. A dozen or so kids looked up at him, rapt.

"Ms. Madeline Kaplan," he said. "Do you know where you are?"

Maddie paused. "A club?"

"A service club."

A girl piped in: "We tutor and do food drives."

A boy added: "We give back to the community."

Maddie looked at them. "What community?" she asked.

"Our own," said another girl. "Fifteen percent of the people who live in this neighbourhood live below the poverty line."

Sophie grabbed Maddie's hand, leading her to sit down. "It's actually fun. You can just sit in and decide later if you want to join," she said. "We're brainstorming."

"Mindsqualling," said the boy.

"Psychegusting," said the poverty-line girl, so proud of this phrase that she tapped it into her phone.

"Synonym nerds," said Sophie.

Maddie couldn't tell if this assessment was affectionate or not.

"All rights, *mes amis*," said Dr. Goldberg. "We need that one big project that will galvanize the student body this year."

"Bake sale?"

Sophie wrote BAKE SALE on the whiteboard.

"Food drive?"

"Tutoring? Our local public elementary school has a forty-five percent ESL rate."

A boy said, "It's so patronizing to assume that just because someone doesn't speak English as a first language, they need our help."

Sophie's hand hovered over the whiteboard, unsure whether to write.

"We do tend to get a bit . . . colonialist," murmured someone else.

The poverty-line girl pinkened and shot back, "Oh really? Are we so PC as to ignore the needs of newcomers right on our doorstep?"

"We don't know what they need," said Sophie. "But we could ask." She wrote TUTORING on the board.

Dr. Goldberg turned to Maddie. "Madeline, any thoughts?"

Maddie looked at him. "I'm still not—what exactly is this club?"

After a moment of silence came a tumble of words. "We're community activists."

"Philanthropists."

"We build bridges."

"We empower."

There was nothing else to do, Maddie knew, but nod and smile. She wondered what it was about suffering that made them all so alert. She had gone along, too, back at her old school, collecting toys for the children's hospital, and selling cupcakes for endangered species. But she wasn't moved from within. She was like a dancer who learned her moves from YouTube. She wondered if she would ever feel real sadness for the world, or if she would just keep nodding along, faking it like the rest of them, right into adulthood.

× × ×

Maddie retreated to the library. She had fallen behind on her work already. There were hundreds of pages to read, dozens of equations to solve. Around her, students stewed in the same panic, surrounded by textbooks, binders and laptops. Maddie began watching Mitch Hedberg videos on her new laptop, trying not to laugh out loud.

An email popped up in her inbox. *Subject: Hello*

Hi Maddie,
You don't know me but we should meet. Write me back.

It was sent to her school account, but if it was from another student, they were hiding behind a generic Gmail address. Probably spam. She considered deleting it, but something pulled at her, and she left it unanswered instead.

When she looked up, she saw Joshua at a faraway table. He

even sat lightly, his fingers turning the page of a textbook. Maddie removed her headphones and shut her computer, opening a book. When she glanced over again, Joshua was typing, eyes locked on a laptop. She looked down, flipping pages. Had he sent the email?

When she looked up again, Joshua was next to her.

"Want to go for a walk?" She grinned, pleased to hear in the timbre of his voice that he was nervous, too.

They walked together through the hall, Maddie side-glancing at his light, clipped stride. When they pushed open the door, a cooler fall light covered the street, the traffic lights caught in its haze.

Maddie had already mined social media for Joshua. He came up in the student directory, with a serious, deep-eyed gaze: *Joshua Andrada. Programmers Club. Born: Quezon City.* That was it. Maddie Wikipedia'd Quezon: Philippines; 7,104 islands prone to earthquakes and typhoons; coups; a place with the very cool name of the Chocolate Hills of Bohol. She had scanned Facebook, Instagram, Snapchat. No sign of him there. Joshua left almost no digital footprint, at least not under his own name.

"Where should we go?" Maddie asked.

"I have to work in an hour."

Back home, her friend Raj worked in his father's restaurant. Some kids worked at camp, and girls babysat. But Maddie didn't know anyone with a real job, the kind that involved bosses and uniforms.

"I'll walk with you." Her sudden burst of confidence surprised her: wherever he was going, she wanted to go.

They passed the football stadium of the university, weaving between tangles of construction. Above them, cranes swung in the wind, piling beams on top of fresh skyscrapers. Joshua offered up simple questions, and Maddie answered in the bland tones she gave her parents. It was another thing she didn't like about herself. *Why do you get so boring when you're actually excited?* she wondered. She was skipping all the interesting parts. He could not possibly be enjoying this tedious walk through this cement city with this pudding of a girl.

"Look," he said, and they stopped in front of a new building, a steel and glass checkerboard bowl. "Do you think it's ugly?" he asked.

Maddie knew the museum. Her family had driven there once to look at dinosaurs. It had seemed like such a long drive to reach it, and now here it was, accidentally.

"No," she said. "But it needs humans in it, or else it's just like . . . a spaceship that crashed here."

"I kind of like it," said Joshua. "My mother thinks it's the ugliest."

"Is she an architect?"

He laughed. "No, she's just judgmental."

They cut through the legislature, over green lawns and past a statue of a king on a horse clutching his helmet. Joshua would take his citizenship oath in that building, he said, hopefully next year. There had been a delay because of a problem with his birth certificate. His grandfather had already mailed him a tie from the Philippines for the ceremony. Maddie pictured Joshua singing the national anthem; he probably had a beautiful singing voice.

"Will you put your hand on a Bible?" she asked.

"You can bring one if you want," said Joshua.

"Could you swear on anything? Like an Archie comic?"

Joshua laughed. She was surprised how easily he moved between laughter and uncanny stillness.

Maddie felt her phone pulse through her backpack. It would be her mother. She ignored it.

They kept walking. Noodle restaurants and shops selling bongs. She had been here before. They were approaching the Lottery Offices. Maddie slowed in the sidewalk crowd, bodies braiding around her. Joshua moved ahead, and she was tempted to call out to him, to explain what had happened to her right here, on this sidewalk, just a few months ago. But she had told no one in the city. When you're a teenager, so much is shameful: the strange new hairs above your lip; how you sometimes can't look your mother in the eye for no real reason. The shame about the money was different. To mention it would be showing off, and there was nothing worse than a girl who got caught looking for attention, Maddie knew.

Up ahead, Joshua stopped, noticing her absence and looking around, anxiously, until he located her, standing in front of the Lottery Offices, considering what to say. He waved her forward, and she went, saying nothing.

× × ×

The air in the food court was gluey. Empty tables were scattered with garbage, and at the full ones, people lifted food from styrofoam boxes into their churning mouths.

"Do you like working there?" Maddie asked, and then burned pink at the question. *Duh*, she thought. At the sub shop where Joshua worked, Maddie saw a bent-backed older woman with plastic gloves and yellow smock, smearing something neon orange on a bun.

But Joshua said, "It's pretty good. Brainless. The boss is nice. He lets me make up shifts if school gets busy."

"Hairnet or no hairnet?"

"No hairnet," he said.

It was time for them to part, Maddie knew, but they stood across from each other, not moving.

"The worst part is the garbage. I always have to do it, because I'm basically the only guy and the women won't go. It's this long corridor, and it gets darker and darker, and more and more of the slime from the bags leaks as you go, so by the time you get to the room, you're basically wading through a garbage river. The bins are so full they don't close. There are rats, too. You hear them more than you see them."

"That's worse. I'd rather see them."

"You wouldn't believe how much garbage is in here. It's like its own planet."

"People are disgusting," said Maddie, looking around at the chewing faces.

"Customers take so much stuff they don't need. It's like: 'Free straws! I'll take three!'"

They shared a moment of repulsion.

Joshua sounded so much like a teenager that Maddie was surprised, but comforted, too. His otherworldly quality receded slightly, and now they were not so far apart.

7

GWEN: BEFORE

When Gwen stopped running that day after the attack in the donut shop, she found herself in the cold at the mouth of the College subway station. She looked down the stairs, and she could not think of a single place to go. Because she was afraid—of what she had seen, of what she had done and not done—she yearned to be comforted, and comfort was still Daniel. He was the thing to be feared, and he was the comfort from that thing. She recognized this split thinking as a form of madness, but still she went back to the professor's house. She told herself that if he showed up, they could make sense of what had happened together. At the same time, she dreaded his return.

The floors of the little house were sharp with needles and bottles and long, circular conversations generated by half-sleeping bodies. Gwen smoked pot and bartered for cigarettes and toothpaste, locking herself into a fog that would allow her to sleep. The little money she'd saved would run out soon. She hunkered down in a sleeping bag in the bedroom. No one bothered her. She was Daniel's still, marked.

She smoked mostly in the bathroom. The white tiles along the wall were smeared with filth, but Gwen liked it in there, alone. She would sit on the edge of the tub and smoke, peering out the small window at the garden covered in snow.

In the ransacked medicine cabinet, she saw an empty Tylenol bottle without a lid and a pregnancy test in an unopened box. How odd that this one item would survive. And then an electric realization coursed through her.

Minutes later, the stick turned blue, and a cross appeared. Gwen caught her breath, checking and rechecking the instructions, the road map.

Underneath the sink, she found a can of Comet, yellow gloves and a wizened sponge. Hazily, she sprinkled the white soap on the floors and flung it across the walls, and began scrubbing. And then she heard the front door open, and a woman's voice screaming: "What the hell is going on? What the hell?"

The professor had returned, at this of all moments. Was it the New Year already? Gwen pictured what the woman was discovering in her living room: mounds of bodies shaking beneath her soft throws. She was seeing pizza boxes and burn holes in the rug.

"Where the fuck is Kristina? Who are you people? I'm calling the police."

Gwen scrubbed faster. She kept cleaning, pushing through the panic. She had smoked so much pot! She pictured a baby with flippers and a heart on the outside of its chest; all the worst things would come to nest in her body. Payback.

The professor was rattling the bathroom doorknob.

"Who's in there?"

Gwen scrubbed.

Because there was no one to tell, she wouldn't have to explain why she didn't get an abortion. There was no moral high ground in the decision, which wasn't a decision. Of course every sound argument was against a baby. The church had no say; Gwen's father thought church was for suckers who wanted to give away their money. Gwen's God, as far as she had one, didn't want women to suffer, or children to be unloved. Gwen had sat in the free clinic waiting room while Laura had an abortion. Laura emerged through the door afterwards with an entirely new face—terror replaced with relief. Gwen had hugged her friend close.

But this was different. Something in Gwen had shifted when the cross on the stick grew darker. A blind over a window snapped up. Light poured in. This swerve in her circumstances was somehow inevitable, anchoring. A change—the most dramatic of all changes—was instantly, entirely welcome. She felt like Laura after the abortion: relieved, and unjudged.

"Who's in there?" The door shook.

If the baby is okay, I'll never smoke again, Gwen thought, scrubbing. *I'll never see Daniel again. I will call my mother.*

A baby would make everything different. She could fire every cell in her being and *do*.

She dropped the sponge. *This part is over.*

She opened the door to the screaming professor. Gwen brushed past her, grabbing her backpack. One by one, the squatters stumbled out of the house into the snow, clutching plastic bags, scattering in the streetlight. Gwen ran down the front walkway, the professor yelling behind her. Police sirens drew closer.

Gwen's shoes were wet, and the cold air clawed at her, as if she were wearing no clothes. Christmas lights twinkled on porches. She was so tired, her mind muddy. Her wet feet took her to Palmer's.

Through the stale beer and smoke, she found Gus in the back room, behind his desk, as if he'd been waiting for her.

"You looking for your boyfriend?"

Gwen didn't answer because she didn't know. Maybe she was making sure he wasn't there. Maybe she was saying goodbye.

"Fucker stole from me," said Gus. "Cops picked him up. He's no genius, that one. Had my seven thousand right in his pocket."

Daniel in a cell. Daniel in a locked box. She should have felt relieved, but it was all mixed up. If he got picked up because of Gus, and not the attack in the donut shop, then he wasn't actually caught. But—okay—neither was she.

And then a prick of a thought: *No one stays in jail forever.*

"What about you now?" said Gus, leaning back, smirking. He was ridiculous. "You gonna work for me?"

Outside, in the bar, there was a smash of glass and yelling, as if someone had dropped a box of bottles. Gus leapt to his feet.

"Goddammit!" He pushed past Gwen, swearing.

Alone in the tiny room, Gwen leaned forward, opened the desk, and without looking behind her, picked up Gus's black handgun. In the split second she held it, it was as banal in her hand as a stapler. Quickly she put the gun in her backpack and was pulling closed the zipper when Gus strode back through the door.

Years later, she would remember the moment that followed, and how she mumbled and got out of the room. In the hall, a man walked by with a guitar case. She nodded at him and kept moving, waving lightly at the bartender, eye on the door, waiting to be stopped. But no one stopped her. She walked right out onto the street.

Once, when she was a child, her father had driven Gwen and

her sister out to the river, lining up beer cans and giving each girl a turn with a shotgun. The first time, Gwen pulled the trigger and the sound made her cry out; the kick threw her shoulder backwards. But the next time, Gwen figured it out, and the bullet hit the can, knocking it to the ground. Nancy wandered around in her red cap, complaining of boredom. Gwen's father stood behind her, endlessly directing. As she improved, she grew more and more aware of how easy it would be to turn around and put a hole in her father's head. Maybe her father sensed it, because after she'd hit three cans in a row, he said, "Come on, now. Time to go." And he never took her shooting again.

Gwen had never owned much, but from apartment to apartment, from those first days with Maddie in student housing, all the way to Shadow Pines, and now, in their new house, she had kept Gus's gun. It stayed wrapped in a dishtowel, bound with elastic bands, at the bottom of the ratty pack that had been with her on the streets that summer. It had stayed there for years, witness to all her changes, untouched but nearby. And loaded.

× × ×

Only a nurse and a doctor were in the hospital room with Gwen for Maddie's quick, bullet birth.

"Can I use this phone?" Gwen asked, closing her eyes to place the call.

The next morning, her mother picked them up, and Gwen returned home to her childhood bedroom in Procter with Maddie in her arms. They lay side by side, Gwen looking up at the popcorn ceiling, plotting her next move.

For those first months, her mother changed diapers, but she still vanished to her bedroom in the afternoons. Nancy, Gwen's sister, was in her final year of high school, with her university acceptance letters stacked up on the kitchen table in order of preference. She would poke her head into Gwen's room and eye-roll at her sister with her half-shaved head, softening slightly to greet the baby kicking on the bed.

Gwen's father mostly kept his distance. He held the baby sometimes, and Gwen was surprised to hear him cooing. But the next hour he would revert to the snap and growl. He looked on every person in the house as a hindrance to order. "Why is there so much plastic crap everywhere?" "Who screwed up the remote control?"

With the bedroom door shut and the cordless phone in her lap, Gwen got ready to start over. Because she had been pregnant and poor, it turned out that she qualified for a special program at the university that accepted high school dropouts. She applied for every grant and every student loan available to single mothers. One morning, with Maddie tucked into a carrier on her chest, she took the bus to the city, paying with coins taken from her mother's wallet during one of her naps.

The grants Gwen earned provided just enough money to afford a furnished, one-bedroom apartment in student housing. She told her mother that she would be leaving while her father was at work, and her mother said sleepily: "Oh, Gwyneth. That's a very good idea. It's awfully crowded in the house, isn't it?"

The apartment was on an upper floor in a worn high-rise on the east side of campus. Maddie got a subsidized spot in day-care. At night, Gwen pushed Maddie's stroller home, looking up at the building she lived in with its rows of lit windows, comforted by the presence of inhabitants united by hard work and patchwork grants, loans and promises, charging toward the future. The elevator took forever to arrive, and in the crowd of waiting tenants were men speaking Russian, and women with regal, bright headdresses. The tenants were either indifferent or kind, stopping to admire Maddie as they waited for the elevator. One Brazilian student left a Fisher-Price schoolhouse outside Gwen's door, faintly smelling of lemon cleaner. Gwen brought her freshly baked bread, and back and forth they went when they could, delivering small gifts.

It turned out that in the city in the early 2000s, there was some benevolence extended to single mothers, as if to make up for earlier mistakes that left pregnant girls dropping fetuses in alleyways, and babies stashed in shoeboxes. Elaine from student services—a stylish divorcee with clipped grey hair—helped Gwen find a part-time job as a receptionist in a dental office near campus.

At the interview, the office manager said, conspiratorially, "I'm a single mom, too."

Gwen was puzzled. "How did you know?" She thought perhaps it was her look—black eyeliner; the rubber bracelets up her arm—but in fact, the woman had been alerted by Elaine. It seemed there was a single-mom underground railroad, and Gwen was lucky—so lucky—to find herself on it, hurtling along.

She took classes in linguistics, studying at night while Maddie slept. There was no particular reason to choose linguistics except that lots of women seemed to study linguistics, and a website listed possible jobs for linguists that included acting coach, airline customer service agent and speech pathologist. All of those seemed preferable to the last years of Gwen's life.

At student services, Elaine held her hand and said, "You're heroic." She invited her to a fundraising banquet where Gwen sat on stage surrounded by university governors and donors, applauded for the mere fact of still being alive, an alive mother of one. She was twenty years old.

But Gwen didn't feel heroic. In the library, with Maddie sleeping in her stroller next to her, she would check databases for reports of a robbery in a donut shop on College Street, or worse—a murder. But nothing ever came up.

She lay awake in the small apartment with its rumbling heating vents and considered her previous life. She could still remember hunger, its slam and monotony. Daniel was somewhere in the world. Only the walls of the apartment separated her and Maddie from that life, and she would not go back. At night, she felt her most fierce. She would slay them all, gut and burn the whole city before she and her daughter would be as forsaken as she had been.

She was twenty-one when Seth came into the dentist's office for a checkup and said, "Can you make sure I get the hygienist who doesn't hate people?" Gwen saw his warm eyes behind his glasses and held his gaze. She exhaled.

The courtship was fast and tucked around the edges of Gwen mothering Maddie. Seth came over when Maddie was asleep, and he and Gwen sat and talked quietly at the kitchen table, and Gwen played music for him on a donated boom box. He listened closely while she explained the story the music was telling. Gwen liked looking at him listening; she had never seen a face so entirely attentive to her.

She had been so serious for so long, but Seth could be silly. He drew faces on oranges for Maddie to find in the fruit bowl. He lightened long, arduous afternoons with a cranky toddler by lolling his tongue and pulling Gwen back from the edge of tears. He showed them both a trick with a stack of coins and a cup. He made the bed, washed the sippy cups. This meant less motion for Gwen on days when she had none left in her—no energy for one more task, one more gesture.

In bed, he was confident with his hands and questions, and looked her in the eyes and made sure she came. To Gwen, her own desire was a revelation: Sex wasn't ruined for her. Love wasn't ruined. There was hope.

They spent nights on the roof of the apartment building after Maddie went to sleep. Someone had put lawn chairs up there, to look down on the alleys and up at the lights in the taller buildings. Gwen would carry the baby monitor, and Seth the bottle of wine. They looked over the city and drank out of the mugs that came with the apartment. Seth asked about her, and she told him more than she had ever told anyone, even though it wasn't the whole story. It was enough so that she didn't feel duplicitous. It was enough so that she could be sure that when they were falling in love, they were two real people.

The dull fact of Seth's stability felt thrilling to Gwen. He had a job that he liked well enough. He had money but not money like the rich men who had walked by her, or worse, when she'd been on the street. He was certain of her, and unafraid of what she'd been through. She held on to him too hard, and left bruises on his back that he pointed out in the bathroom mirror with a laugh and concern. "Stay," she said, and he did.

On a rainy spring day, Seth and Gwen got married at City Hall, holding Maddie's hands. The very next week, Nancy called to tell Gwen that their mother had died. Her thirteen-year-old Toyota hatchback had been sideswiped on the highway by a semi. Nancy didn't know where she'd been headed. Remarkably, this had happened three days earlier.

"I thought someone should tell you," said Nancy brusquely, letting Gwen know it was an obligation she resented.

Gwen had been scrubbing a mixing bowl in the sink. If she turned, she could see Maddie sitting cross-legged in front of the TV in the living room, her bare toes wiggling. Gwen liked that she could see her from the kitchen; it was one reason she'd wanted to rent this little apartment in an Italian neighbourhood north of downtown.

At the age of sixty-three, her mother had died, and no one had told Gwen. It made the new configurations official: Gwen was the mother. The washed bowl was still spotted with batter, she noticed, and then her knees buckled for a quick second.

Maddie looked over. "Mama?"

Gwen pulled herself straight, smiled at her daughter and turned back to the mess.

When Gwen was pushing a stroller, she expected to see Daniel around every corner. She had looked it up: theft over $5,000 would get, at most, five years, or ten, but sometimes, a few months and a fine. She avoided Chinatown. Surely he wouldn't appear in this quiet part of the city where Gwen, Maddie and Seth lived. She tried to tell herself she was safe, and he was disappeared. Poof.

Gwen didn't say that she wanted to leave the city because she felt him around her, waiting. What she did say was true, too: she did not want to return to work, or finish school, or do anything but hold Maddie close and sing her songs. Financially, the place that allowed this was Shadow Pines. Gwen's salary at the dentist's office was barely more than the cost of a nanny. She called Elaine at the Women's Union to tell her, thank you for your help, but she was married now and would be officially dropping out of school. She didn't need the job at the dental office either.

The line was quiet, and then Elaine said, "I'm happy for you, of course. But . . . have you considered what it means to give up your studies at this late stage? The implications—your job? There are so many options—you're a thinking person . . ."

Gwen excused herself and hung up.

What were the implications? Well, Maddie wouldn't have to spend her days in an institution (Gwen started using the word "institution" instead of "daycare," to anyone who was listening, hoping to conjure exactly that picture: row upon row of snot-covered, screaming babies in beds of tattered sheets, neglected by hardened old women leaning indifferently along the perimeter of the wet-walled chamber, smoking). Instead, Maddie would have a mother and a backyard, and a picture window in the living room. If she stood on a chair, Maddie could see the top curve of the roller coaster at the amusement park across the freeway.

Then came Eli. Gwen experienced motherhood as she had never been permitted to the first time. Now, with the second baby, in the quiet of Shadow Pines, the days were soft and dream-filled. Eli was an easy baby, a series of naps and awakenings, with joyful, skin-to-skin feedings in between. Gwen slept too, deep and dark. She had slept with one eye open for years, and now she made up for lost time.

At 3 p.m. they walked to pick up Maddie at school, and their world expanded to three. Maddie clutched her papers (like a businessman, she always carried papers: finger paintings and art pieces of cardboard and papier mâché) and talked in staccato bursts about her crayons and the class rabbit. With Eli in the carrier across her chest, Gwen showed Maddie lavender, how to push it through her fingers and smell it on her skin. By spring, Eli was looking around, and reaching out at passersby.

Seth was the anchor, but he was also incidental, a guest star at night and on weekends. He worked long hours, so his invisibility was normal. Gwen reported Eli's milestones on the phone, each one reached exactly on schedule. Gwen was there to document.

In curlicue script, in a leather-covered notebook, she wrote: *Tuesday, Sept. 3: Eli says "Da" before "Ma" but smiles at me so it's okay! March: WALKING!!!!* There had been no such book for Maddie.

The kids never questioned why she didn't work. The Shadow Pines women, even those who had jobs, rarely commented on it. Once, her neighbour Eleanor, trudging slowly down the road from the GO Train station after a long day working on Bay Street downtown, briefcase dragging from a limp wrist, caught sight of Gwen and Eli in the yard. She stopped to make small talk, and as she departed, she said: "You're not missing anything, you know. I'm sure you think you are, but you're not." Eli had been little, up to Gwen's knees, and was running around the front yard in his underpants, howling like a wolf. Gwen murmured that everyone was different, and how wonderful difference was. But she knew, smugly, that Eleanor's two preteen daughters were latchkey kids, and they were waiting at home alone, probably playing violent video games. During those early days, Gwen was quietly righteous. She saw herself as a massive success, like a top-tier corporate lawyer, only her field was motherhood.

Even so, sometimes the intensity of her own self-guided transformation surprised her. In a window, she would catch a glimpse of a woman whose entire demeanour radiated motherhood—stretchy pants; smear of applesauce on a competent, determined jaw—and then start, realizing it was her. The dark girl in the mosh pit had been replaced, inch by inch, bone by bone, with this whirling, ferocious she-beast. That girl was missing, and unsearched for.

At night Gwen would put the kids down, and with the kitchen cleared of dinner dishes, she would make the rounds of the house, checking the arrangement of stuffies on pillows, testing doors and locks, noting Seth at his computer, back to her. If all the domestic labour was complete, and a tiny pocket had opened up in which she could reflect, she allowed herself to grieve a little for that girl. It was shameful to do so; she could never explain it to Seth, or anyone. It made no sense, to long for a terrible past. Did she miss being hit, strangled, followed? Yet she could, in fact, put aside the violence and yearn for her youth anyway. She missed desire. She missed noise. She missed chaos. Maybe she missed her own small, unoccupied body, without the wavy stretch marks on her belly. Her new body belonged to everyone, and was a thing to be sucked at and snotted on. It was also a body to be held, she reminded herself, returning to the warm shadows of her home.

But it had been a long time since she'd felt smug around working moms. Neither Gwen nor Seth had known exactly what would be sacrificed with this exchange of Gwen's adulthood for their children's endless childhood. It would be many, many years before they knew.

Gwen took Seth's name, and gave it to Maddie, too. Seth said: "Are you sure?" He was flattered. He didn't know that some women took the names of men as a form of disguise, masquerading as devotion. But Gwen told herself that she wasn't trying for Gatsby-like reinvention, waves against the current and all that. She thought of "Kaplan" as a place for all of them, a cave to hide in. Gwen felt safe inside its walls.

She didn't let herself think about the blanket she was dropping over her past, putting out the flames. It was for Maddie's sake, she decided. All of it for Maddie.

There was never a conversation about keeping Daniel a secret. Gwen had crouched down at the courthouse and said to Maddie, "This is your daddy." Maddie, barely three years old, looked at Seth, and Gwen did, too, nervously, as realization passed over his face. Maddie smiled her tiny-tooth smile, excited. It was true already, Gwen thought; he was her daddy.

Seth looked at Gwen and nodded, and as he leaned down to hug Maddie, Gwen felt the brick of her past slip off her, her spine uncurl. The decision to stick to this story would require a little work along the way, but she was up for it. She would skim details, and craft for Maddie—for all of them—a narrative of safety and love. It would become real because she said it often, and came to believe it. This was the covenant. It did not feel like a lie. She was ready.

8

MADDIE

Maddie avoided Clara and Sophie. She began to study with the same aggressiveness that she'd engaged two summers ago when she stopped eating for a week. Joshua found her in the library after school and they sat at the same table. She proofread his paper on Cormac McCarthy. He showed her a game engine he was developing in the computer lab. On the days he worked, she walked him to the mall after studying.

It was a routine that became formalized without discussion. But Maddie, alone in her bed at night, wondered what occupied Joshua the rest of the day, and night. She wondered about his bed, the food he ate. She wondered when they would be together doing nothing but being together, but she didn't know how to ask for that yet.

Then, one day after school, Joshua appeared at the table with his thumbs hooked into his backpack straps, elbows bent. "I have to take care of my sister," he said. "My mom has to work tonight." He didn't look at her, keeping his eyes on a display of books on Remembrance Day just over her shoulder. "Do you want to come?"

× × ×

The rain poured down in great grey sheets. On the subway, they left puddles in the aisle. The bus ride from the train took them north to a part of the city that Maddie didn't know, far up Bathurst. Strip malls and plain brick apartment buildings bracketed lanes of traffic. By the time they got off, the rain had become even heavier, and Joshua turned to Maddie and said, "Let's run." They ran past an empty parkette, then a strip mall with a bagel shop and a giant cartoon pig with the word LECHON on its belly. A mannequin wearing a hot pink nursing uniform had been pulled in from the rain and blocked a doorway to one store, her arms bent at the elbows, lifting something invisible. Maddie smelled bread baking.

She was a fast runner and felt like speeding up, beating the rain, so she did. She stopped at a crosswalk and Joshua caught up, panting. He looked at her and smiled.

"You're fast," he said.

"Yes," said Maddie, suppressing an instinct to deny it.

Joshua said, "Cool."

They came to a low-rise building with a jungle gym humped in the centre. From the outside, the apartments varied in tone and attention: one had flowers in small baskets lining the window and white lace curtains; the next had a car's bucket seat resting on a porch.

Joshua used a large key at the door. Maddie stayed behind him as they climbed three flights of stairs to the top floor.

At 3B, Joshua unlocked the door. The sound of television flew at them immediately. Maddie followed Joshua's lead, taking off her shoes and placing them on a clear rubber mat with other shoes, all their snouts facing the same direction. Joshua gestured her forward, into the living room. A girl sat on the floor, photocopied worksheets spread out in front of her on the glass coffee table.

"Turn it down," Joshua said, and then did it himself. "Alexis, this is Maddie. Maddie, Alexis."

Alexis looked at her suspiciously, then smiled.

"Nice to meet you," Maddie said. The TV was playing a talk show with a bunch of doctors in scrubs hectoring a crying woman.

"Mom's working late," said Joshua.

"I know," Alexis said.

"I'm cooking."

"Tacos?"

"Sure. You shouldn't do homework with the TV on."

"But this lady is getting her stomach stapled, and I have to see her get skinny!"

Joshua laughed affectionately. Maddie vowed to be nicer to Eli.

"Are you staying?" asked Alexis.

Joshua looked at Maddie expectantly. "Sure?" said Maddie. She texted her mother.

"Alex, we're going to study for an hour. Don't come in," Joshua said.

Alexis nodded, writing in her notebook while glancing at the screen.

In the kitchen, the linoleum counters curled at the edges, separating from the seams. They walked past a bedroom with a large bed covered in pink, shimmery fabric. Then Joshua opened the door to a small room with two twin beds and a desk. Alexis had covered her wall with posters of pop singers, class pictures, a drawing of a koala bear eating a flower. Both beds were taut as drums. Joshua's had a navy blue cover. On his wall was a map of the world.

Joshua sat on the bed, and Maddie didn't know if she should, too. It seemed strange to do it and strange not to, so she stood still in the middle of the room, deciding.

"I like your map," said Maddie.

Joshua gave her a sceptical look. "Want to sit?"

Maddie did, and she could feel the pulse of him, his shallow breath. She noticed a flush on his cheek. And then he leaned close and kissed her. The kiss was hard, and their mouths were misaligned; teeth snapped against each other. But when he pulled away, Maddie felt lightheaded, hungry. Joshua put his hand on her shoulder, then dropped it to her breast, where it stopped, frozen. Maddie moved closer.

Then came a knock at the door. "Joshua, can we eat? The show's over."

They pulled apart.

Maddie felt a surge of power: she was going to be in love, maybe, someday. Or maybe not. But either way, she was going to have sex, and for now—maybe this was almost better—in this weird new place, she had made a friend.

Oh God, she thought, cringing at herself: You are *lame*!

GWEN

Tom stood on the dock, grinning whitely.

"You made it!" he barked.

Gwen's limbs noodled as she made her way down the slope from the parking lot, her bags swinging.

On the bobbing dock, Gwen anticipated the quick descent of Tom's hand on Seth's back. Sure enough, down came the man-slap. Seth's body quaked along with the dock.

Tom and his grin hopped in and out of the boat lightly, grabbing the suitcase, tote bag and the large picnic basket that Gwen had packed. Seth imitated Tom's dexterity with slightly less assurance—bounce, bounce, stumble—while Gwen struggled awkwardly with the gunwale, her midsection flopping over the edge at one point like a towel on a rack. Tom caught her and placed her lightly on the banquette. Gwen stiffened at the touch of another man's hands on her torso.

At the wheel, Tom called behind him, "You guys don't need life jackets, do you?" He winked, and the boat's engine roared, drowning out any possible answer.

The bow tipped upwards and Gwen gripped the seat.

The boat accelerated through black water. Seth gave Gwen a smile from his seat. Another boat went by, and the driver beeped and waved, which Tom reciprocated.

"Water levels," Tom shouted back to them, slowing the boat through a narrow channel. Water lines were etched one atop another on the rocks, markers of the lake's past. How low could the watermarks go? Gwen wondered. How many years or months until the mucky bottom revealed itself?

The leaves were a whorl of yellow and red, as promised. The entire weekend was predicated on the fact that the leaves were changing, and this was worth observing. Seth had assured Gwen that also, it would be fun. But on the drive to the dock, she worried about Eli and Maddie. It would be their first time at home alone for the night. She had made Maddie walk next to her through the house with a man in a jumpsuit showing them how the new security system worked. He stopped at several windows and doors, shaking his head in disbelief at how much danger they were in, repeating the phrase, "Point of vulnerability."

It wasn't just business, Seth had pointed out, but a chance to get away, to maybe make some new friends to go along with the new life.

The boat lurched forward, and Gwen flew up, her hip slamming into the wall. Neither man noticed, gesturing toward a dock that moved closer, until the boat bumped up against it.

Tom swerved and cut the engine. "The abode," he said, hopping out, rope in hand.

Gwen was surprised: the house was new but quite modest, and attached to the dock.

Out of earshot of Tom, Gwen said to Seth, "It's smaller than I thought."

Seth laughed. "That's the boathouse."

Gwen looked again. A staircase jutted up the rock face, and on top of the cliff, a house peered down at them. It wasn't a cottage, a word from fairy tales and England, a place for gnomes and trapped children. It had sleek mass, grey polished stone, with decks on all sides. Either it had just been built or just been polished, because the windows gleamed beneath the birch trees. On one of the highest decks, a woman in gym clothes—a woman too solidly built and casually dressed to be Julia—stood flanked by two little boys. Gwen squinted: a nanny. Gwen waved at the children, but they didn't wave back. The nanny did.

× × ×

Gwen tried to look as comfortable on her lounger as Julia did on hers. It was turning cool, but Julia's pale legs, free of bumps and nicks, were in shorts. People used to call women's legs "pins," Gwen remembered, and thought it was appropriate: Julia's could pop a balloon.

Gwen wore linen pants and a floppy hat that she'd purchased for the weekend. She had not anticipated how much she would like to shop, turning out to possess a high tolerance for change rooms, and quietly enjoying the subservience of salespeople in expensive stores. She preferred earth-toned fabrics with wizard-y sleeves and wide ankle cuffs. All those years in yoga pants and sweatshirts had made her crave release. She felt, in this new unbinding wardrobe, like a strong wind could turn her into a kite, her clothes flapping crisply in the sky, and she might go anywhere.

"It's a beautiful place," said Gwen, for the fifth or sixth time, sipping her white wine.

The men had gone out in kayaks, and Julia had suggested that the women read on the dock. But Julia wasn't really reading; she was clicking away on a laptop, flipping between it and her phone. Gwen had her paperback, a nothing historical romance that she had picked up at the bookstore because it was on the table marked "Inspirational Bestsellers."

Gwen recalled with a wince the awkward presentation of the picnic basket upon arrival. In the kitchen, the nanny, Flor, had been tenderizing steaks with a tiny hammer—*thap, thap*—as Julia unpacked the items Gwen had brought, one after the other, gasping excessively at each. "Seth should have told you not to bring anything! Look at all the work you did!" Jam. *Gasp*. Baguette. *Gasp*. Cheese. *Gasp*.

"I just did some baking . . ." said Gwen, realizing that she had cemented her reputation as a housewife. She had brought homemade muffins and cake. Goldilocks's grandma's food.

"Oh my God!" said Julia, removing a plastic Tupperware dome.

Thap, thap, went Flor, who glanced over at the uninvited baked goods with a little hostility. Gwen didn't disagree: the cake looked ridiculous now, a hulk of white icing and fondant flowers. A birthday cake without a birthday.

"You're such a Martha Stewart!" said Julia. "I'm so embarrassed. I could never do anything like this."

"Anyone can bake. It's just chemistry."

Julia shook her head. "We had a cook where I grew up."

"Where was that?"

"British Virgin Islands, for a while," said Julia.

Of course. A plantation. Julia as a child, arms extended in a lacy white dress, spinning through fields of sugar cane.

On the dock, with her nurse protagonist lusting for a wounded soldier, Gwen asked Julia, "Where are the twins?" She was beginning to wonder if she'd actually seen them at all.

"Nap time," said Julia absently, frowning and pounding at the laptop. She looked up. "I'm being rude. I apologize. We have a little crisis. Work—it doesn't stop, really. I keep thinking it will but it doesn't. Not ever."

"Let me leave you to it then. I think I'll go for a walk."

"Is that terrible? Am I being an awful hostess?"

Gwen knew the answer she was supposed to give to these uptalking rhetorical questions that women asked. She remembered the ways of the Shadow Pines mothers, seeking affirmation when none was needed; performing insecurity when they were, in fact, fiercely in charge—fiery lead singers who required no backup at all. Gwen murmured that no, no, Julia was a great hostess.

"Oh, Gwen, you're so sweet," said Julia.

Gwen felt hungry to find the kids. She needed someone to watch over.

There seemed to be a path along the edge of the water, a rug of pine needles and moss. It *was* beautiful. Seth had been telling the truth. On foot, the landscape cancelled out the opulence of the house. Leaves rustled on the edge of falling. In the distance she could see Seth and Tom, bobbing in two tiny red kayaks.

An island across the water stood uninhabited. The shoreline was too craggy, too rocky. No one could build there, Tom had pointed out, but they'd bought it anyway, just to make sure no one tried to.

Gwen turned back to the house, feeling good. Seth had been right: a little break was important. A step away from things, to make sense of all that had happened in such a short time. She should stop resisting so much, stop being so outside of every-thing and appreciate her great good fortune and this beautiful place, the grace of an invitation. Look where she was! Crazy!

Halfway up the path, she saw a shape—a crouching figure. Gwen halted, swallowed, turned up the brim of her hat to see better: it was a kid, one of the twins presumably, shoeless, wear-ing only shorts, his naked upper body covered in dirt. He looked at Gwen and grinned, revealing soil-smudged teeth.

Unattended children set off Gwen's panic centre. Gwen thought of pinworms from the dirt in his mouth, and the deep lake where a body could sink. "Hello, are you Louis? Or Henry?"

Henry nodded. "Hen. Louis is my brother."

"Where's your—where's Flor?" Gwen asked, scanning the woods for anyone else, a real adult.

"Nap time," said Hen, licking his lips.

"I'm Gwen. I'm a friend of your parents'."

Henry wiped his face with the back of his hand, getting even dirtier, and looked at her neutrally.

"Maybe we should go up to the house and get you cleaned up. I don't think you're supposed to be out here by yourself."

Hen stood up. He held out to Gwen a plastic bucket of dirt, pocked with branches and leaves.

"I made a cake," he said. "Pretty yummy."

"It is. You know, I made a cake, too."

Henry's eyes lit up. "What kind?"

"Do you want to come see it?"

Henry nodded. He gave Gwen the bucket to carry, then stuck out a hand for her to take, as if they had known each other forever. Gwen had missed this, her hand folding over his gritty little one. She wanted to scoop up Hen's small body, to have him rest his arms around her neck. She hadn't carried one of her own kids in a few years, and wished she had commemorated the last time somehow, with a photo or a poem. No, she wanted an oil portrait, a Madonna and child, titled: *The last time I carried Maddie. The last time Eli sat on my shoulders.*

At the back door, Hen dropped Gwen's hand, split away and ran inside. Gwen followed, entering a gleaming white mudroom, with baskets of plastic beach toys and a row of coloured raincoats on hooks by the door. The scale of a small shower confused her: too small for any regular sized human. Henry stepped inside.

"It's for dogs," he said. "We aren't allowed to have a dog, though, so Louis and me use it for our feet."

He stood in the shower expectantly, and Gwen realized it was she who was supposed to clean his feet. So she unhooked the hose and knelt down, running the warm water over Henry's muddy legs, soaping up his toes, rinsing his muddy cheeks. He giggled.

They sat next to each other at the kitchen island, eating their cake in the silent house. Henry talked about the dog he imagined they would get (a rescue who needs a home, black because no one wants black dogs). Out on the lake, Gwen couldn't see the kayaks anymore.

Flor rushed in, bleary-eyed as if she'd just woken up.

"Where did you go?" she demanded.

"He was with me," said Gwen. "It's okay."

But it didn't look okay. Flor's face tightened, and she lashed out. "I only sleep for twenty minutes! He knows better!"

Henry, unaffected by this outburst, said, "Flor, would you like some cake?"

"Wow, Henry, you have excellent manners," said Gwen.

Flor looked at Gwen expectantly. These transactions were another addition to her life, Gwen thought. The built-in deference. The bitter-edged interactions where Gwen was perceived to have power over someone who was paid to make her life easier—*did* have power, she corrected herself. And with it, something like responsibility, a responsibility to be kind, if nothing else. Kindness was a sort of power, too, perhaps.

"Yes, please, Flor, have some cake," said Gwen.

Released from the need for consent, Flor resumed her slightly haughty tone and said, "I'm going outside to clean the mess." But she took a piece of cake with her onto the deck, placing it on a table, pointedly uneaten. Henry followed, babbling while Flor gathered toys.

A bird made a loud sound, and Gwen watched Flor stop for just a moment, looking up at the sky, hand above her eyes to block the sun. She said something to Henry, who stopped, too, imitating her gesture, hand on his forehead, gazing upwards.

× × ×

Tom tended the firepit on the beach. Gwen was on her third glass of wine, very good wine, she thought, noting that she had learned to tell the difference. Tom, beer in one hand, poker in the other, was proud of the cast-iron firepit, and Seth asked many questions about its construction. Men and gadgets, Gwen thought. The two had already discussed at length a machine that emitted sound waves to deter mosquitoes. Seth and Eli could spend hours playing video game basketball, as if the obligations of the day weren't calling. Last week, Gwen had come home from grocery shopping, and there was a brown box in the foyer. What was more exciting than a brown, unopened box, really? Gwen cut through the cardboard to reveal a small stainless steel, glass-fronted object, like a small refrigerator. It perplexed her. No grooves for wine; too small for food. When she called Seth, he told her, sheepishly, that it was a humidor.

Gwen didn't know what to make of this. "Do you smoke cigars now?"

"That's the next step," Seth had said.

Gwen thought of her own new toys: the soft wardrobe, and the Danish dining table that she'd bought. Even when they didn't have a lot of money, Seth wasn't chastising, or controlling. He was matter-of-fact before, and matter-of-fact now.

"Did you solve your work problem?" Gwen asked Julia, who was wrapped in a silky shawl, her bare feet tucked under her, as tightly bound as a French pastry.

"Oh, it doesn't stop. You put out one fire and then there's another one."

"Julia's always working," Tom said. "Gwen, you must like being at home." He and Seth were moving around the fire side by side, avoiding the smoke.

"I did, when they were younger," said Gwen.

"Well, I think it's important, a woman who's so committed to her family like that. My mom sure as hell wasn't. Julia doesn't make it home for dinner most nights."

Gwen assumed that the same could be said about Tom. She snuck a look at Julia, waiting for marital crossfire. But Julia looked relaxed, smiling.

"I'm making up for lost time professionally," Julia said, and then, to Gwen, "I lost a few years in my twenties."

"Julia had a lesbian party-girl moment," said Tom, almost proudly.

Julia rolled her eyes. "Bi, actually." She jutted her chin, that thin clavicle poking out from beneath the scarf.

Seth cleared his throat, drank from the beer bottle.

"Does—do you just stop being bisexual?" he asked.

"You get married, and you make a choice," said Julia.

Gwen wondered if Tom was threatened by Julia's sexuality, the sheer vastness of it. But Tom didn't seem threatened, not ever.

Julia had dropped out for a while, lived in Paris working as a model. But no matter how skinny she got, it didn't make her taller. While she was in Paris, she met a woman, a photographer from Morocco. "The sex was phenomenal," said Julia.

Gwen's spine straightened. She saw Seth drink quickly.

"Jesus, Julia . . ." said Tom, but he looked a little pleased.

"Well, it's true."

Gwen tried to imagine what current ran back and forth between them. Her own sexual experience was limited, curtailed by young motherhood. Seth had had a few girlfriends before her. Two of them were math students. One left for grad school, and he didn't want to move in with the other. Lukewarm relationships—until Gwen, he'd told her.

"What about you? What's the best sex you ever had?" Julia asked, looking right at Gwen. "You can't say your husband."

On the beach, the fire flickered. Seth sometimes rushed in to protect her when conversation got too close to her past. "Gwen's private," he'd say.

But tonight, lake pulsing gently, wine in hand, Gwen didn't feel private. "I haven't slept with many people," said Gwen. "I was . . . I left home young. I was on my own at seventeen."

"Intriguing!" Julia said. She smiled in Seth's direction.

"Where did you go?" asked Tom, dropping down in the chair next to Gwen.

Seth remained standing, clutching his beer. He looked different in the fire shadows, his face in and out of light, his hand hooked in the pocket of his jeans. He was handsome, Gwen thought. So was Tom, next to her, with his jaw tilted expectantly. And Julia—beautiful Julia. They were all so good-looking, she thought, her mind sprawling from the wine.

"I was homeless," said Gwen.

Tom tilted again. "Oh, wow," he said.

"Oh, wow" wasn't much, but Gwen preferred it, maybe, to "I'm sorry." With an apology, Gwen imagined a second part, unsaid and steeped in blame, *I'm sorry you're such a mess.*

Julia asked, "How did you . . . leave that situation?"

The true answer—"I got pregnant"—would have dragged the whole family into the light, revealing Maddie's background, launching questions about her birth father. The real story was too enormous for anyone to hold, and too many people depended on the version Gwen had written long ago. To tell the truth would be a betrayal.

"I went back to school. I just—I had to change my life," said Gwen. "It wasn't long after that I met Seth."

"Ah," said Julia, a little triumphantly. "Mystery solved. That's why your daughter is so old, and you're so young. Young mom."

Tom looked deeply at Gwen. "That must have been tough." He put a hand lightly on her arm and held it there.

Suddenly Seth said, "My best sex was with Gwen. Is, I should say."

"Awwww!" said Julia.

Tom removed his hand.

The wine thickened Gwen's thoughts. She heard the three of them drop the topic, moving on to real estate. Gwen leaned her head back. Strangely, it had felt good to speak just this little bit, this variation on the truth. It was more than she'd said in years, out loud or to herself, and it had wrung her out. She was exhausted. Now she would let the three of them talk, and she would listen. She looked up at the stars, feeling the chill.

9

GWEN

On a cool autumn Saturday, Gwen drove Eli to the suburbs for a hockey tournament. High on a hill, after another strip mall, Gwen caught a glimpse of a housing development in process, backhoes and tractors stilled for the weekend. From above, Gwen could see inside the tiny half-finished houses with their roofs missing, walls and staircases already inserted.

Eli was watching a movie on the screen suspended from the ceiling in the back seat. Suddenly he said, "Conrad's dad collects Porsches."

"No, he doesn't."

"Swear. He showed me pictures. There are only two at the house, but they have this place somewhere in the country where he stores them."

"What a strange hobby."

Gwen pulled into the parking lot. The arena contained six rinks. TV monitors told parents which dressing room to go to, as if they were passengers waiting for flights. Eli scuttled off with his huge bag on wheels.

Gwen wandered between the rinks with a styrofoam cup of herbal tea, scanning the players hidden beneath their helmets and swollen with gear, trying to find the Everwood team. She took a seat low in the stands, surrounded by parents in brightly coloured outdoor clothing and winter boots. Shearling poked out of the top of one woman's leather mittens. Everyone looked ready to hit the lifts at any moment.

But once the puck dropped, Gwen was confused. The cheering was backwards; yays should have been awwwws; nos should have been yeses. The woman next to her stamped her feet with joy when an Everwood boy missed the net. Gwen realized that she had sat in the wrong section of the stands. These parents wanted Eli and his teammates to fail.

Gwen moved to the correct side. She recognized a few faces from drop-off at Eli's new school, and gave a brief, stiff smile over the edge of her tea, generating some nods in return. There were more fathers at the game than she had ever seen in the row of idling SUVs that circled the school's driveway. They were stomping and clapping, necks whipping back and forth, brows twisted.

"On it, Dylan! Come on, Dylan!" Dylan's father was furious. "Ref! Offside, Ref! COME ON! Are you blind?" He smacked the Plexiglas divider. Dylan, who was number fourteen, Gwen deduced, skated in a circle, head down. Dylan's mother, presumably, sat silently checking her phone. At the stomping of her husband's feet, the bench she sat on bounced up and down ever so slightly.

A tall woman in a parka appeared in front of Gwen, blocking the game. "We met the other day. Elizabeth Morton, Conrad's mother." She smiled, extended a downy mitten. Gwen remembered Conrad chatting with Eli at pickup—another boy with short badger-cut hair, blazer and tie. Elizabeth Morton had gathered him up and shaken Gwen's hand firmly before rushing back to her car. People were friendly enough, but Gwen kept wondering if her sudden appearance at the school would be questioned. She expected to be called out any day. *So, how exactly are you affording this school? You couldn't afford it last year, could you?* But among the moneyed, no one discussed money. She had heard that somewhere.

"I wanted to ask if you might be interested in joining the Art Night Committee. I don't want to pressure you, of course."

"Oh—"

"The event is at Christmas, or as we call it now, 'the holiday season.'"

"Mmm."

"I'm not looking for anyone to reinvent the wheel, but I could use some administrative support."

In Shadow Pines, Art Night meant a trip to the Dollar Store for face paints and googly eyes for the craft stations. Gwen wondered if there might be a possibility of felting with the Everwood boys. Perhaps there was a sensitive one who might want to make some felt woodland animals.

Elizabeth Morton continued, "I've seen three boys pass through the school, and I know that when Art Night is unsuccessful, it's usually a result of poor planning."

"Conrad is your fourth?"

"Yes, four boys."

"What's that like?" asked Gwen.

Elizabeth sat down, reaching into a soft leather tote. She pulled out a tablet. "Exhausting. A lot of talk about erections. It didn't help that we sent them to a school called Everwood."

Gwen laughed. "I never thought of that."

Elizabeth hit a button and the tablet hummed. "I'm the kind of person who doesn't waste time," Elizabeth said, as if to underscore that the previous flicker of personality was an anomaly, nothing to get used to.

Gwen nodded. She herself probably radiated wasted time; why else would this woman point it out?

Elizabeth Morton informed Gwen that she had already written up a list of tasks. "I'll email them to you right now. Ready?"

Elizabeth sat very still, expectant. Gwen stared at her, and then realized she was meant to get out her phone. She dug around in her purse and heard a ping, but couldn't find it beneath the wadded Kleenex and her wallet, overstuffed with receipts and family photos. Finally, she fished it out. Elizabeth watched as Gwen struggled to log in.

"Can you see it yet? How about now? Did it come in? The subject is 'actionable items.'"

"Come on, Ref! You don't know offside! What are you— blind?" Dylan's dad pounded the Plexiglas. His wife bounced.

Gwen's phone was painfully slow, with a spidery crack on its face. She was tempted to shake it like an hourglass to make it go faster. She would buy a new phone tomorrow. This was another difference between the before and the money: the ability to meet every whim. Organizing upgrades was Gwen's new job. She spent days corralling service people to bring in new appliances, change the landscaping, install high fibre-optic cable. Now blinds could close and heat could be adjusted with the click of a button. There was now, Eli had pointed out excitedly, the possibility of opening the bedroom blinds from blocks away, via phone, revealing someone half-dressed.

Finally, the document popped up. Elizabeth's list of actionable items did not include felt foxes. Number one was the name of a well-known local architect who had designed the ceramics museum.

"Do you know Nobu?"

"No—I mean—I know his work," said Gwen.

"His son is in Year 8, so he's willing to contribute. He wanted to do something involving geocaching and a public art tour." She raised an eyebrow. "I talked him down. He's donated a painting. It's quite a prize, the largest item of the silent auction."

The father was cupping his hands over his mouth and shouting, "Dylan! Head in the game! Dylan!" His wife had left.

"I'd love to give you flowers," said Elizabeth.

"Oh!"

"Flower pickup."

"Right," Gwen said quickly.

"Could you take on pickup at the florist and delivery to the school by 5:30 p.m. at the latest?"

Gwen agreed enthusiastically. Once this task had been decided, the women sat side by side, facing the ice. They kept their eyes on the game, cheering lightly.

Finally, when the silence grew too thick, Elizabeth asked, "Where do you cottage?"

At that moment, Dylan scored. Gwen looked over at the dad. He had his hands jammed in his pockets and a small, grim smile on his face.

During the three-hour break before the next game, while Eli ate pizza with his team, Gwen drove to a mall. She didn't know this suburb, but she intuited where a mall would be. Nearby, probably east of the subdivision, north of the hockey complex.

She was correct. Oh, the consistency of new places, she thought, padding across the parking lot. All suburbs, like all happy families (or was it unhappy families?) were the same.

In the mall, between the teen mannequins with their midriffs showing, and the matronly mannequins clutching their little pocketbooks, Gwen could not find her tribe.

And then she saw the store. She had been in this chain once before, in the city, before the money. She had walked in, checked a price tag and walked out.

But now she went in and let the doors close behind her, locking her into a cool, dark room scented with jasmine. A happy song played in Spanish. Her eyes focused in the dark: tables of folded sweaters and shirts, everything a little beaded, a little "ethnic." A clerk spun by, gossamer in her blouse, tinkling from her silver jewellery—"LetmeknowifIcanhelpinanywayma'am"—and then vanished.

It was a grand act of theft, Gwen knew. A Navajo blanket pattern popped up on the asymmetrical front of a shirt. A sudden burst of beadwork around a neckline hinted at Africa—tour bus Africa, she suspected. Gwen fingered silks and wools, soft and seamless. She lingered at the perfumes, arranged on what looked like an old wooden box, found washed up on the shore. Many smelled vile and food flavoured—a new trend?—but one was lovely: clear blue, in a small glass bottle like the kind a lady of the manor would have on her dressing table, in an atomizer, with a tiny balloon to squeeze. It smelled like air and ocean, and bougainvillea. The price was more expensive than she would have spent on groceries in a month back in Shadow Pines.

Gwen thought of all the dinners she'd made, and the fevers she'd vanquished, the bums she'd wiped, the carefully folded laundry she'd placed in drawers. She thought of the long, slow hum of the Shadow Pines years. She hadn't resented it at all, or she'd never believed that she had. But now, in the store's half-light, she thought: *I deserve this.* She took out her credit card and bought two: one for her, one for Maddie.

In the blank air of the mall, swinging her tiny bag of perfume, Gwen stopped in front of a hair salon, its interior sparse and white. She regarded the white tulips in a clear glass cylinder, reflected in a mirrored wall. Then another reflection, and on and on and on. She walked inside.

"We've been waiting for you," said the man behind the desk, who was wearing mascara. "You're twenty minutes late."

Gwen was about to explain that she didn't actually have an appointment, but instead she said, "Remind me—how long did I book for?"

He sighed and read from the computer impatiently. "Three hours: cut and colour."

That would be enough time. A woman walked by, paused slightly at the salon entrance—Gwen felt a little anxious—and then continued on her way. Gwen exhaled.

"So Shelly can get started, then?" said the receptionist.

Shelly had short, platinum blonde hair. She pulled out Gwen's long greying locks and spread them in the air like bat wings.

"So what's the plan, my dear?"

"Something like yours," said Gwen.

The stylist made a happy clapping gesture without actually allowing her hands to touch. She put all of Gwen's hair in an elastic band first, and then sawed through the horsetail. Gwen felt nauseous, suddenly, to see the bodily waste that was her hair, severed and held in a stranger's hands. She had kept locks of the kids' hair from their first haircuts in a little cardboard jewellery box. Then as they got older, she accumulated enough hair to fill a shoebox, stealing from their hairbrushes. Finally Seth said, gently removing the box, "This is getting to be like something a serial killer has in his closet."

"Ta-dah!" Shelly waved the slab of grey in the air. "We can donate this."

"Who would want grey hair?"

"Oh, you'd be surprised. Everybody gets cancer."

As Shelly cut, and bleached, and coloured, and cut again, checking her watch as the hours ticked away, Gwen thought about the woman who had reneged on her appointment. The stranger had missed an opportunity for change, and Gwen had seized it. That woman would never know what had happened, but Gwen looked at herself in the mirror, boyish and foreign, white blonde, and sent a thought to this shadowy, forgetful person: thank you.

× × ×

When the tournament ended, and the boys had lost, Gwen made her way to Eli's dressing room. As soon as she pushed open the door, she knew she shouldn't have. A dank, damp synthetic sweat smell overtook her. There were no parents, only boys, sitting and standing in various states of undress. Their bodies were surprising in their pronounced differences. Some chests belonged to little boys, smooth and narrow with the nipples of toddlers. But there were a few who had broadened and coarsened, hair sprouting on legs and poking out from armpits.

The team was bereft from the loss, and therefore quiet and angry. One boy threw his glove across the room. He looked at her in a way that Eli's friends had never done until that moment.

He looked at her the way a man would look at a woman, appraising and dismissing in a single beat.

Ah, there was Eli—off in the corner, head down, gathering gear for his bag. He still had his hockey shirt on. He wouldn't get naked in front of other boys, she knew. He had put his sweatpants over his long johns. *I know everything about you*, she thought. *For now, I know everything.* He looked up and saw her in the doorway. His eyes widened and darted. She raised her hand to her new hair, and saw herself as he would see her: a woman in a costume.

She could feel in her son the tension between his instinctive love and the impossibility of expressing it here. She could feel him breathing fast, trying to blow away the social transgression of having your strange-looking mother in the locker room. All of this happened so quickly. She took it in, her son's pain, caused by her, and walked backwards out the door.

Gwen leaned on the snack bar, using her phone to avoid eye contact with the other parents. An unfamiliar email address popped up, but that wasn't surprising. Pleading emails had continued to trickle in from strangers, guessing at her Gmail address. But the subject line was odd: *Meet up.*

I'm hoping this is you, it began.

Gwen scanned, then went back and reread it, her chest constricting. *It's not quite right to say congratulations when it's only luck that you won and someone else didn't.*

It was happening, then. The walls had been breached. Gwen's eyes went in and out of focus, and then landed on the neon line: *I wouldn't want anyone to get hurt.*

She had left her kids alone for the weekend, all weekend

while she and Seth were drinking by the firepit with Tom and Julia. He could find where they lived. No one was impossible to find anymore, and they had been there, in that big, new house, alone for two nights.

Gwen rushed back into the change room. Eli was the last boy, zipping his bag. He was small again, nothing manly about him. He smiled when he saw her.

"Cool hair. You look like an avatar."

"We have to go," said Gwen. As Eli grappled with his gear, another email popped into Gwen's inbox. Heart racing, Gwen opened it. He had sent a postscript, an afterthought.

Gwen, I have a question about your daughter, the one the article said is seventeen. I looked at the calendar and figured it out. It's bold to keep a secret like that. Did you tell her about me?

Cold came over her. "Hurry up," said Gwen, grabbing Eli's bag.

"Hey—I can carry it . . ." he said, following.

I wanted to say also that I did love you.

MADDIE

Maddie stood outside the house with Joshua.

"We just moved here," she said. "It has a stupid heated driveway." She hadn't thought of it as stupid until precisely that moment. She unlocked the door, knowing that no one was home. Gwen had taken Eli to hockey, and Seth was always at work these days.

They took their shoes off and walked across the shiny wood floors.

"Do you want something to eat?" The kitchen had a second, smaller fridge just for drinks. Maddie looked inside. "My mom won't let us have pop, but we have juice and water."

"This is a really nice house," said Joshua plainly. He never said anything to her about money, or envy.

She passed him a can of mango juice and watched him take a sip, looking out the window at the empty pool.

"Let's go upstairs."

Her bedspread was perfectly made, courtesy of a housecleaner. A housecleaner! Her name was Lana, and she came every Friday. Maddie had overheard Gwen outlining her "expectations" (her teachers at the U loved this word, too) on Lana's first day. Gwen's expectations seemed pretty basic to Maddie—i.e., clean the house—but Gwen broke it down in agonizing detail: the baseboards; the inside of the refrigerator; the folded laundry in three baskets, one for each kid, one for Gwen and Seth. She asked Lana a bunch of questions about her life in Serbia, which Lana answered curtly. At one point, Gwen said, "Oh, we're exactly the same age." Sometimes Gwen was so oblivious.

Lana had lined up Maddie's three teddy bears so they looked like they were holding hands. Maddie threw her jacket over them. She didn't want to think about Lana, or the driveway, or the fact that she had borrowed this whole life, checked it out like something from the library she would soon be expected to return. She just wanted to think about Joshua's black hair, the softness of the sleeve of his T-shirt that she'd brushed accidentally on purpose with her hand.

Maddie and Joshua spread out their binders and laptops on the carpet and sat across from each other.

Joshua read, "A certain lake has an irregular shape. In order to estimate the area, the north–south distance across the lake is measured every fifty metres down an east–west line . . ."

It sounded like music because it was coming from him. Even as she wrote down her solution, her body was linking to him, cell by cell. But she didn't know what he was feeling, with his head down, working the numbers.

She'd heard that with certain guys, the girls had to do the hard labour. She was almost certain that if she made the first move, he would turn animal. She wanted that, too. Her breath sped up.

Maddie placed her laptop on the bed, and sat up on her knees. It was awkward; he was cross-legged, so she was taller now, looming above him. Joshua looked up. Maddie dropped down so her knees were to the side, close to him. Joshua tilted his head, raised his eyebrows in a question, and Maddie leaned in. But then he suddenly did something unexpected: he leaned down as she went forward, smashing the top of his head into her torso. It wasn't a sexy brush against her breasts. It was bony and brutal, a collision.

"Oh," said Joshua, rubbing his head.

Maddie was only fortified. *Now*, she thought, and she leaned in and kissed him. The kiss was deep and familiar, and she had been right: within moments, he was frantic, pulling her to the bed, as if it were his. She lay on her back. He hovered on one elbow, hand on the zipper of her jeans. He stopped, looked her in the eyes.

"Okay?"

"Yes," she answered, with a glinting memory of a sex ed class about "consent." He's a good student, she thought. She pulled his T-shirt over his head, and took in his smooth chest, the wiry muscles in his arms. His jeans came off quickly, but she couldn't get a full look, because he was at an angle, his face next to hers.

He used his hand first, slowly, until she was shuddering and slick, the familiar feeling she gave herself early in the morning, between the alarm and school, with the door locked.

"Wait . . ." he said, and went to his backpack.

Maddie saw his whole body now, the long, lean legs, the bones of his hips, the hard penis. The sight of his body made her defiant, determined.

He held up a condom and waved it around sheepishly. "I guess I'm, uh, an optimist."

"Have you . . .?" asked Maddie.

"Once. You?"

"No," said Maddie.

Joshua said, "It wasn't . . . important." Maddie smiled. It doesn't matter, she wanted to say. Everything that came before doesn't matter.

Joshua looked at Maddie with flashing eyes as he entered her—sharp, blunt. She had a biologist's distance on the moment, surprised at how fast he moved. It almost made her laugh. She knew she was supposed to close her eyes and make a lot of noise, but she didn't; her body didn't. Her body wanted to look at him, and he looked at her, too. He looked at her with such wonder— such appreciation!—and that collapsed into the animal part of her, the part that wanted to rip his bones from beneath his skin, consume all of him, and he was perfect, it was perfect.

But then there was a shot of pain—oh God, it hurt, and Maddie cried out. Joshua probably confused it for ecstasy, she thought. He slowed, but she didn't want that either, pulled him deeper. He stiffened and gasped for breath. This was "coming," she thought, and as all the energy left his body and he collapsed onto her, she thought, *I chose well.*

Afterwards, they lay in the shadow of evening, their clothes off, the quilt pulled up to their necks. All her confidence was gone, and Maddie was cast in a strange feeling, not of loss but panic: *That was just the first time. I'll be doing that forever now, and not always with him.*

She curled onto her side, facing away from him, and Joshua put a palm on her hip. She should try to steer the moment away from that future loss, to pull him closer, she thought. The lottery. She had been holding it in for so many months. Her parents had never said not to talk about it, but doing so seemed hideous. You can't be that tacky, or that mean to people. Saying out loud what you have is like asking a question: So, what do *you* have? Or maybe: What *don't* you have? But he was different. Safe, she thought, feeling his hand on her hip.

To the wall, Maddie said, "None of this is real."

She rolled onto her back, acutely aware that his hand had moved onto her stomach.

"What do you mean?"

"This house. My family. We won the lottery."

"Yeah, everyone who lives in this city should probably admit that."

"No—literally. We won ten million dollars last summer. That's why I'm suddenly at your school. Why we have this new house."

Joshua was quiet for a long moment. "What were you like before?"

Maddie considered this question. She had no real answer for him, so she pulled the quilt higher. She looked at the clock. Eli and Gwen would be back from hockey soon.

"I should be grateful, I know. It's just—there was nothing that really needed fixing. Everything just got bigger. Like Peter Parker in the lab or something—we got amplified."

He looked up at the ceiling. "You just made me realize something: I've never met anyone who won anything. You know those raffles at school? Or a door prize? I never really think I'll win, and I never do."

"Do you ever buy lottery tickets?"

"Nah. My mother thinks it's gambling. It's against God."

"And your father?"

"I don't know what he thinks about."

He turned to look at her, pushed her hair out of her eyes, which made Maddie smile; no one but her mom and dad had ever touched her hair like that before.

"Don't feel bad about having money. It's not yours anyway. We're all just pushed along by our parents."

Maddie nodded, deciding that was the nicest thing anyone had ever said to her.

Joshua looked thoughtful. "What's really crazy is that in this city, it's not even that much money. That party we were at? That house probably cost close to your ten million. Your friend Clara went on this cruise last year, and she was telling everyone how her family stayed in a special section of the boat where they had their own, like, butler, and they didn't have to interact with the other passengers."

Maddie wasn't sure what she was supposed to say. Maybe he was trying to comfort her, telling her that while the money set her apart from him, there were all these other people who were apart from her, trussed to even greater sums. Maybe you're supposed to feel good about that. She didn't really.

Downstairs, Maddie heard the front door open, followed by footsteps, and Eli calling, "Anybody hooooome?"

They rose quickly and stood in the dimming light, not looking at one another's bodies, covering them item by item. She put a finger to her lips, and they walked silently to the top of the stairs. Eli had turned on a TV, and sports sounds drifted up at them. Eli's presence meant Gwen was home, too, but Maddie didn't want to deal with her, so she went down first, scanned the hallway and then gave Joshua the signal to descend.

Maddie opened the front door, and he walked straight out of the house, his coat and bag over one arm, onto the porch. She pulled the door closed behind her softly and was watching him head down the walkway, when he turned back suddenly and returned to the stoop.

He stood in front of Maddie and said, "Thank you," and then blushed. "I mean—not thank you but . . ." He kissed her on the cheek.

A cheek kiss was a weird, grown-up move, so sexy that she trembled. They studied each other, smiling over what they had shared, and as he finally vanished out of sight, Maddie looked to the sky and suppressed a scream: *Holy fuck! THIS PERSON! I LOVE THE WORLD!*

When he was out of sight, she re-entered the house, slipping upstairs to her room. She shut the door and stood at the window, grinning madly.

Maddie could sense Gwen outside the door before she saw her. Her mother burst in.

"Blonde!" cried Maddie. With her new short hair, her mom was someone else, not younger, but someone from a fantasy book—someone in possession of a Pegasus or a sword. "I like it," said Maddie, but Gwen was wild-eyed; the drapey sleeves of what Maddie secretly called her mom's "pillowcase wardrobe" flopped at her sides.

"Was someone here?" Gwen asked.

"No," said Maddie quickly.

"You have to keep the door locked."

"We have the security system—"

"I'm not kidding. There are break-ins in the neighbourhood. You're not used to the city—"

"Points of vulnerability. I heard the guy."

Maddie didn't want her mother to ruin this. She didn't want to tell her or anybody what had just happened, minutes ago (minutes!). Surely her mother would sense it, smell it. She was scanning Maddie so intensely that Maddie wrapped her arms around her body.

"Can I do my homework now?"

Gwen checked the windows, and then left Maddie standing in the room. Maddie unwrapped her arms, putting her mother's panic out of her mind. She danced across the room, goofily, and immediately the good feeling returned and settled all around her.

GWEN

After the kids had said goodnight, Gwen sat in bed with her laptop, reading and rereading the email. Finally, she typed: *Where are you? What do you want?* Then she erased it. Her phone rang. She seized it, but it was just Seth.

He talked and talked, oblivious to her simmering alarm. He told her that he loved LA. He loved that in LA, it didn't feel like fall, and the sky was a sheet of baby-blanket blue. Tom drove the rental car they were using, which meant Seth got to look at the other cars out the window; so many cars—fast, gleaming cars with Voodoo engines. Gwen had never been to LA.

She managed to speak, "Did you get any investors?"

Seth was less exuberant then. "We'll see. Tom's positive. We had a few guys tell us there's 'location risk.'"

"What's that mean?"

"We're not in the right city."

Gwen's unease deepened, even as Seth talked on, describing meetings with barely thirty-year-old guys who bought companies and sold companies and invested in new companies and built and tore down and started up over and over. He hadn't been dressed right, he realized, and went shopping with Tom, replacing his jacket with a garment like a hoodie without a hood, but not a sweatshirt. As he pinged, exhilarated, through his stories, Gwen decided that telling Seth about the letter from Daniel at that moment seemed impossible, like sending a message between planets. There was no common tongue. But she was bursting, too, so she finally interrupted him:

"Seth—I don't think we should have left the kids alone the other weekend."

"Why not?"

"It's just—it's not safe here. We don't even know our neighbours."

"We should have people over. When I get back, we'll invite some people—"

"No one lives here. Half the houses on the block aren't even occupied."

"Offshore money."

"We don't know who's actually coming and going—and these crazy lottery people—they could find us—"

"Oh, come on, Gwen."

Behind him, Gwen could hear traffic. She wished it were the ocean.

"Where are you?"

"We have another meeting. I'm in a parking lot. In fact, I should get going." She said nothing. "Gwen, please don't worry."

"I'm not crazy." It was a sentence women said just before being institutionalized or abandoned.

"I didn't say you were. I get it. It's a new place. It'll take time. It's normal to be anxious. But we can't lock up the kids." He spoke as if they had had this conversation many times.

"Maybe we should," said Gwen.

"Don't scare them, okay? Don't scare yourself."

After hanging up, Gwen prowled, checking the rooms, testing the battery on Eli's sleepwalking mat. She turned on the lights by the pool and looked out from the French doors off the kitchen. She would need to call someone to get the pool drained. A row of juniper trees hunched below the tall fence. She turned off the lights.

Upstairs, at the threshold of Maddie's room, Gwen looked at her daughter lying in bed, and thought about her snark at the door. Maddie didn't know bad things could happen, not really. Gwen climbed in bed with her, but far away, not touching, because if they touched, Maddie would surely push her away.

Being near Maddie calmed Gwen, and she fell asleep, waking sharply in the pitch dark. Outside, she heard something—a bang, and then the sound of objects falling. Gwen went to the window, heart racing, but it was hard to see anything in the dark. Shapes, black and hulking, vertical and horizontal. Just trees, she told herself. Just trees.

WINTER

10

MADDIE

The front door of the building was propped open by a brick, so Maddie walked right to Joshua's apartment and rang the bell, as they'd planned the night before. Shuffling sounds and a wet, loose cough came from behind the door. Maddie stood back as steps closed in.

The door opened, and Joshua's mother stood before her wrapped in a blanket, smiling, her eyes watering. "Please, come in."

Maddie hesitated.

"I'm Madeline. I came over to study . . . with Joshua—"

"Yes, yes. Please, I will explain. Joshua has gone. He couldn't find his phone. Boys! He had to hurry so he could not call. He told me you would come. I will explain." She coughed and moved to the side of the hall, gesturing for Maddie to enter.

Classical music played in a faraway room. "Come, come," said Joshua's mother, pulling Maddie by the arm, leading her to the couch.

Maddie sat on the very edge of the cushions.

"Tea?" asked Joshua's mother.

Did she have a name? Could Maddie use it? She decided on Mrs. Andrada in her head, and nothing out loud. Maddie wouldn't have minded tea with Mrs. Andrada—maybe she would learn more about Joshua—but she declined, because it seemed more polite to do so, and because she had never had tea before.

Instead of sitting across from her, Mrs. Andrada sat down next to her, smiling, still clutching the blanket around her. She reached for a Kleenex and blew her nose hard, but she was still smiling.

"I'm sorry. Rude," she said, tucking the Kleenex in her sleeve.

"It's okay."

"I'm sick. I should not sit too close." But she was sitting extremely close. "So Joshua has gone to my boss's house. He is me today."

"Oh," said Maddie.

"I cannot work because I am sick. I don't want to make the baby sick. But you can go, too. The baby won't mind. My boss is a very good woman. And when the baby is sleeping, you can study, just like you do here."

She stood up, so Maddie did, too.

"Sit, sit. I will get paper." She patted Maddie on the shoulder and smiled at her. Maddie sat down.

"You work as hard as Joshua?" she asked, moving across the room slowly, swaddled in her blanket, feet snouting out of the bottom edge. Maddie looked around, stopping at a photo of Joshua as a young child, against a backdrop of a forest. Crooked bangs and grinning.

"I try. He's a really good student," said Maddie.

"I know!" Mrs. Andrada exclaimed, laughing. "He works all the time. Too hard, I think. I worry. I tell him: You are just a child! Have fun! Go with the pretty girl!"

Maddie felt herself redden.

Joshua's mother wrote an address on a piece of paper. "But I am proud, of course. I want success for him. He must be successful. I always say: my children are my only property."

Maddie struggled to make sense of this statement, its coldness next to Mrs. Andrada's warm smile.

"Alexis was born here, at St. Michael's Hospital. Did you know?"

Maddie shook her head.

"I went home to get Joshua, in Quezon, and I had one night, just one, with Joshua's father." Maddie nodded. "Poof! Baby." She giggled and kept smiling.

Heat spread across Maddie's cheeks. A warning had been issued.

Mrs. Andrada rubbed her nose with the handkerchief. "You understand. Everything I do is for my children. My children will finish school, go on to university. I did two years of university. I was a track star. Very fit. I was almost in the Olympics. One hundred metres." She put the handkerchief back in her pocket. "Alexis is a citizen just because she was born here. Not the same for Joshua and me. We're visitors." She laughed again.

Maddie found Mrs. Andrada's laughter disorienting, like looking at a face where the eyes go in two different directions.

"But you're citizens."

"Permanent residents."

"But you will be citizens."

"Yes, yes. But it's very slow. One letter from the government was never delivered. I was missing one document—we had to start over twice. Whole process again. Two extra years. Still no papers." She blew her nose.

Maddie wondered if it was possible that Joshua really was just a tourist, after thirteen years in the country. It made no sense: she and Joshua were the same.

"Your parents are proud of you, too," said Mrs. Andrada.

Was it a question or a statement?

"I think so," Maddie said.

Maddie wanted to leave. She wanted to stand up from the slippery couch and flee the strange smell (squash, was it?) blowing in lightly from the kitchen, and the photo of Joshua's stern, faraway father who looked like he might punch his way out of the frame.

"Here," said Joshua's mother. She handed Maddie the piece of paper and smiled. "You warm enough?" she asked, reaching out and touching Maddie's jacket.

"Thank you," said Maddie, putting the address in her coat pocket. She stood to leave. "I'm warm enough, thank you. It was very nice to meet you."

Her fingernails on Maddie's arm were short and clean. Maddie had heard that you could tell everything you needed to know about a person from her fingernails. She looked hard at Mrs. Andrada's hands, but she had absolutely no idea what that everything was.

× × ×

Maddie almost laughed when she saw the house. She had thought that the house where she'd been to the party was big, but this one eclipsed it. The house was a giant cube, with smaller cubes on the top and at the sides, all blonde wood and glass. If the house dropped from the sky, bottomless, it would swallow three of Maddie's new house.

When Joshua opened the door, Maddie said, "Did you shrink?"

He gestured upwards. "It's the ceilings."

Maddie padded across the floor in her socks. She stopped in the living room, in front of floor-to-ceiling bookshelves, spines arranged by colour. The back wall of the house was glass, over-looking a ravine, a tangle of vines and shrubbery. In this huge room, the cube felt precarious, jutting out over the forest floor like a branch that might snap and tumble.

"Look," said Joshua, and he leaned into the glass, pressing his head against it, his arms wide, as if he were flying.

Maddie did the same and could feel the ravine pulling her down into its thorns.

"Whoa," said Maddie, standing up, dizzy. They looked at each other, and Maddie was overcome, fevered: Could they have sex on one of the long grey couches? Could they run up the wide, shining staircase to a bedroom? Everyone talks about your first time, thought Maddie, but surely it was the second time that mattered, the time without the airplane going through the sky trailing its banner announcing: HEY, WE'RE HAVING SEX! This time, it would be only the feeling, that quick feeling that she had tasted so briefly last time, of sinking and being gone.

Joshua looked at her, and Maddie leaned in, mouth open, her arms falling around his shoulders. He pulled her tight against him, crushing her against the glass. The mossy tree outside swayed. Then, somewhere in the depths of the house, a baby began to cry. They pulled apart.

"I should take him to the park," said Joshua, backing away, flushed.

Maddie touched her bruised mouth, nodding.

Getting Carter the baby ready involved changing his diaper first, which Maddie watched Joshua do from a distance.

Carter's bedroom featured a giant black-and-white photo of

him when he was smaller, his fists curled and eyes closed. It took up most of the wall opposite his crib.

Carter could walk, it turned out, and he toddled along to the top of the stairs, muttering, "Out?"

"He knows it's park time," said Joshua, moving him away from a possible fall.

The stroller was perplexing: a long stick on wheels with an egg-shaped seat and a robotic hood.

"How does this . . . What?" Maddie pushed buttons, watching the hood move slowly back and forth. A word with an umlaut ran along the side of it. While Joshua examined the stroller, Maddie followed the baby as he staggered across the foyer, pointing at things and looking back at her.

"Chair," he said, pointing.

"That's right," said Maddie. He got to the wall of books and pulled one out.

"Boo," he said, flinging it to the floor.

"Don't throw," said Maddie. She tried to put it back.

Carter didn't like that. "No!" He shook his head, then pulled another book. "Boo," he said. This one was heavy; he tried to heave it, then dropped to his bum. Now he was eye level to the books with black spines, and he began pulling them, grunting and straining. Giant art and design books fell, one by one.

Maddie gathered each discarded book and made a pile. She felt Joshua looking at her, measuring, assessing her skill with this baby. Maddie didn't like it. She didn't want to seem like a good mother to anyone.

"Carter is very advanced. He's already reading," said Maddie.

Joshua scooped up the baby, who screamed and kicked. "Outside, we're going outside." Carter relaxed as Joshua strapped him into the egg-cup part of the stroller.

They took up the whole sidewalk as they walked, but there were no other pedestrians, just the occasional gently humming luxury vehicle. Maddie thought: *We could be a young couple, a teen pregnancy cautionary tale.* And then: *We are not that much younger than my mom was when she had me.*

The wind whipped through the park, surrounding children and nannies. The nannies hovered around the picnic table, some with strollers and sleeping babies, others whose charges were off in the sandbox, or chasing each other around the perimeter of the park. The nannies were everything but white, Maddie noted, and most were Filipina.

Maddie followed Joshua toward the table, and the women smiled. One called out, "Hello! How is your mama?"

A small woman in an oversized pink ski jacket stood rigid at the side of the table, unsmiling. She examined Maddie from head to toe, then looked in at the baby in his stroller.

"He needs to walk," she declared, and Carter laughed and kicked.

Joshua unstrapped him and put him on the ground, where he paused and then accelerated toward the other kids. He picked up a truck and flung it across the sandbox. A nanny rose from a bench to cuddle a crying child.

The woman in the pink jacket spoke to Joshua in Tagalog, and Joshua spoke back. It was strange to hear his voice but not understand him; for all she knew, he was someone else entirely in that language.

The woman was gesticulating, and she handed Joshua a piece of paper. He translated, reading it back to her. Her face darkened. She nodded. Maddie saw tears in her eyes, and then she turned away, to be comforted by another woman.

Joshua moved away from her, and introduced Maddie to the women around the table.

"Nice to meet you," Maddie said several times, and she was greeted with wide smiles.

But when they turned and spoke to each other in their own language, the smiles were different, or gone entirely. Maddie supposed it made sense; they were away from the houses where they worked for only a little while, and they probably had a lot to say to each other in the time that they were free.

It soon got too cold to stay, and Joshua strapped Carter into his stroller. He put a hat on him, too, and a blue pom-pom bounced on his head.

"Who was that woman who was so upset?" asked Maddie, as they began to walk.

"Susan. She's been waiting a long time," said Joshua.

"For what?"

"To bring her kids over."

"They don't want to come?"

Joshua exhaled. "It used to take two years of working full-time, and then you could bring over your family. But they're changing the law." He sounded impatient, as if he shouldn't have to explain. "Too many came, and now it takes years. Backlog."

Tentatively, Maddie asked, "She has kids?"

"Three kids. She hasn't seen them in six years."

Maddie looked behind her, as the park retreated. The nannies were still talking and laughing. One was checking her phone, indifferent to the small hands on her pant leg. And there was Susan, crouched and hugging a crying toddler. She held the child tight, kissing her little wool cap, making it all better.

GWEN

Gwen parked in a small lot a fair distance from the park. Maddie would not be able to see her, in all likelihood, the minivan's licence plate obscured by a low wall of decorative rocks. Tracking was easier with the new phones she'd bought for the kids.

But she had been good; she hadn't tracked Maddie since that first day of school, and hadn't checked in on Eli at all, even though the phone meant she could always see where he was. But she had never followed him as often. Eli didn't need it. He was of the world and permanent in a way that Maddie had never seemed. Hours after Gwen gave birth to Maddie in the hospital, the social worker came in and peered down at Gwen in the hospital bed, Maddie on her breast. The woman saw Gwen's black streaked hair and arm of rubber bracelets caked with afterbirth, and asked, "Might we discuss adoption?"

Now, once again, Maddie was under threat. Gwen was a mother making sure her daughter was safe, that was all.

She scanned the park. How much did Daniel know? And what if he did find her? She didn't know what he was capable of, but when it came to her kids, not knowing was unacceptable to Gwen.

Gwen watched Maddie pushing a stroller. A boy appeared. He was Asian, tall and slight in tidy jeans unlike the baggy sweatpants most boys wore. Nothing about him struck Gwen as cool. His floppy hair was the sole teenage gesture, the kind of hair that could make a girl swoony. The boy went off to talk to one of the nannies. So many nannies! They were clustered, their chatter drifting back to Gwen. She could see each nanny's eyes darting to the kids in her charge, each woman connected to one or two toddlers. Every few minutes, one of the women, mid-sentence, would rush over and pull up a hat, remove a sand shovel, offer a kiss. Experts, Gwen thought admiringly. Expert mothers.

In the back of the van, the vases of flowers sat covered in cellophane, wilting.

Maddie hovered near the baby she had removed from the stroller. It was walking in circles, pointing and talking. One day, perhaps Maddie would be a mother. The idea of it almost made Gwen laugh. *Don't do it!* she wanted to call out. Or at least: *Wait. Just wait.* A child is born, and funeral bells ring. You make a little life, and you make a little death, too. From the moment they're born, they're leaving, and it's unbearable.

Gwen knew she shouldn't think like this. She should bend toward the light, to the dailiness of motherhood, where the joy was. She made a list: cupcakes, glue sticks, beach vacations, teenagers in the basement in Shadow Pines dancing to hip hop and Gwen and Seth at the top of the stairs, grinning and recording on their phones—the light, the light. Would she really want Maddie to miss all that? Would she advise her own daughter away from motherhood? No, no, childlessness seemed unbearable, too. (Still she wondered about a life without children, sometimes with envy. Solitary and strong. Or maybe just limbless; a helium-filled human, bouncing through her days . . .) Why, Gwen wondered, couldn't she picture the in-between, where one was a mother, but also unbroken, unsacrificed?

The boy put his hand lightly on Maddie's back. A ripple of recognition ran through Gwen. So it really was romance, then. She was excited for her daughter, but afraid, too. The boy's hand dropped. Gwen could see Maddie turn to him and Gwen was embarrassed, suddenly, to be intruding, so joyful was the look on Maddie's face. It was time to leave.

She had time for one more stop before picking up Eli at hockey and getting the flowers to Everwood, didn't she?

×××

Outside the mission in Moss Park, a line of men was forming for dinner. Men appeared from around corners and out of doorways, emerging from downtown crowds that kept moving past the church. Men gathered, and more men joined the line. The door at the side of the church—SUPPER 5 p.m.—stayed closed, and the line got longer.

Gwen walked along the sidewalk directly across the street, trying to be inconspicuous as she scanned their faces. Beards. Eyes lowered. Hoodies. Baseball hats and toques. Only a few spoke to each other, loudly jostling. Others bent and shuffled, separate.

Gwen didn't know if she would recognize Daniel if she saw him. She had no photographs. No one took photographs before smartphones. He was something locked in her head from back then, an unreliable police sketch.

More hoodies. She was looking for a young man with long hair, but Daniel would be old, maybe bald. Men didn't wear their hair long anymore. These men all seemed old and grey, even the young men.

One looked up: black eyes beneath the hoodie. From all the way across the street, he caught her eye and froze her in place. They shared a glance, then Gwen looked away.

She felt caught out. A tourist. A white lady who paid twenty bucks to park her minivan behind a chain-link fence.

She would not find him this way.

Gwen walked back to her minivan, where a woman moved the chain-link gate and gave her a nod. Her phone lay on the front seat, chirping and vibrating like a panicked rodent. Gwen wrestled its jumping form, looked down at the numbers: Eli, Eli, Eli. She had forgotten Eli.

"Shit, shit, shit," said Gwen.

She swerved onto the road, but it was after five, and the city was gnarled with traffic. At a red light, she texted Eli, but there was no answer. She attempted to call Seth, looking up from her phone to the street, trying not to kill or get killed. But Seth wasn't picking up. Gwen pushed through the sludge of rush hour, slamming her hand on the wheel at every red light.

Gwen was an hour late when she finally arrived at the arena. A few streetlamps spiked the parking lot with light. There were no families left; she had missed the post-game milling.

Right away, Gwen could see Eli by the doors, sitting on his big hockey bag at the curb, stick upright like a shepherd's staff. He had a toque pulled down low over his forehead and somehow this hat catapulted him right out of childhood. He could be just a short man waiting for a friend, thought Gwen as she pulled up in front of him, pressing the button to open the sliding doors of the minivan.

In the rear-view mirror, Eli heaved the bag inside the vehicle and slammed the door. He climbed in the back, removing his hat and fixing his gaze out the window, sliding his body to the edge of the seat, loudly silent.

"I'm so sorry, honey," said Gwen.

Eli didn't answer.

"Do you want to sit up front?" she said, and then backpedalled: "I got stuck. But there's still time. You have your uniform with you, right? You can change at school. We'll go straight to Art Night." Silence. "Where's your phone? You didn't answer."

Still silence. Gwen remembered parenting books and articles in magazines that all advised not to push. *Let them come to you,* experts said. But she'd never been able to do it. She was forever charging at her children, storming their rooms, their homework, their Instagram accounts. She had been entirely and absolutely present for seventeen years. Now she had missed a pickup—a single pickup—and there was her son, sullen in the back seat, hating her. Hating her for trying to protect him, to protect all of them from—from—someone. Something.

She had a new thought, one that she'd never had before about Eli: *Fuck off.*

"You don't have to be rude," Gwen snapped. "Everyone makes mistakes."

Eli locked into her in the rear-view mirror, and his eyes were filled with tears.

"Eli," Gwen said, immediately ashamed. They were stopped at a red light, and she turned her head back to him. "Sweetie . . ."

"I thought you died," he said. Tears rolled down his cheeks. "I thought, no one knows I'm here."

"I'm so sorry," said Gwen, and she was crying, too, because he was still a child, and the great unrest that was roiling in her, faster and faster day by day, was instantly stilled by his tears. She reached for his hand, but a car horn beeped, and she had to move along.

✕ ✕ ✕

Fairy lights arced from the high vaulted ceilings in the halls of Everwood. The children's artwork hung framed along the mahogany-boned corridors with even, gallery-perfect spaces between. Boys in ties and navy blazers wandered among the parents, dutifully offering pastry puffs and skewers of bocconcini and tomato. The parents moved slowly, murmuring and assessing each artwork, holding their phones aloft. In front of a water-colour of a golden retriever, Gwen scanned a code and a screen popped up on her phone: "Edwin Graham is ten years old. Says Edwin: '*My Dog* is inspired by the baroque masters who painted animals to demonstrate their portrait skills and pay tribute to the most noble companion of all classes.'"

Gwen stared at the dog's eyes, which were uncannily human. It was a terrible painting perfectly executed. Oh, Edwin, thought Gwen.

Elizabeth Morton came up and put her hand on Gwen's shoulder, breaking her reverie.

"Not exactly Dürer," she said, removing her hand to cradle her glass of red wine.

Elizabeth was looming, even taller in high heels and a short black skirt. It hadn't occurred to Gwen to dress up. She was wearing jeans and a knee-length blouse, beige. Gwen caught a glimpse of herself in a trophy case and realized she looked like someone in a barber's cape.

"Do you think a ten-year-old really said that about the baroque masters?" asked Gwen.

"He probably heard it on that trip to France last year. They're little parrots," said Elizabeth. "Thank you again for your help. The flowers are beautiful."

"I'm sorry I was so late—"

Elizabeth waved her hand. "It's Art Night. No one really notices the flowers until the spring gala— Hi, Julia!"

Julia breezed up to the women, leaning in to Elizabeth for a two-cheek kiss. Gwen watched carefully—right cheek first—so she would be prepared when Julia came for her.

When the women had untangled from their greetings, Julia said, "I'm hoping this event lands my kids a good art dealer."

"They don't have one already? In kindergarten? Late bloomers," said Elizabeth.

Gwen laughed. She wondered how many glasses of wine Elizabeth had had.

"I was just telling Gwen that all this work amounts to nothing."

"That's ridiculous! It's beautiful, Elizabeth. You're a master," said Julia.

Elizabeth smiled.

"It does look pretty damn good, doesn't it? Gwen did the flowers."

"No—I just picked them up."

"They're beautiful," said Julia. She lowered her voice. "Can I complain for a second? I had the most shit day. On top of my own workload, I've been helping Tom—well, Tom and Seth . . ." She nodded to Gwen, as if the two of them were in on something. "So I missed a deadline, and one of my bigger clients accused me of 'neglect.'"

Elizabeth offered Julia counsel ("Fuck that," she said). Gwen was surprised, happily so, that these women with their thin wrists and red-painted fingernails could swear so casually.

Gwen had a strong suspicion that Julia was the most competent of the BuzzSwitch team. Tom's breeziness would be a problem. For him, it didn't matter if BuzzSwitch didn't work out; there had already been other BuzzSwitches in his life, and there would be more. He had the air of a man wandering in a sun-soaked orchard dangling with opportunities, abundant and ever perpetual. For Tom, any losses would be temporary. Seth, in contrast, was in possession of hard-earned competence, and inherent doggedness, but also the very human potential for failure. Julia, though—Gwen remembered her tapping away on her laptop at the cottage, slicing through one problem after another.

If BuzzSwitch worked, Julia would be the reason. Were her professional triumphs the corollary of maternal neglect? Gwen might have believed so, at one point, or needed to, to comfort herself. But those feelings were long gone. Gwen thought of Eli alone in the arena parking lot, and neglectful mothers everywhere.

The women were standing in front of a sculpture that appeared to be simply a stack of tin cans. A small trophy stood in front of it: ECO AWARD.

"I wonder what will happen to these kids when they join the real world and realize that they're untalented," said Elizabeth under her breath.

"Oh, they'll probably never have to find out," said Julia lightly.

United, the three women sipped their wine and scanned the room. The dads seemed to have arrived together, all at once, their suits ranging from grey to dark grey and back again.

So smoothly that Gwen hardly noticed it, Elizabeth facilitated a merging of their threesome with another group of parents. A short, handsome man was on the edge of the new group, but somehow, he was at the centre, too. This was the famous architect, recognized by Gwen before Elizabeth introduced them. She feared a two-cheek kiss, but he grabbed Gwen's hand and shook firmly. His square silver glasses occupied 90 percent of his facescape. The power he threw off was entirely different from Elizabeth's but just as forceful—coolness in place of her heat.

"Nobu donated the Lawren Harris," said Elizabeth to the group.

Nobu turned to Gwen, unblinking. "Do you like the piece?"

"I haven't seen it yet," said Gwen.

"It's a study for a minor work," said Nobu. "But Harris is having a moment, for what that's worth."

Gwen didn't know about Lawren Harris's moment, and when everyone had finished murmuring their agreement about it, she asked the architect, "What grade is your son in?"

"Eight," he said. "I fear this place will make a banker out of him. It was his idea to send our son here."

Gwen was then introduced to Nobu's husband, a younger man with blond hair and a blinking, dumbstruck expression.

"Oh, Nobu," said Elizabeth. "Look around. These kids are so creative. You know the Everwood slogan: 'Building the whole boy.'"

Nobu touched the upper rim of one lens. "Such a strange campaign. It works on the page, but when spoken, it sounds like 'hole boy'—*h-o-l-e*. Which is at once vaguely obscene and slightly tragic."

Gwen pictured a boy with a hole in his chest, a perfect pie-pan circle straight through his tie and dress shirt.

"What year is your whole—*w-h-o-l-e*—boy, Gwen, or are there more than one?"

"Eli. He's in Grade Five. My daughter goes to the U." There were approving murmurs about Maddie's school.

"Ah," said Nobu. "They still love you when they're ten."

"And then?" asked Elizabeth.

"And then—" Nobu put a fist in the air and opened his palm quickly. "P-chuu!" He made an explosion sound. His husband nodded sadly.

Gwen decided she disliked Nobu. His ugly, theoretical buildings would live forever in the city for generations to walk past and rarely step inside.

"Will you excuse me?" said Gwen, breaking away.

She walked down the hall, through the noise of parents, feeling bereft. In a few years, she would be forty, and she knew almost nothing about Lawren Harris, or how eighth graders become bankers. She was thirsty and hot inside the cone of her big shirt.

Looking for more wine, Gwen wandered into the library. Tables had been set up for the silent auction, and Gwen joined the parents winding between the stations, bidding on an iPhone, Raptors tickets, an evening with a prominent author. Stacks and stacks of books surrounded them, up to the mahogany ceiling beams. Gwen took great comfort in these books, running her hand along the spines and looking up to see if she could locate the top of the stacks. Doing so, she walked smack into a giant metal box, crunching her hip. She reeled, stinging, and looked more closely at the thing that had attacked her: a 3-D printer.

She rubbed her hip where she'd hit it, and through watery eyes she saw someone waving at her, a man standing by the back wall beneath a banner: WE ARE NOT PREPARING KIDS FOR THE REAL WORLD—WE ARE PREPARING THEM TO CHANGE THE WORLD. He was in a blue suit, which set him apart: Daniel, she thought. Daniel in a suit, in a grown-up world, his hair cut short.

But it wasn't Daniel. The hair was curly, and the wave was her husband's. It had finally happened: she was seeing things. She was officially a crazy lady. Gwen caught her breath and headed over.

"Hey," she said. "Should I bid on tennis lessons at the Boulevard Club?" It was comforting to see Seth here. She gave him a kiss on the cheek.

"Did you look at the painting?" he asked.

Seth led her to an easel, and there it was, a painting the size of a magazine cover. It was a strange picture, just a few strokes away from something that might be airbrushed on the side of a van: a tiny house, trapped on an iceberg, caving at the sides. The sky in thick marshmallow slabs all around it. The ground electric blue.

The iceberg striped like the pleats on a whale's jaw. Gwen thought it was one of the most beautiful things she'd ever seen.

"It's just a study," said Seth. "But still . . ."

Gwen thought of Shadow Pines and how their life there had been, without them knowing it, a study for this one. But actually, it had been beautiful in and of itself. She couldn't imagine how the artist's next painting would be any more valuable than the one it grew from.

She looked around the room, and then at Seth. "Where's Eli?"

× × ×

Outside, a heavy cold had descended, and Gwen zipped her parka quickly. She followed voices and an electronic hum by the clock tower. A drone flew overhead, spider-armed and mechanically falling and rising against the night scrim. Blazers were strewn here and there on the football field. In their dress shirts in the cold, a group of boys moved frantically. Some of them appeared to be wrestling, some of them kicking a soccer ball. Others were just running in all directions, screeching.

Gwen spotted Eli because of his stillness. He stood next to a boy with a remote in his hand, their necks craned to the night sky, looking up at the drone.

"Eli . . ." called Gwen. She could hear him talking as she moved closer.

"I'm getting one of these for Christmas," Gwen heard her son say. "But mine's got 1080p video. Japanese."

Gwen moved more quickly.

"Eli—"

Some of the boys got out of her way, pulled themselves up from the field to stand, watching.

"No offence, but this one kind of sucks," she heard Eli say

in an unfamiliar deep voice, an agonizing brag—the tone of a tremendous asshole.

"Eli!" Gwen strode forward, propelled by two competing instincts: to snatch him up and hold him close to her; but also, to grab him by the ear, drag him like a cartoon mother with a bar of soap in her other hand. Eli looked up, bewildered. But then he saw her and grinned happily, and Gwen softened. Her transgression at the arena had apparently been forgiven.

"Hey, Mom," he said, excited to share something with her. "Did you see the drone?"

Gwen remembered all the things he'd wanted to show her over the years. Small Eli: *Mom, come look . . .!* Butterflies. Sketches. A jump shot.

She nodded.

"We're leaving," she said. "Get your blazer."

"It has a GoPro!" He followed her quickly across the field, blazer wadded under his arm.

When they reached the parking lot, out of earshot of the boys, Gwen turned to him. "Why did you tell those kids you were getting one of those things for Christmas? What possible reason would we have to get you one? It's ridiculous. What do any of them even need it for? To take pictures of what?"

Eli lifted his finger to his mouth.

"I dunno," he said.

"Don't bite your nails," said Gwen. Eli dropped his hand. "You don't know what it's for, or you don't know why you were lying to those boys?" She closed her eyes, awash in fatigue. "Why, Eli? Why would we ever buy something so stupid for you?"

He looked up at her, and asked it as a question, entirely sincere. "Because we can?"

11

MADDIE

They were high up in the bleachers, away from everybody, shoulders and knees touching. Joshua was reading and Maddie was watching him read. She couldn't concentrate on her textbook; she'd been staring at a section about suffragettes, starting and restarting. Below them, the girls' volleyball team ran laps in a circle, one after the other in their coloured T-shirts.

Suddenly Joshua looked straight ahead and said to the air in front of him, "What do you think your parents will do with that moncy?"

Maddie separated her leg from his.

"I don't know," she said. "It's not that much, like you said. If you're starting a business, like my dad is, it's not that much." She was quiet. "And they bought that house."

Joshua nodded and looked back down at his book.

She added, "I mean, I know it's an obscene amount, by almost all standards." She was supposed to say this often, she felt, even if only to herself. She needed to genuflect, even though a little part of her thought: *We didn't do anything wrong.* Clara was born into a house nicer than hers, and Clara didn't walk around all day feeling like a half-human inside a giant mascot suit, head lolling on her shoulders.

Joshua shut his book. "I have to go drop off some papers."

Maddie tingled nervously. Had they just had a fight?

She didn't want him to go away from her. "Can I come?" Joshua looked at Maddie, which made her think of his eyes during sex, and made her feel like she was being skinned alive, in a good way.

"Really? It's far."

"Really."

They took the subway and two buses to East York. The buses were filled with people, pressing against one another in their thawing winter coats, the air heavy with melted cold. A man sneezed loudly and violently on her shoulder. Joshua pulled her out of the way and mouthed, "Gross." Maddie leaned against him, under the arm of his jacket. She looked around to see who had noticed Joshua's declaration, his connection to her.

They got off the bus by the side of a six-lane street. Then they walked, turning away from the traffic onto a road of high-rises.

Susan opened her apartment door. "Come in, come in," she said.

Joshua spoke to her as they walked deeper into the apartment, and Maddie followed, stopping in a small living room with a large TV and a couch made up like a bed. Maddie could see inside a room off the living room: two sets of bunk beds where bodies slept, lumps beneath sheets and blankets.

Susan shut the door to the room of sleeping people. Maddie and Joshua didn't sit or take off their jackets. Joshua talked quickly but quietly, trying not to wake the women. As he showed Susan the papers that would help her get her children back, Maddie circled, peering in the slightly ajar door of another room. Two more bunk beds, empty and tidily made, with flowered sheets and bedspreads, the brightly coloured patterns of little girls' rooms.

Susan pointed to the room where the women slept. "They are only here part-time. They pay one-fifth rent." She shrugged. "Too many people. I'm never alone!"

The walls held photos of children and old people, formal and posed. One frame was shaped like hands praying, cupping a picture of a baby squinting on a blanket. Another was of two white girls, twins in matching pink overall shorts.

"My first *alaga* in Canada, Olivia and Kate. Sweet girls," said Susan, touching one head, then the other. She sighed. "I miss them."

At the door sat an open cardboard box about the size of a small refrigerator. Maddie peered inside: bundles of new socks with the tags on; a giant box of Smarties; a three-pack of men's shaving gel; a stuffed moose with a tiny plastic hockey stick glued between its paws.

Susan saw Maddie looking and explained, "For the family. It's expensive to send. My new boss is bad, he stopped paying me. I owe four hundred dollar."

"'He owes me,' not 'I owe,'" said Joshua. Maddie had never heard this edge in his voice before. "'Dollars,' not 'dollar.'"

Susan sighed. "He *owes me* four hundred dollars," she said. They were all looking at the moose with the hockey stick on the top of the box.

"Cute," Maddie offered. "I'm sorry about your boss."

"It costs a hundred and ten dollars to send," said Susan. "I have to wait."

The vanilla smell of potpourri wriggled in Maddie's nose. She excused herself to use the bathroom. By the sink, beneath a mirror edged with rust, stood a row of water glasses, each with a toothbrush inside, like flowers in pots. More than the bunk beds, more than the moose or the smell of potpourri, these separate toothbrush glasses made Maddie feel anxious and sad, like she was somewhere she shouldn't be.

Maddie reached into her backpack for her wallet, pulling out five twenty-dollar bills, all the money she had with her. She placed them carefully by the toothbrushes.

When Maddie came out of the bathroom, Susan offered pop and invited them to sit on the couch.

"Stay," she said, smiling kindly.

Joshua looked at Maddie expectantly.

But Maddie was prickly with discomfort, the vanilla smell burning in her nostrils. She had been in so many new places lately, around so many new people. Where were her Shadow Pines friends right now? What would Emma make of this apartment, of Joshua? Probably, Emma would think it was cool. Maddie wanted to think that, too. But the performance required to get her through the days was wearing her out. She stood up.

"Thank you, but I have to get home."

At the bus stop, Joshua asked her, "Are you okay?"

There was no way to talk about any of it, so Maddie leaned into him and said nothing. He took her hand while they waited.

GWEN

I didn't hear from you. Don't you want to see me?

My plan is to move west. I know a guy who's a rig hand in Alberta who says they still need people. Fourteen days on then seven days off. Good money. But getting out there costs a lot. What do you think about helping me out, Gwen? 30K could get me set up.

I know what you got going on now and I'm guessing you don't want me showing up. But the truth is I can't leave unless I find some way to get out there.

I saw Maddie, Gwen. She looks just like you. I don't want to wreck anything for you. Can we meet?

Gwen stared at her phone. *I saw Maddie.* He knows her name.

Gwen flew to the front door. Locked. Upstairs to the kids. To Maddie's room—empty. Eli's door stood ajar and there was Eli at his desk, headset on, gripping a video game controller.

Gwen asked, "Where's Maddie?"

Eli murmured something, clicking away. Gwen snatched the headset off, and the controller fell from Eli's hands to the ground.

"Mom!"

"Eli, I need you to tell me: Did anyone come to the house while Daddy and I were away at that cottage? Did anyone knock on the door? Or come in?"

Eli gripped the arms of his desk chair, a nervous flicker in his eyes. Gwen had become thirty feet tall, her giantess voice shaking.

"Tell me, Eli. Did something happen?"

"Yes."

Gwen froze. She waited. Why was he so slow to speak? "Eli— who was here?"

"Nobody, I don't think—I don't know." He talked fast. "Maddie was away. She was out and she said she was coming back but then I woke up and I was in the kitchen. The clock said 2:34. I had the fuzzies. Remember how I used to get the fuzzies?"

Blood thumped in Gwen's ears. "Yes, of course."

"And then I saw something in the pool. Or I thought I did."

"But the pool is empty," said Gwen, dry throated.

"I know. It was a person, maybe. Just standing there. I tried to call Maddie but she didn't come. And I went upstairs but she wasn't in her room. I didn't want to tell you . . .," said Eli, and his face twisted, on the edge of tears. "But I did want to tell you."

"It's okay, Eli—"

"Maddie told me not to."

Gwen couldn't fit the pieces together. "Not to what?"

"In the morning. She was back and she said, 'Don't tell Mom.' She made me promise to keep the secret."

Gwen tried to make sense of this, and her son's contorted face, his wobbling lip. He was expending so much effort just to stop himself from crying. Gwen had the thought that she needed to free him from his own containment. She crouched down on the edge of the bed, facing him.

"You can cry, Eli," Gwen said quietly. Immediately, a tear rolled down his cheek. She wiped it away with a finger.

"I went upstairs and put my head under the covers. When I woke up, it was morning."

"That must have been scary," said Gwen.

"What must have been scary?"

Gwen looked up. Maddie stood in the doorway, her jacket and backpack still on, carrying with her a plume of the outside cold. Her hair had grown longer. It hung below her shoulders, flat. Like her father's, thought Gwen. Like Daniel's.

Gwen kissed Eli on the head and left his room, gesturing at Maddie to follow. When they were in Gwen's bedroom, she shut the door and turned to face her daughter.

"What the hell, Mom . . ." said Maddie, thumbs hooked on the straps of her pack.

"You left your brother alone when we were away?" Gwen asked in a voice coiled with anger.

Maddie dropped her thumbs. Her gaze shifted to the floor.

"Why would you do such a selfish thing? He's ten years old."

"He's eleven," Maddie said to her running shoes.

"He can't be alone all night."

"I didn't mean to. I fell asleep at Clara's—I was home by three."

"Oh, Maddie. Stop it. You were with that boy from the park."

Maddie's head snapped up.

"What?"

"I saw you. In the park, with a hundred nannies and a boy."

Gwen immediately regretted saying it: she had undermined her power by admitting to the stalking. There had been a family meeting about Gwen's habit last year—a kitchen table intervention back in Shadow Pines. Seth had facilitated, gently saying, "You know your mother loves you, and she worries," and "You know Maddie is trustworthy, and you need to stop."

"Wait—you're still tracking me?"

Gwen pushed ahead. "I wanted to know where you were, and that park popped up on my phone—I don't owe you an explanation. You've just demonstrated that you're unable to look after yourself yet, let alone another person."

Maddie glared.

"Has anyone approached you? Or—have you been followed?"

"Only by you, Mom," said Maddie. She raised her voice. "I think you are seriously losing your shit alone in this big house all day. You should probably get a job or something. Go volunteer at a soup kitchen."

This was a new way of speaking. It wasn't the adolescent eye rolling. It was adult contempt, rock hard, tossed down from on high.

Gwen exploded. "I have a job! My job is keeping you and Eli safe! My job is holding this family together!"

"You suck at it, Mom." Maddie walked out.

Gwen stood, shallow breathing. Maddie wasn't wrong. It had been a very careful performance: a normal mother; a normal wife. She had made herself a woman without a past, which is what motherhood seemed to require. A clean white space. She had excelled at it, too. It was the one thing she knew how to do. But now her daughter hated her, and would soon be leaving, and her family was in danger. She wasn't very good at that one thing after all.

Panic surged in her chest, and she followed Maddie into her room. Maddie's pack and coat were strewn on the ground, and she was sitting at her desk. It was all backwards. Gwen was the one who should have been sulking. Gwen was the misunderstood kid with the crazy parents. She saw herself sneaking cigarettes, leaning her torso out the window to exhale.

She stood in the room, at a loss as to how to repair the breach. Maddie's head hung low, her chest caved and heaving, waiting.

What would a grown-up do? Gwen thought. She would act like a grown-up, saying calmly, as she did, "We need to meet this boy. Invite him over for dinner." Then she added, "And when you're out—don't talk to strangers. I'm not kidding. Things are different now."

Maddie sighed loudly. "I'm not five, Mom," she said.

Gwen left the room on shaky legs, walking down the hall while choking back tears. *I'm not five.* In the park, five-year-old Maddie came running up to her with the stem of a dandelion that had lost its fluff, distraught that there was nothing to blow, calling, "Mama, it's not working!" *Come back*, thought Gwen, bracing herself on the hallway walls. *Come back.*

× × ×

Later, Gwen fed them dinner. She ran a bath for Eli, and when he was soap-scented and in bed, she read to him as if he still wanted to be read to. Maddie kept her door shut.

Night settled around the house. Gwen checked the security system. She moved between the kids' bedrooms, squatting close next to their sleeping bodies to watch the duvets rise and fall.

She texted Seth, who was on a night flight back to LA to make a morning meeting with Tom and the angel investors. Then, when everything had been secured, Gwen climbed in bed with her laptop and composed a response to the email from Daniel.

Outside, the first snow of the season fell, thin and uncertain.

Gwen watched the snow dropping, vanishing before it touched the ground, and hit Send.

12

MADDIE

Maddie circled the foyer, waiting. Joshua was never late on purpose, but he would be coming from work, so he could get delayed. She hoped he wouldn't be wearing his work shirt with the brown plastic sheen, even though she knew it wouldn't bother her parents. She tried not to let it bother her.

He rang the bell for just a split second before Maddie flung open the door. Joshua's hair was wet from a shower, and he was carrying a clear plastic container.

"I brought cookies. Alexis made them. I brought my school stuff, too. We could do History after?" He turned to show Maddie his backpack, sagging with weight. He peered past her, into the house. "Where are your parents?"

"Let's go upstairs for a second," she whispered.

Joshua hesitated. Maddie nodded, coaxing him into the foyer. She hadn't planned to take him to her room, but he looked so beautiful with his box of cookies and his showered skin smooth as glass (he never had a zit—not ever!) and his nervousness that implied this meet-the-parents thing mattered.

Maddie led him up the stairs, with that feeling moving black and wavy in her middle.

She locked the door behind her and turned to him, a boy standing in her bedroom with a box of cookies in his hand. Joshua's eyes widened in a question mark, and Maddie took the cookies and placed them on the bed. He threw his backpack next to the box, and they moved toward one another at the same time, hands and mouths reaching.

"Fast," whispered Maddie, and she leaned against the window.

Joshua moved behind her, pressing his hips into her extended body, reaching around and unzipping her jeans, running his hands between her legs. This was almost enough, just the brush of him, and Maddie said it again, louder, "Faster," which he generally was anyway, fast and slightly surprised. (Maddie knew she was supposed to make fun of him for that, but it was fine with her; she was fast, too.) As she listened to him unwrapping the condom, Maddie stayed bent over, her hands against the Juliet windows, head bowed, hair curtained. As he entered her, breathing quickly, she wondered if there were neighbours looking up who could see them. She wouldn't mind. But when she looked down at the empty grey lawns waiting for winter, she saw no one.

× × ×

When they walked into the kitchen, Seth was there. He pushed up his glasses as if to see Joshua better, and then held his hand out.

"You must be Joshua. I'm Seth, Maddie's dad."

"He knows who you are," snapped Maddie, instantly regretting it. She was nervous. But Seth didn't blink.

"Right. You said he was sharp, didn't you? I forgot."

"Thanks for having me," said Joshua, offering the box.

This went wrong: Seth had his hand extended, but instead of shaking Joshua's, he took the cookies and placed them on the counter. When he turned around again, Joshua had his hand out, like he'd been waiting. Finally, they shook. Maddie noticed that Joshua's handshake was strong.

Seth fussed around the kitchen, crushing a tin of tomatoes in a pot. Her mother wasn't cooking much these days.

Stirring, Seth said, "I just got back from California, so you'll have to forgive me if I'm a bit spaced, Joshua. Jet lag."

"Where were you?" asked Joshua.

"Los Angeles. Have you ever been?"

"No. I've never been west."

"Well, perhaps for you, all of this country is the west, isn't it? For immigrants, wherever they land is the frontier, I suppose."

The word "immigrant" rolled through Maddie's head like a rock in a canyon. The word "they." So it had only taken a few minutes for that to come up. Jesus.

"Maybe. I don't know," said Joshua.

"My family came from Russia," said Seth. "Just before the war."

Oh God, thought Maddie: *this* story (even though she'd always kind of liked this story, it seemed transformed into something different by Joshua's presence).

Seth moved around the kitchen, stirring and chopping, telling Joshua about how his grandmother paid a priest for safe passage to New York with a diamond ring. While Seth's grandparents were waiting at the train station, the priest's wife appeared with a loaf of bread wrapped in a tea towel, and wished them luck. When the wheels of the train had been grinding for hours—the first train of many, toward Lisbon, and the ship that would deliver them to New York, and finally, the train to Montreal—Seth's grandmother bit into the hunk of bread, thankful for the generosity of the priest's wife. Suddenly, she screamed in pain (Seth raised the tomato-soaked wooden spoon, for emphasis, spattering red into the air). She had cracked a tooth on a hard object. The priest, or his wife, or both of them, had hidden the ring in the dough.

"The generosity! The risk!" Seth exclaimed.

Joshua nodded encouragingly.

Seth was placing them side-by-side, Maddie thought, trying to get some imaginary version of his grandparents and some imaginary version of Joshua's Filipina mom to link arms and kick together in some conga line of history. She swung between pride at Seth's sincerity, and mortification at his cluelessness.

But Joshua, with his sombre brow, was polite. He asked questions about Russian geography as he carried the salad to the table, following Seth.

Eli was already seated. He greeted Joshua. "What's shakin', bacon?"

Gwen appeared. Maddie took in her mother's strange transformation. It wasn't just the white David Bowie hair. She had abandoned the mom uniform of Shadow Pines, and was wearing a kind of sandwich-board-shaped silk dress, layered with a woolly garment that made Maddie think of a cape. It seemed like something a medieval peasant would wear, but Maddie had seen the tags: the new wardrobe was shockingly expensive. Maddie remembered how Gwen used to order most of her clothes for the year at online Boxing Day sales, because everything was on sale. She bought her bathing suit in December just to save fifteen dollars.

"We're so happy to have you here, Joshua." Gwen smiled, inviting, but she was pale and seemed distracted.

She had always checked out from time to time, vanishing into herself with a shuttered expression. Where did she go? Maddie wondered. Her mom's past was a series of dead ends: left Procter for the city, went to university, met Seth too young, had a baby, dropped out of school. Those were markers; few details on what happened in between were offered. "Oh, I used to love this song," said Gwen once from the driver's seat, when some punk girl band came on the radio. In the back, Maddie and Eli looked at each other and burst out laughing. How could that song have ever mattered to Gwen?

Seth and Gwen occupied either end of the table. The table in the old house had been circular. Now, seated at the giant rectangle, everyone was spaced far apart, as if another family could have joined them, sliding between the chairs like black piano keys.

Seth did most of the talking, and Joshua responded politely. *Favourite subject? Neighbourhood? Movies?* Maddie found the questions parasitic. Her parents were taking bites out of Joshua, which meant there would be less of him for her.

Gwen moved her food around on her plate, back and forth, barely eating. She was somewhere else, Maddie thought.

"So what are you reading?" Seth asked, which he always asked Maddie's and Eli's friends.

"*Blood Meridian*," said Joshua.

"Ambitious. You reading that too, Mads?"

"No. In our class it's *The Handmaid's Tale*. These women have to make babies for the state."

"And does *Blood Meridian* float your boat, Joshua?"

Maddie winced at "float your boat."

"Dad, what'd you do to your teeth?" asked Eli.

Seth quickly curled his lips over his teeth, clamping his mouth shut.

"Nuffin'," he said.

"They're like Tic Tacs," said Eli.

Gwen was listening after all, because she slowly turned her gaze to her husband.

"What does he mean?" Gwen asked.

Seth's lemon-puckered mouth slowly came undone. He sighed, resigned. Then he grinned, his lips pulled back in a growl, and there they were: glistening and blinding, snow white teeth.

"Whoa! Dude!" said Eli.

"His teeth aren't usually like that," said Maddie to Joshua.

"They look good," offered Joshua. "Supremely clean."

"You did something in LA," said Gwen, astonished.

"It's no big deal, is it?" asked Seth. "They do it at the airport when you land." Flustered, he inserted long pauses between thoughts, a tic Maddie hadn't heard in a while. "They won't let you into LA with Canadian teeth." He paused and swallowed. "They call it 'Canadian yellow' and make all Canadians bleach their mouths at port of entry."

"Wait—is that true? Are you joking?" asked Eli.

"It's no big deal," said Seth again, but his cheeks were pink, and he was tapping his knife on the table rapidly. No one spoke. "Lasers, okay? Walk-in."

Gwen continued to stare at her husband with a look that suggested betrayal. Maddie did not recognize this look.

Joshua put his fork down, cleared his throat. "I do find it

violent," he said, and everyone looked at him. "The book. It's violent, but its violence serves a purpose."

"What purpose is that, Joshua?" asked Seth. Her parents kept saying his name like he might not know it.

"Well, there's the Kid, and he's violence incarnate, just a teenager who kind of like kills to kill, just all about the bloodshed. Then there's the Judge, and he thinks killing is inevitable, that death and rampage is our natural state. So McCarthy wants us to think about that."

Eli said, "Where do I get this book?"

Maddie thought that Seth would volley back his own interpretation, and they would sit at the table discussing this book that she hadn't read. But Seth's phone was vibrating, and he cut short the conversation, murmuring, "Yes, yes, I think you're onto something, Joshua. I'll get dessert."

He grabbed his phone and stood while Gwen continued to sit in front of her uneaten food like a toddler.

Something was wrong with Gwen tonight. Lately, Maddie had been catching her in an expression of pure mourning, like she was memorizing Maddie's face before the casket closed. But right now, Gwen seemed like she was avoiding looking at Maddie at all.

Annoyed and hurt by Gwen's pointed withdrawal, Maddie stood to clear the dishes, and Joshua followed her lead. He moved efficiently, stacking and carrying. In the kitchen, he smiled at her and shrugged, which she didn't know how to interpret.

Seth brought out a Whole Foods box.

"We'll put out your cookies, too, Joshua," said Seth. "You two get the forks and plates."

In the kitchen, Joshua pulled open a drawer. "Empty," he said.

He tried another one, and another, all embarrassingly empty. They had too much space, Maddie knew, too many drawers.

"Over here," said Seth, who had found the cake forks.

Joshua brought in the plates, Maddie the tray of Alexis's chocolate chip cookies, and Seth carried the cake. It was white, with coloured macaroons on the side floating like balls of bubble gum.

"What is that?" said Eli, forlorn. "I like angel food cake."

"It's called a Marie Antoinette—ironically, I suppose. I thought Gwen would like it. It's panna cotta."

"But Mom usually makes the cakes, remember? Her cakes are awesome," said Eli.

"You never bake anymore, Mom," said Maddie.

"I think we left the pans behind when we moved," said Gwen.

"Just buy some new ones," said Eli.

"We can't just buy everything we think of," said Maddie. "It's wasteful."

"They're cake pans! Mom just bought a twelve thousand-dollar table!"

Seth looked up, knife still nestled inside the cake. "This table?"

Maddie, disgusted with her family, blurted, "Joshua's dad is in the Philippines. He works in a factory."

The cake pieces circulated.

"Wait until everyone has a piece, Eli," said Seth. "What kind of factory is it, Joshua?"

"Jet engines."

Maddie was embarrassed that she hadn't thought to ask what kind of factory. She had assumed he worked in a sweatshop, packing fruit or sewing clothes—jobs that people over here felt bad about.

"Is he an engineer?" asked Seth.

"He oversees an assembly line. He should have been an engineer."

"Why doesn't he come here? He could probably do that here, for more money," said Eli, eating his cake.

"It's not that easy for people to get here," said Maddie. "In fact, they're trying to send them back these days. We met this nanny who's probably getting deported, because she was caught babysitting." She sensed Joshua glancing at her sideways.

"So what if she babysits? She's a nanny," said Eli.

"It violates her visa requirements," said Maddie.

"That's terrible," said Seth. "The government is ruthless."

Maddie didn't know which one he meant, here or the Philippines.

Seth's phone vibrated again. A cloud passed over his face as he looked at the number. "I have to take this, please excuse me." He left the room.

The rest of them ate quietly, and the weight of social expectation tilted toward Gwen. Maddie wanted her to wake up and take over Seth's abandoned duties, and show Joshua that they weren't greedy, clueless white people.

As if she heard her plea, Gwen asked, "Joshua, would you like your dad to come here?"

"Mom . . ." This question seemed embarrassingly personal to Maddie.

"He's trying." Joshua cleared his throat, redirecting the conversation with a question to Gwen. "And what about you? Do your parents live nearby?"

Maddie straightened. Gwen's parents were off limits. Apparently Maddie had met her grandmother when she was a baby, but she had no recollection of this. There was a car accident soon after, and she died. Gwen's father was alive, but he was "not a good person," Gwen had said, explaining why they didn't see him, even though he lived a few hours away. But that description covered such a span of possible behaviours that it told Maddie nothing: A guy who didn't replace the empty toilet paper roll? A guy who locked his daughter in a closet? The family didn't talk about Gwen's parents.

"My mother died suddenly around the time Eli was born," said Gwen slowly. "My father—we aren't close." She shut the door on the conversation, lifted her napkin to her lips and pushed her plate away. Then she smiled at Joshua kindly. "Water under the bridge."

"What bridge?" asked Eli.

GWEN

Gwen couldn't sleep. She lay in bed on her back, listening to Seth's cell phone murmurs floating from his office into the bedroom.

She had no plan. Waiting wasn't a plan, but she had become very good at pretending it was. She could just pay him off—but why? *Because he could go to the police and implicate you in robbery and assault. He could tell Maddie that she was raised by liars. He could toss a lit match into your home.*

She lay there, travelling backwards through the night that had just passed, moment by moment, thinking about the enslaved women in Maddie's book, with fetuses planted in their bodies like flags. She was surprised Joshua had asked about her parents. He was a thoughtful person. She loathed him nonetheless.

When the doorbell rang at the beginning of the evening, while Seth was cooking and they were awaiting the arrival of the boy from the park, Gwen had been upstairs, on the bed with her laptop, googling private detectives. Two sets of footsteps moved quietly up the stairs and into Maddie's room next door. No speaking. A door locked.

Gwen had stayed on the bed for a long time, looking up at the ceiling, wondering if she should go next door and alert them to her presence. Perhaps she should just open Maddie's door, armed with a stack of laundry.

Such silence.

Gwen had put down her computer, risen from the bed. She stood in the centre of the room, then slowly walked to her bedroom wall. She spread her hands, then pressed her ear against the white wall (she could still smell the paint, giving them all cancer), catching her daughter's voice like a safecracker catching clicks.

After a while, Gwen backed away. Maddie's door opened. Two sets of footsteps padded downstairs. Gwen could hear Seth exclaiming faintly from the kitchen, "Nice to meet you . . ."

Maddie's door was open, and Gwen went inside. She inhaled, but it was just the same faint mix of scented candles and shampoo. Maddie's binders were in the usual tidy stack on her desk. A worn black backpack lay on the made bed—the boy's, Joshua's. Gwen unzipped it and pawed through the contents. Joshua's binder, textbooks, a calculator, sandwich wrappers. *I'm invading again*, Gwen reminded herself, aware that if anyone walked by— She shut Maddie's door, locking herself in.

In the front pocket, Gwen found his wallet. She opened it up: fifteen dollars. A bus pass. She pulled out a photo of a woman who must be his mother. Gwen admired her muscular, determined face and unapologetic blue eye shadow.

Gwen put the picture back, and her fingers hit something plastic in the wallet's fold: a condom. She stared at the package in her hand, black and yellow writing promising Extreme Pleasure. Gwen hesitated before putting it back. Bristly fury gathered in her gut.

Then Gwen pulled out the boy's history textbook. She opened it up to the centre and ripped out a single page, listening to the tear, hearing not paper but steel on steel—glass shattering. She crumpled the page into a ball and stuffed it into the pocket of her pants, hidden under her swishing dress.

Gwen replaced the textbook, carefully slipping it between the other items in the backpack. She zipped the pack. Now her anger melted into sadness, and Gwen knew it would sit astride her all night, through dinner, into the sleeping hours. The ache wasn't just that she and her daughter were separating. The convergence frightened her, too. Perhaps Maddie would be at once reckless and submissive, a girl with fierce cravings, as Gwen had been at her age.

Gwen had turned out Maddie's light and made her way downstairs, to the sounds of dinner, the smell of Seth's tomato sauce, voices rattling in the kitchen. Dinner was what to think about. Her family was what mattered. She would call on her better self: *arrive, arrive.* She descended the stairs.

But Gwen couldn't stop the remembrance of Maddie's voice. She kept hearing it, the one word she had been able to make out with her ear pressed to the bedroom wall before dinner, close enough to capture her daughter's whisper: "Faster."

Seth came into the bedroom and went straight to the bathroom, bringing with him a nimbus of overwork and heavy breathing. At his side of the bed, Seth's phone flashed. Gwen reached for it, taking in a notification: *Julia.*

Gwen called out, "What exactly is Julia doing for you and Tom?"

The tap ran in the bathroom. "Just some consultation on marketing." The tap turned off. Seth stood in the bathroom door in his boxers and clicked off the light.

"You're thinner," said Gwen. "Richer and thinner." She shored herself to say something, to tell him at last about Daniel.

Seth dropped on the edge of the bed in the dark, checking his phone. He sighed deeply, then threw his phone on the bedside table, flopping backwards, head on the pillow.

"Oh God," he said. To the ceiling, he added, "We're having a few setbacks." He talked about angel investors who had backed away, and the dollar weakening.

Seth looked so distracted, so thin. Gwen couldn't say anything right now, and really, what was there to say? *Maddie's dad is extorting me. How's the new humidor working out?*

Gwen made comforting noises at her husband, with sincerity, assuring him that Tom would figure it out. Tom had never floundered at anything. Tom had the cottage, and the jaw.

Seth took Gwen's hand, and the casualness of it—the millionth time-ness of the gesture—animated something in Gwen, an urge for confidentiality.

"I should tell you something—" she said.

Seth's phone vibrated. "Just a second . . ." He dropped her hand, rolled and clicked. "I'm turning it off . . ." he said, and returned to her.

These little digital interruptions that defined her interactions with her husband reminded her of the loons at Julia's lake: skimming the water, then ducking down and vanishing.

"Okay, what were you saying?" Seth's white teeth flashed. His eyes were on the ceiling, distracted.

It was not the right time. But still, Gwen had to say something, so she said, "Maddie's having sex."

"Are you sure?"

Gwen told him she'd heard them (but didn't mention the textbook, or the specifics of what she'd heard). Seth was quiet. She wondered if he, too, would succumb to a kind of Victorian moral panic; if he, too, would want to scream and break something.

"Huh," Seth said finally. "Well, he seems like a nice kid."

Gwen frowned. Every once in a while when they were raising Maddie—not often—she had the thought: he cares just a little less because she's not his. Why else did he approve the late curfew request, or let her drive with the glazed-looking kid who had had his licence for less than twenty-four hours? But Gwen shook away those thoughts, because in almost every instance, she knew that he minded less only because she minded too much. That was their dance. He loved Maddie. He was her father.

Seth continued, "There are probably worse guys to choose for the first time. Assuming it's her first time."

"It is her first time. Of course it is, Seth," said Gwen. But then she had to think about that.

Seth rolled onto his side to look at Gwen. "I know it wasn't great for you. But Maddie has it better than we did. I hated all the sneaking around, guilty all the time. She should enjoy sex, right? Isn't that the way we're supposed to think about it now? Emphasize the pleasure? Not punish them for what's normal?"

Gwen rolled her eyes. "Did you read that somewhere?"

"Damn straight."

Gwen tried to take comfort in Seth's reasoned responses. She did, usually; it was why she'd chosen him. But she hesitated to fling her arm over his body. *Julia*, the phone said.

Sleepily, Seth put a hand on Gwen's neck, and she jerked, as she always did. She could bear the children's hands around her neck when they were small, convincing herself that their touch was healing old invisible marks. But when Seth touched her neck, she flinched. "You okay?" he would ask, and she would apologize by taking his hand and moving it to her chest, her breast. He would never hurt her, she knew this in her brain, but to her body, the size of his hand was the size of all men's hands, of Daniel's hand. It happened each time: Daniel's hands circled and bore down on her neck. A gasp and thrash—and then the liquid black.

Gwen gulped for air. Seth murmured and rolled away, oblivious. She lay with her heart pounding. She pictured a bird flying overhead, readying to land—hulking, claws out.

13

GWEN

From the top of Spadina, her vision only slightly impaired by a furry snowfall, Gwen saw the old neon palm tree sign for Palmer's. She paused briefly, then shrugged off the fear, striding purposefully down the hill from College Street. Little had changed in Chinatown. Signs above restaurants and stores were still in slightly bumpy English (IMPORTS TRADES CO, THE PEOPLES BOOKSTORE). Overhead, electrical wires made webs between the poles, prettily iced over in patches.

In a small, streaked glass display box by the door of the bar, the marquee advertised bands Gwen hadn't heard of. Cigarette butts littered the sidewalk, bleeding yellow into the snow. It was afternoon, exactly four o'clock, as per the plan.

Gwen pushed hard through the doors. Inside, it was dark; bars existed in perpetual night. Her boots dripped. Gwen looked around at a handful of people day-drinking in shadows. He wasn't there yet, but still, she put her hand on the bottom of her purse where the outline of the gun pressed against her fingers. Gun or money, she reminded herself, depending on how it went. She felt agile, fit. Her reflexes tingled. The music wasn't loud, but it was a good song, an old song, with a buzzing curtain of guitars and a woman snarling. Gwen took it in, let it fortify her.

"Sit anywhere," said the bartender, an older woman scrolling on her phone. Exactly where the bartender stood now, Harsha the dishwasher had stood, shyly pulling glasses from the machine, his eye black and green. She could picture Gus leaning there, his belly sagging. "That's your boyfriend's work. He's a fucking maniac."

"Does Gus still manage the bar?"

The bartender looked up from her phone. "Who?"

"Gus. It was a while ago."

"Don't know him. In spring, the whole place is going to be torn down. Condos. They want to keep the neon sign, though."

Gwen bought a watery pint, and turned, scanning the room for a table. Then she stopped. She had missed him somehow. But it was Daniel, without mistake. His cheeks were scooped and his hair short. A white T-shirt pressed tight across his upright shoulders; he was broader, more muscular. The eyes were the same, black and unquiet. Over the years, she had thought she'd seen him many times, but always in places that he would never be: the stationery aisle at Walmart; a motel in Pittsburgh where Eli's hockey team was staying for a tournament. But she had been seeing young men, and he wasn't young anymore.

This older version of Daniel was still beautiful. She put her hand to her hair, then dropped it quickly. She had put on makeup. She had chosen tight dark jeans. Crazy, Gwen had told herself as she applied lipstick in the mirror. *This is not a reunion.*

It's a shakedown. But when she stepped in front of him, she knew that she would become seventeen for a moment, and she wanted to be dressed for it.

Daniel stared.

"Blonde," he said.

Gwen sat down, unbuttoned her coat, her fingers shaking slightly. She felt him watching her, and experienced twin flickers of shame and desire. It was, in a way, wondrous to see this man again, her first love, the keeper of her troubled youth. A little part of her wanted Seth to see him, too: *Look at this!* they could marvel, like they did at the painting at Art Night. Evidence of something previously inexplicable.

Someone had turned the music up for the band's most famous song. Her entire history with Daniel pitched through her. Her body contained all of it, went back through it and suffered it all over again in the chair, in the ambient beer stench.

Daniel, holding up his glass, said, "Club soda."

His voice was scorched, deeper than she remembered. He told her it wasn't easy, staying straight, but he was doing okay. He was crashing at somebody's apartment, but he needed to leave, go to where he could get a decent job. The city was too expensive.

"You can afford it here, though, huh?" he said, and Gwen recognized an echo of the vague threat of the emails. He stared at her.

Gwen looked down, heart racing, locking on the glass. He was big, much bigger than her. She froze, unable to speak.

"What do you think, Gwen?" he said. "Can you help me get out of here?"

In that question, his voice softened. He became someone to pity. An addict, a broken person. Maybe he could get better.

A little money had helped her when she was starting out with Maddie. *Mercy*, she thought suddenly. Her body held the pain, but it held the love, too. She could feel her curved back tucked into his stomach, his groin, as they lay on the grass in their sleeping bags. Daniel walking next to her as they moved through the city together, bound by the sadness of their young pasts. It had passed for family. This, too, remained.

She reached into her purse, and her hand hovered between the manila envelope and the gun. Her fingers lightly brushed each. The gun was there to provide her a choice. An option to meet a threat with a threat. But the other choice was money, which might end things, once and for all. Gwen's breathing accelerated. Now she was confused. He had always made her uncertain of herself, fuzzy. She should have decided before—she should have walked in the door with a plan—

And then, suddenly, Daniel's hand reached across the table and grabbed her wrist.

Gwen stood up, but he kept his grip, his fingers tightening, her shoulder jerked toward the table. She was off-balance, panicked: now she couldn't reach the gun. Or the money.

His grip tightened around her wrist, but it might have been around her neck. She gasped for air.

"Tell me what she's like, Gwen, my daughter," he said.

He said it like she owed him. But she had no debt here, and with a surprise surge of strength she wrenched her wrist away. Around her, the sleepy eyes of the day-drinkers found focus, landing on the scuffle at Gwen's table.

Gwen backed away and reached into her bag, searching. She hesitated, then pulled out the manila envelope, placing it on the table. Slowly, she said, "Leave us alone."

He stared at her for a moment, a small smile on his lips.

"Or what, Gwen?" he said.

He was smirking at her weakness, which he would remember well. She had been the girl too frozen to do anything; too frozen to leave him, too frozen to help an injured man.

He tapped the envelope with a long finger. "You don't want your family to know what you got up to, and now you don't have to worry about it. We're good." He put the money in his back pocket and leaned back. He was calm, settled. He cocked his head and asked it again: "So what's she like?"

At the mention of Maddie, the gun seemed to grow heavier at the bottom of Gwen's bag, its heat spreading to her hip where the bag rested—available to her with just one gesture. But what could she do, really? She glanced around the bar: a slack-faced old man at the closest table stared into space. Hadn't she done enough now, by handing him the money, by taking him at his word that she was buying his vanishing?

Shaking, she leaned close to Daniel's face, breathing in his scent, lips to his ear. "Don't ever contact us again." Gwen stood to her full height, gripping her bag where the strap met her shoulder. "And Maddie is miraculous." Then she turned and walked fast to the door, feeling his eyes on her with every breathless step.

SPRING

14

MADDIE

All through winter and into spring, Maddie revelled in the fact of her first boyfriend. Every morning, she awoke and remembered, holding up a telescope to survey her life and ensure the discovery was still visible. Despite Gwen's hovering, and the love of both her parents, Maddie was aware—had always been aware—that at the beginning and end of every day, she was fundamentally alone. But now there was this other person in her near orbit, this satellite human who was with her always, even when he wasn't. At night, they texted each other to sleep. In the day, Joshua's tall frame waited for her by the locker between classes. They weren't stupid about being a couple, though; some girls got stupid, Maddie had seen it. But not Maddie and Joshua. They didn't hold hands to make other people feel bad, or have reality-TV–perfect fights in the hallway. Joshua didn't grab her butt (not even ironically) or ask for nudes. What they had was private, maybe even invisible to other people, Maddie imagined, which made it more sacred and a little superior.

Mostly, she had someone to do stuff with. When Joshua could get away, they walked a lot, far from each of their homes, through new neighbourhoods in the city that Maddie was still learning. He knew the streetcar routes, and the ravines that spidered beneath the roads and apartment blocks. They walked over the Bloor Street Viaduct, looking down at traffic through the webbed net meant to catch jumpers. In the woods below the Don Valley freeway, they spotted ducks in the Don River, and through the trees sometimes, they would spy a tent, tightly zipped.

One day, Maddie stayed home with a cold. Gwen was on a field trip with Eli's school, and at 11 a.m. on a Wednesday, the bell rang and there was Joshua, who never cut class, on the stoop. He looked nervously from side to side, and held up a plastic takeout bag.

"Pho," he said. Maddie must have looked confused, because he said, "Vietnamese soup."

They ate soup in front of the TV. They talked about school, and Joshua showed her a new comedian on his phone, a woman who said, "Say WHAAAAT?" at the end of each joke, which was kind of hilarious. They watched a show about a family in California where everyone was good-looking, and the grown kids lived in the guesthouse, and the big problem was whether or not one of the teenagers was going to continue being nice to her much older boyfriend, who had been fighting in Afghanistan. Outside, on a bench in the big backyard, the girl had a talk with her dad, who was grumpy but kind.

Maddie, foggy from her cold, was enjoying the fast-food high of mediocre TV when Joshua turned to her and said, "I don't actually know my dad."

"Okay," she said.

"I don't know why I said that to your parents, about him coming here." Joshua straightened the soup containers on the coffee table. "He probably has another family now. My mom came to get me when I was four, and when we got back to Canada, she was pregnant with Alex. We haven't heard from him since. Alex never even met him."

Maddie took this in, but she didn't feel too bad for Alexis. Instead of a dad, she had Joshua—a fair trade. He sat cloudy and serious, arms wrapped around his knees.

"She still sends money to his parents, though."

"Why would she do that?"

"You just have to. *Bagong bayani*—all the OFWs who move here and send money home."

Maddie looked at him blankly.

"Overseas Filipino Workers. She works two jobs, and sends half of what she makes back there to her parents, and his parents, and my aunt and her family. Then I give her my money from work. The big pass-along."

Maddie glanced at the empty containers of takeout soup. She should offer to pay him for the food.

"I need to keep my grades up," he said.

"Because of your scholarship."

"No, it's not that . . ." He frowned, irritated.

She was getting it wrong, which was scary. She needed him to be happy with her.

She tried again. "Because you owe your mom?"

"Because she's—it's been hard for her. I'm the son. I take care of her." He leaned back on the couch and shut his eyes.

In that position, he looked to Maddie like a man, in the worst way possible, like someone just barely hanging on. He looked like her dad frantically typing at his computer late at night. He looked like the zombie dads in Shadow Pines getting out of their cars at 6:30 p.m., faces baggy, briefcases dangling from the sleeves of their winter coats.

He opened his eyes and looked at her. "You and your mother—you could be sisters."

He smiled then, and so she could, too, relieved that the moment of distance between them had passed. She rested her head on his chest.

"You're hot," he said, feeling her forehead, and she tried to make a joke about being hot, but was too dizzy.

Joshua drew Maddie a bath, while she waited on the edge of her bed. When it was ready, she went in alone, shutting the door, taking off her pyjamas. She eased herself into the water, lying with her hair floating on the water, imagining drifting down one of those fake rivers at a water park, until a bout of violent coughing forced her to sit up. Joshua came in and put his hand on her back until the coughing stopped, averting his eyes from her naked body. Then he left again.

Maddie came out of the bathroom in her robe. He had made her bed and was sitting on the soft chair in the corner. It was light blue, and Maddie had never sat in it, because why do you need a chair in a bedroom anyway? Her mom had bought it without asking. But there was Joshua, with a book in his lap. He looked up and smiled at her, and she felt entirely safe with him there as she fell into sleep. When she woke up, he was gone.

× × ×

Carter's family was known to call at the last minute when Mrs. Andrada was already working at another home, so some afternoons, Maddie met Joshua in the park in Leaside with the kids and the nannies. Maddie made sure Carter's head was covered in the cold, and as the snow melted, she made sure that he wasn't too hot in his padded jacket.

What did they talk about? At night, in bed, reliving her time with Joshua, Maddie sometimes couldn't even remember. They talked about videos, and school. They talked about their pasts, and Maddie was surprised to find she had one. Shyly, she offered impressions of her life in Shadow Pines: the time she was babysitting at the Chen's and found a bunch of bookmarked porn on the desktop computer; the time she and Emma poured Kahlúa into their iced mochaccinos and went to the mall; her favourite feeling when the first snow fell.

He was a good listener. After she rambled on, he would say, "Huh," in this serious, thoughtful way, like he was putting all her pieces together to see her fully.

Maddie asked him about the Philippines. It was faint, he said, kind of abstract.

But he did remember taking the bus to visit his grandparents on weekends, out by a half-dead lake away from the city. Joshua always knew he and his mother would be getting off the bus soon when the rice fields came into view, striped rows of bent-backed women, arms in the mud. Soon after, his grandfather would be waiting at the side of the road, holding a plastic bottle of bubbles. The visit seemed serious at first, with his mother bowing, putting his grandfather's outreached hand against her forehead, and his grandfather shy. Then Joshua would blow bubbles, and his grandfather would laugh, applauding the biggest ones. One time, after a weekend visit, Joshua's mother told him that she would be leaving without him. "I'll come back for you." He cried as her bus left, leaning into his grandfather's legs. His mother didn't return for a year.

Maddie made murmuring sounds to tell him she was sorry, but in a tight voice, Joshua told her that he didn't think too much about that place. Last summer his mom and his sister rode the subway to a Jollibee in Scarborough for peach-mango pie, like this was such a big deal that Jollibee had finally come to Canada. But the pie was way too sweet. Only Alex really liked it, and she'd never even been to the Philippines.

But the hum beneath all their time together, if Maddie was completely honest, was sex. When and where and how, and when they couldn't and where they couldn't. Never at Carter's house (that was work; Joshua got paid). Sometimes at Maddie's, but they had to be careful there because Gwen had everyone on lockdown these days. When Alexis was at the community centre for choir, and Mrs. Andrada was picking up an extra shift—which was pretty much all the time—they would go to Joshua's bedroom. Then they would pick a playlist and have sex. The more they did it, the better it got. This was a surprise. Maddie had thought sex was like eye colour, a constant. But as she lost her doubt and they began to talk to each other, just a little ("This?" "Yes . . . this?"), she watched Joshua's expression buckle because of her, and she thought, "Hey, I'm figuring this out."

And then, in April, Joshua vanished.

× × ×

For a week, he wasn't in school. No texts, no social. Dr. Goldberg told Maddie that he had called in sick, but it didn't make sense. Nine days, including weekends. Maddie was swollen with anxiety; at night, she didn't sleep. Her mom tried to find out what was wrong, and her sympathy and hungry curiosity made Maddie recoil. All she wanted was an answer, not more questions.

She hoped that maybe Joshua would show up for Give Back Day, so on a cool Saturday morning, Maddie entered the auditorium. The event was just getting started, balloons bobbing and inspirational pop music blaring: "*You lift me up, up, up! You make me the best, best, best!*" Kids in Homes for Humanity T-shirts were hammering at wood planks, building what looked to be a doghouse. They wore shiny, newly purchased tool belts.

Maddie, already exhausted with worry, found herself further irritated. Since Joshua—since sex?—her eye on the world was surgical, and she was diagnosing some serious bullshit here at the U.

A kid came up to her and tried to get her to sign a petition for something. Maddie felt as accosted as she did by the cell phone salespeople and perfume pushers at the mall. She signed whatever it was, scanning for Joshua.

Maddie moved past a Hurricane Relief booth (precisely which hurricane required relief was unclear), and a massage table (20 DOLLARS = 1 MASSAGE!—read the banner—PROCEEDS TO REFUGEES!). Across the room, in front of the stage, Clara sat at a long table covered in clipboards of petitions and info sheets. She waved at Maddie and pointed to the sign above her head: CHILD RESCUE. Clara rolled her eyes and lolled her tongue. The song continued: "*You lift me UP UP UP!*" Maddie made her way through the dance-a-thon in the middle of the room, looking for Joshua.

She felt grim: *You are doing the girl thing, the thing of songs and movies. You are being that girl who stalks and sulks.* She wanted to be the other kind of girl, even though she wasn't sure what that kind was exactly.

Maddie felt a tap on her shoulder and turned around quickly, but it was only Ms. Harrison, the guidance counsellor. A tattoo leaked out of her T-shirt sleeve, wrapping her right arm, a black spiral of thorns and petals. Along her forearm, the words: "By any means necessary." "*UP UP UP!*" went the song.

"Madeline, nice to see you," Ms. Harrison said, her straight red hair flapping, her black-rimmed glasses low on her nose. "Any word on your applications?"

Maddie didn't want to tell her that she hadn't been thinking about her university applications at all. She'd used Seth's credit card to pay the fees and handed in exactly the same package to each school.

"Not yet," said Maddie.

Ms. Harrison looked at her, weighing her next question.

"Madeline," she said finally. "Would you mind—if I can ask you something off the record . . ."

Maddie tried not to look at the flower twisting around on Ms. Harrison's arm, so of course it was all she could see.

"Okay."

"Is it true that your family won the lottery?"

Maddie not-looked at the tattoo. "Yes. It wasn't a huge amount."

"Well, good for you." Ms. Harrison was trying to catch Maddie's eye, and Maddie refused to give it to her. "You didn't mention it on your application essay."

"No. It didn't seem . . ." Maddie paused, and Ms. Harrison jumped in: "Sympathetic. Good instinct." Then Ms. Harrison added, "You know, some people think the lottery is immoral."

"Uh," said Maddie, growing hotter, wondering why grown-ups did this, pranced around with "Some people" when what they really meant was "I."

"You've heard that argument, I'm sure. The lottery is a tax on the poor, because they pay to play but they never win. It's an economic shakedown. Yada yada yada."

Maddie watched the thorns and petals emerge and retreat from the sleeve. Maddie didn't know why Ms. Harrison was bothering. She already felt guilty; she didn't need this woman to smack at her with this particular broom.

"I had an aunt who spent her welfare cheque on the lottery, week after week, and then had to go to a food bank to feed herself."

Maddie frowned. "If she was your aunt, why didn't your family feed her?"

Ms. Harrison cleared her throat. "Well, we did, of course. But sometimes when people are ill, or addicted, you have to just—let them figure it out."

Maddie looked up at the rafters, anywhere but at Ms. Harrison.

After a pause in which Ms. Harrison seemed to be expecting something (an apology? Maddie wondered), Maddie asked, "How do you even know that about the lottery?"

"Is it a secret?" asked Ms. Harrison.

Maddie didn't answer. She made the right sounds to escape Ms. Harrison, only to turn and find Dr. Goldberg in her path.

"How's the altruism, Ms. Kaplan? Is the world rightly cured of its ails since your participation in the dance-a-thon?" he asked.

At that moment, in the wake of Ms. Harrison's earnestness, Maddie welcomed Dr. Goldberg's default archness.

"Listen, Maddie—" he said, his voice dropping. "You hang around with Joshua Andrada, correct?"

Now he had Maddie's attention. "Yes." Even the teachers knew she was with Joshua, then.

"Have you heard from him this week?"

"No," she said. "Why?"

"I shouldn't . . ."

Dr. Goldberg looked around, and with that shifty gesture, it occurred to Maddie that they were under surveillance, that school was another kind of authoritarian regime, like the ones they studied in Dr. Goldberg's class. This explained the wormy feeling she carried with her every time she walked the hall. She was tempted to look above her for a camera's eye in the auditorium rafters.

"We haven't heard from him since Monday, or his mother." He looked at Maddie kindly, the tenor of his voice gentle. "The administration is working on it, but I thought you should know. Will you tell me if you hear from him?"

This was the first time Maddie considered that Joshua hadn't just left her; he had left everything. She knew now that something was wrong. She strode to the exit, through the dancers, past the charity tables.

At the double doors to the gym, Maddie was blocked by Sophie standing with a little girl, holding her hand.

"Hey, where have you been? You didn't come help us tutor—" said Sophie. "This is Jennica, my reading buddy."

Jennica held up a picture book with a tiger wearing a hat on the cover.

Maddie looked at Jennica, then up at Sophie. "Does it ever get to you? All this? Rich kids fattening up their university applications?"

Sophie, who had a way of curling herself small, straightened to her full, minimal height, tipping her chin up. "Well, I'm not rich," she said. "I'm on financial aid. I used to go to the school Jennica goes to."

"Charles Tupper Junior," said Jennica, not looking up from her book.

Maddie was surprised. She'd seen Sophie and Clara as two-headed, and assumed that Sophie's house would be as vast as Clara's, her holidays as luxurious. "I didn't know—"

"I'm not embarrassed about it. But this stuff . . ." Sophie gestured around the room. "I know it seems . . . fake, but people mean well."

"Do they? What do they mean?" Maddie asked the question sincerely, but even to her ears, it sounded sarcastic.

Sophie gave her a harder look and said, "You don't know everyone's story, Maddie. Not everybody is an insider."

Clara danced up to them, arriving in a plié. "*Bonjour, mes amis,*" she said, gushing lightly over Jennica, who showed her the tiger book with the same solicitude. Clara then turned her attention to the others.

"I hope Sophie's giving you hell for being such a ghost, Madeline," said Clara. "You missed, let me see . . ." She began counting on her fingers: "The spring gala, Andrew D.'s house wrecker, the DJ Rav show . . ." One finger was left: the pointer, perfectly manicured and wearing a familiar green ring.

Maddie stared. "Where did you get that ring?"

Clara rolled her eyes. "Duh—where do you think?" she said. "I'm kind of a genius shoplifter."

Maddie's jaw seized. She looked to Sophie, but Sophie was heavy-lidded now, biting her lip.

Maddie turned to leave.

"Wait, Maddie—" Sophie called.

But Maddie had shoved open the doors, pushed through them onto the field, into the light—and was gone.

× × ×

Maddie banged on Joshua's apartment door until someone shouted from behind a different door to shut the fuck up. It was not her first visit.

Then she took the streetcar to the food court. At 11 a.m., it was still quiet. Grey cages covered the unopened stalls. A woman swept. A few people sat alone at tables.

Behind the counter of the sub shop, an older woman held a clear plastic bag the size of a pillow. She turned it over one of the silver trays and shook out the snowy white lettuce.

The woman smiled at her. "I know you. We met that time," she said.

Maddie didn't remember but nodded and smiled, trying to make up for not remembering.

"Joshua hasn't been at school—"

The woman's smile vanished. "His mother is very sick," she said. "She's in the hospital. I tried to get them to hold onto Joshua's job, but I don't know. They don't like us taking holidays, you know? Even if it's Joshua. He's such a good worker."

Maddie caught her breath. "Which hospital?" she asked.

The woman told her, and said, "Do you want a sandwich? No charge."

"No, but thank you."

"Just a bun?"

Suddenly, Maddie couldn't remember the last time she'd eaten.

"Okay," she said. "Thank you."

The woman wrapped the bun gently in a napkin and handed it to her with concern. As Maddie walked to the hospital, she ate it up in three ferocious bites.

× × ×

At the hospital, Maddie signed in as a relative of Mrs. Andrada's. It was easy. She had thought it would be more like a prison somehow, with patients like inmates.

When Maddie got to the door, she saw the nameplate: *Andrada, S.* She realized that she didn't know what the "S" was for. When she opened the door with her sticky, disinfected hand, Joshua's mother lay directly in front of her. There were three other beds in the room, but only one other person, shapeless on her side.

Joshua's head was down, reading a book. After all that worry, Maddie couldn't believe that he was just there in his body, sitting in a chair.

Joshua's mother's head poked out of the sheet, eyes closed. Maddie was relieved: his mother suffering was better than Joshua suffering, she thought, even though it was cruel. A machine beeped, and on the fourth beep, like it was a musical cue, Joshua looked up, directly at Maddie. He frowned when he saw her, and his jaw clenched. Somehow Maddie had expected a joyful reunion, but instead, she was making him angry, just by being there, by being an intruder.

"What are you doing here?" he asked in a whisper.

Anger didn't suit him, but there it was, burning in the narrow line of his mouth. He didn't stand up, so Maddie stood in front of him stupidly, looming above his tiny mother.

"Everyone's worried," she whispered. She felt like crying, but only a little for his sick mother, mostly for Joshua, and for herself. She wanted him to stand up now, and touch her, like before. She wanted to be enfolded.

"She has a kidney infection."

"Oh no," said Maddie.

Joshua rubbed his face in his palms. He looked tired. A little red zit glowed on his cheek.

Maddie asked, "Both kidneys?"

Joshua stood up finally, close to Maddie, and looked down

on his mother's sleeping body. He exhaled, gently whispered something to her that Maddie couldn't make out.

"Can she hear you?" asked Maddie.

"She's so drugged she keeps thinking I'm her dad." Joshua moved his hand to the sheets, just above where his mother's waist would be. He reached under the sheet and pulled briskly, like a magician doing the reveal.

Alarmed, Maddie said, "Don't . . ." She didn't want to see anything. Whatever it was could not be unseen, and it was bound to be something terrible. "Please . . ." she said, but Joshua pulled back the sheet and the side of his mother's gown, revealing a waxy mannequin torso.

"Look," said Joshua, and Maddie forced herself to look where he was gesturing, at his mother's side, below her ribcage. She saw a long white scar, gruesome and badly stitched. It hugged her side, leading to her back.

"She sold one," said Joshua in a hospital-quiet voice.

Maddie stared at the scar.

"Sold one," she repeated.

"It paid for my plane fare and my paperwork," he said.

"I don't—"

"She sold a kidney so I could leave," said Joshua. "So I could come here."

Maddie had seen a documentary in Philosophy class last year. In a poor hot country, men—wasn't it mostly men?—would sell their organs for money. Livers and kidneys. The cellophane-wrapped dregs of the grocery store. She couldn't for the life of her name the country.

Maddie's mind sprinted past all she knew about organs. "Can't someone donate—?"

"She's way down on the list," said Joshua. Mrs. Andrada's

scar moved up and down with her breathing. Joshua pulled the gown over his mother's torso, tenderly. Then he tucked her in, leaving her arms outside the thin blanket.

"Can't you give her one?" asked Maddie.

"Alex and I are both type A. Mom's O."

"Alex? She's twelve."

"Kids are allowed to donate, with permission," said Joshua.

Maddie forced herself to look at his mother's inner arm, at the drinking-straw shape of a fistula beneath the skin. Around it, the skin was puffed and meaty and punctured with holes. She wanted Joshua to see that she was strong, so she didn't look away.

He told her that the wait list for a new kidney, one that could do its job machine-free, went on and on, like a scroll, like a roll of paper towel, name after name after name. Joshua's mother's name was somewhere in the bottom third for this province. That meant years, he explained. It meant you waited and waited, and they evaluated your life on a point system, and if other people mattered more and earned more points, you dropped down on the list. A younger person might apply, someone with more life left; or a better patient, one without a chronic condition like Joshua's mom had. Point getters. Line cutters. Or maybe not enough people check the "organ donor" box on their driver's licences, and you go even farther down the list because there just aren't enough kidneys to go around. Turns out that no one wants to part with themselves, even after death. We get greedy, hoard our bodies, just in case we need them later. So down, down on the list she goes. The scary part, Joshua said, was that it could happen, she could get called up, top of the scroll—but maybe, when it happened, it would be too late. Her one kidney, operating at "twenty-three percent" (he said it like he was answering a math question), could have stalled out by then, too far gone. The engine stopped.

His mother had been on dialysis for months. She would come to the hospital and get hooked up to a washing machine that pulled out the blood and cleaned it, then put it back. She had been doing this three times a week, six hours each visit. All those times that they had been with Carter happened because Mrs. Andrada was here, at the hospital. Her body was her other job. And Maddie never knew that this cloud of fear and sickness was what Joshua lived beneath. All their conversations (all that *sex*)—and she knew nothing.

"Why didn't you ever tell me about this?"

"She didn't want me to tell you," he said. "She thought they'd take me and Alexis away."

"They," Maddie repeated.

"That's what my mom said." He couldn't tell her, because Maddie was the "they," a white girl who would bring scrutiny, inviting Children's Aid, social workers.

Joshua's mother's hand lay on the sheet, its holes illuminated.

He led Maddie out of the room, shutting the door. At the end of the hallway was a floor-to-ceiling window, looking out over a parking lot. He stopped there, and she could tell that he wanted to say something. Joshua rubbed his finger along the glass, looking at the cars. Tears welled up in his eyes.

Maddie moved toward him, but he put his hand out—stop.

"I can't see you anymore," he said. The tears snapped back.

Maddie stared. "Why not?"

His eyes stayed on the parking lot. "I can't think about anything but my mom right now. There's this social worker—she thinks we're staying with friends, but she's going to come by the apartment soon."

"Come stay with us," Maddie said, eager to solve it. "My mom wouldn't mind. Our house is too big anyway—"

He didn't let her finish. "She said 'foster care.' I can't let that happen. I have to take care of Alex." He kept tracing the same line on the window. "I don't know how I'm going to do it, get through school—pay for university. I don't have parents to cut me a cheque. It's not the same for me."

The bitterness in his voice was unfamiliar, and seemed directed straight at her. Maddie wished she had never told him about the lottery. No—she wished they had never won the lottery at all. Maddie felt as if a hand were holding her head under water. She was flailing.

"Dr. Goldberg can help—the U has counsellors . . ."

Out the window, where Joshua's eyes fell, every single stall in the parking lot was occupied. "Sometimes I hate that school," he said. "I've been there for six years, and you're the first girl who's ever looked at me as anything but a lab partner. Charity case."

Maddie wanted to pull him back from this rare bout of self-pity. "Sophie's on financial aid, too—"

She put her hand out to take his and he recoiled. Her touch had repelled him. What if he never touched her again? She couldn't bear it. Her body wouldn't stay intact. She would shatter.

"You can still study," she said. "We can study together. I can help with Alex. You can move in with us—"

"My mom might die," Joshua said. "Can you believe that?"

Maddie shook her head. She moved to him again, and he backed away.

All of a sudden, he asked, "Why did you leave that money at Susan's?"

"What? I . . ." She tried to remember. She couldn't read his expression. Joshua seemed much older than her.

"She needed the money. I had it."

"You should have just talked to her. She wanted us to stay.

Remember? But you wanted to leave. You practically ran out of there."

Maddie frowned. "So what if I gave her money? We should all just stay in our little bubbles? Aren't we supposed to take care of each other if we can?" She knew she sounded like a celebrity vlogger, but she believed it. She loved being in Joshua's bubble. She wanted to behave like a generous person, even if she didn't always feel generous. It was a hundred dollars. It was nothing. It was everything.

"You have to go," said Joshua, looking away again, definitively.

It was because she always listened to him, because everything he said was true, that she stood for a moment longer, and saw from his rigid back that there was no way forward. The change in him was a thing, not a feeling. A large, cement object now sat between them. Maddie couldn't get him to go around it. He wouldn't even try. He was far away, bound only to the great injustice unfolding at the centre of his life.

She turned and stumbled down the corridor.

At the elevator, Maddie put her hand on the wall, her knees buckling. If you are going to fall, fall in a hospital. Hands lifted her. People murmured their concern.

"I'm okay," she told these strangers, through her tears. "I'm just visiting someone, and it's sad."

When she was at last outside, away from the acrid hospital smell, she made a decision. She could not do nothing. She just had to figure out what the something would be.

15

GWEN

Chickadees scrambled between the newly budding shrub roses in the backyard. Sunlight streamed in the windows, climbing the kitchen walls. Gwen showed up on time at Eli's pickups and drop-offs, and kept her eyes on her children's phones, tracking them several times a day. But there were no strange sightings, no threats.

The most thrilling change was Maddie's return. She was in the house more than she had been, quiet and shadowy, but *around*. Of course, Maddie's presence sprang from a loss: Joshua seemed to have broken up with her, but this topic was firmly off limits. Once, though, when Gwen had knocked on her bedroom door, Maddie had let her in and collapsed in her arms, sobbing. Gwen held her, in awe, revelling in her touch: she could still comfort her daughter.

Seth didn't notice the money Gwen had taken, a testament to how little Daniel had asked for and Seth's work distractions.

After the win, Seth had set up the family at a new bank in the city, abandoning their old bank where the profits from the sale of the last house (after taxes, lawyer and agent fees) still sat. That account had once held all their money and been the axis of their days, telling them what they could and couldn't afford to do. But now the account was entirely neglected, waiting at the bottom of a to-do list to be closed.

Three times Gwen drove back to their old branch, parked in the strip mall and made withdrawals until she had the money for Daniel. On the third visit, when the teller called over the manager to ask about the reason for the withdrawal, Gwen said, "Construction project." The manager leaned in and said, "Congratulations on your good fortune, Mrs. Kaplan."

Months passed, and there was no word from Daniel. Maybe the money had worked. Gwen had handled the situation correctly, after all, and having done so, she gradually felt less tormented. She put away the sound of Steve's wheezing as his body thumped to the floor, put away the image of some girl watching him, dumbstruck. She could do this—punch the airbag back into the steering wheel—put it all away like it had been locked up those many years. Slowly, slowly, Gwen let herself breathe again. A new, airy mood descended, as if she were sleeping in the sun.

On the night of Maddie's birthday, when Maddie walked in the front door, Seth had the three of them waiting in the living room. Gwen was searching her phone for a cab number. Eli was rolling a soccer ball with this foot, untied shoelaces clacking.

"Surprise!" Seth called. "Keep your coat on. Did you read the card?" He had put a small gift in Maddie's backpack that morning, as he did every year.

"Yes, thank you," said Maddie.

Gwen saw her touch her ears, where diamond studs glittered. Last year the school gift was lip gloss in a little plastic pineapple. Gwen watched Seth hug her. Maddie softened in Seth's embrace.

"Mom picked them," Seth said. "The bird reference on the card. Did you get it? It's the other part of your present. You're about to have your mind blown."

"Do up your shoelaces, Eli," said Gwen.

Eli had worn Velcro for so long that he came late to shoelaces. He crouched down and attempted the laces slowly, his hand moving through space like a mime, his face grimacing, recalling the steps.

The three of them stood with their jackets, waiting until Gwen finally dropped to her knees and did the shoelaces herself. "One, two, three, FOUR," she said, and they were done.

× × ×

They ate in a wood-fired pizza restaurant, part of a chain that had come to Toronto from New York. A big round light hung over the table as if they were in an operating theatre.

The whole extravagant evening had been Seth's idea, but Gwen was glad; she needed a night out, away from the silent neighbourhood, the big house with its slippery floors. Seth had started planning the party a few days ago, stumbling into the bedroom after getting home late, a little drunk, maybe. "It's expensive, but screw it, right? She's only eighteen once. Let's enjoy these last days before the horsemen arrive!"

The server brought salted caramel tarts. Seth proclaimed, more than once, that the meal was "amazing."

"What, no candle?" asked Eli.

"Your university fund matures today, Mads," said Seth. "The money's in your account now, so don't panic if you see a high balance. We'll talk about moving it to GICs."

"You're rich!" said Eli. "What school are you going to any-way?"

Gwen and Seth both leaned in.

"Don't know yet." Maddie poked at the tart.

"There's not much time," said Seth. "You can't make a bad choice, really."

Maddie nodded, taking a small bite.

"Let's not talk about choices tonight," said Gwen.

× × ×

The Town Car was waiting outside the restaurant. Gwen opened the back door to an interior coated in black: black leather seats, black windows, a driver in a dark suit nodding his hello. They climbed in. Eli adjusted the TV to a sports channel.

The car sped along the freeway, the daylight fading. Gwen could feel Maddie growing anxious next to her.

As they turned onto the road to the airport, Maddie asked, "Are we going on a trip? Because I didn't pack, and I need some things . . ."

"Do you want to know?" asked Seth, turning around from the front seat.

"Yes," said Maddie tensely.

Gwen had reminded Seth that Maddie hated surprises. Then the Town Car pulled up in front of a sign: TORONTO HELI TOURS.

"Oh," said Maddie.

"Yes!" cried Eli.

"It's very safe," said Gwen, though no one but her was seeking reassurance.

"We'll get to look into the skyscrapers, see how other people live," said Seth.

Maddie smiled, and Gwen took this as a positive. She walked behind her down the corridor, Seth and Eli up ahead.

The helicopter was surprisingly plastic. Gwen had expected it to feel more substantial. Before they could enter, the pilot delivered a lecture about the possibility of nausea, and the benefits of "inertial relief," a phrase that Gwen liked, chewing on it.

Gwen sat next to Maddie, Eli sat next to the pilot, Seth sat in back, all of them in bulbous black headsets that sat aside their skulls like fly eyes. As they ascended, the plane jerked and heaved; the blades hammered loudly.

Over the headsets, the pilot explained what they were seeing: the lake to the south; the distant lights of Niagara Falls; the TD Centre towers. He had mistaken them for tourists, and no one corrected him, because they were still tourists, in a way, even though it had been nearly a year since the money.

As Seth had planned, they were flying inside the dusk. The light was pink, and fading quickly. The pilot slowed in front of a massive glass building face, so close that Gwen didn't know what they were looking at. He hovered there and explained almost tenderly, despite his electronically distant voice piped into their ears, the origin of the building. It had been built to be the tallest in the world, but then someone else in another city had the same idea, and now it was fourth. He sounded disappointed.

The sky darkened, and specifics gave way to shapes, long rectangles and pointed pencils. They were yanked back up into the sky to look down at the snaking lights of the night, just flickering into steady lines. The city turned electric. Gwen looked down on the neglected tops of the buildings. Air vents blew puffs of white smoke.

She felt a tap on her knee: Maddie pointed out the window, excited. Gwen strained to see what she was seeing.

"Mall!" she mouthed. Gwen nodded at the glittering block. Maddie pressed a button so that her words could travel out into everyone's ears. "That's where Joshua works!" she said excitedly.

Gwen nodded, gave her a thumbs-up, and then she sat back, thinking, *Oh no, it's not over at all.* Whatever had happened between them, whatever severing Joshua had attempted—Maddie hadn't accepted it. Her daughter was madly in love. Gwen could feel its residual heat on her. For this, there was no motherly comfort to be offered. *You will suffer these losses, and I can't help you*, she thought. Gwen patted Maddie on the knee, and Maddie kept her face close to the glass.

Seth's voice crackled through the static in her ear. "Hey," he said. Gwen turned around to look back at him. "I'm going to have to go back to the office as soon as we land," he said into his mouthpiece, holding up his phone by way of explanation, grinning. "Tom has big news."

Gwen nodded, trying not to be annoyed at Seth's constant absences. "He does it for us," her mother had said once, when Gwen complained about having to tiptoe past her father sleeping on the couch after work, beer on the coffee table. But Gwen had never really believed it: he did it for himself, so he wouldn't have to be around the three women. Men worked so they could be silent and elsewhere, recused from the boredom and mess of the quotidian, which was left to the women. Even the women who worked full-time—Julia, or Eleanor, the Bay Street financier back in Shadow Pines—never entirely stepped out of their families in the way of the men. Gwen was almost positive that they didn't get to be war heroes after work, crashed on the couch, absent when present.

She looked at her daughter. Gwen knew that Maddie was searching the skyline, as if she might see Joshua there, and he might see her, floating above the city in her bubble.

At that moment, Maddie looked over at her mother and dropped her hand on top of Gwen's. Gwen looked at it, bewildered.

Maddie's voice came through the headset. "Thanks for a really nice birthday, Mom." She smiled and Gwen swelled with joy.

"Happy birthday, hon."

MADDIE

The email looked, at first, like junk mail. It didn't have a subject line, and the address featured a weird series of numbers. Maddie almost hit Delete, but then thought maybe it would be something surprising, like a note from Joshua—

Dear Madeline . . .

As she read, her centre of gravity shifted. By the time she was finished, she was some other girl, sitting at her desk in her unfamiliar bedroom on her eighteenth birthday.

Happy Birthday. I hope this doesn't come out of the blue.

You never know what's normal. You never know what other people's families are like. Emma's mom, back in Shadow Pines, could remember everything she wore on the first day of school of every single year of her education, from Grade 1 to Grade 12. The summer before Maddie and Emma started high school, Emma's mom pulled out her old journals. Together around the kitchen table, the three of them sat looking at a stack of pink notebooks from the '80s, tiny broken locks flapping. They were boring ("I

235

got a shaker knit sweater at Le Château. I got blue but wishing it was white. Paul T. super cute today. See ya!"), but Maddie was fascinated anyway. Details were what her mother never shared.

Maddie had rushed home and asked Gwen, "Do you have any journals from high school?" Gwen clouded over as if nothing had been asked. It was the same blocking she did when Maddie asked about her grandparents, or Procter. Seth would always step in between Maddie's questions and Gwen. "It was a hard time for your mom. Let's talk about it later." But there never was a later.

Maddie had mentioned to Raj once that she didn't really know anything about her mom's life before becoming a mom, and he'd shrugged and said his own mom never talked about India either. "It's an immigrant thing," he'd said. But what world had Gwen emigrated from? What planet had expelled her? She was her own cold star.

Maddie had just accepted it. All her life, the dead space between dates and facts—she was an idiot. Maybe she had always known. It didn't take a genius. There was Eli, with Seth's curls, and there was Maddie, with Seth's nothing.

Splinters of images came back to her with new meaning. She was tiny, sleeping with her mother in a bed in a strange room with a desk by a window. A dream she'd had over and over. Then there was her little yellow dress, and holding Seth's hand. That was the first photo of the three of them after the others were lost—she stopped. The photos weren't lost, though. They didn't exist. Just the one of her and her mother in the hospital— newborn Maddie in a blanket, her mom's black rubber bracelets. Where was this guy, this Daniel guy, that day? Daniel. Where was her dad when she was born?

Maddie stumbled out of her bedroom. The house was dark, except for a light in the kitchen. Seth was still out, at work, but as Maddie went down the stairs, she could see her mother in her pyjamas, perched at the island, pulling a sagging teabag from a mug. Seeing her mother dangle the brown, wet teabag from a string was revolting. Maddie's expensive dinner flipped in her stomach.

Maddie placed her phone in front of her mother, pointing at the email.

As Gwen read, weather passed over her face: fear, sadness, a kind of submission. Probably her mother had been waiting for this reproach forever. She must have known it was coming. How strange to always be waiting, Maddie thought, almost pitying her mother for just a moment, and then letting fury overtake that generosity.

Gwen said numbly, "He was supposed to leave." She stopped on the email's last line, which was a request. "No, Maddie—you can't meet with him."

"Why not?"

"He shouldn't be here . . ." Gwen looked up. "You can't see him."

Maddie stared at her, the most direct look she'd given her mother in months.

"I know it's hard to understand, but we did it to protect you. He's not a good person. I wish he were. But Maddie—he's not . . . safe, for you—"

"Did he rape you or something? Is my father a rapist?" This question came to her suddenly as a plausible explanation, the ramifications of which were too cosmic to consider, even as she asked it.

"No! God, no," said Gwen.

Maddie stared. She felt like Truman in *The Truman Show* when he figures out the conspiracy. All of them, in on it.

"We made—I made—a decision, a long time ago, to try to make it easier for you."

Nothing about this was easy. Maddie couldn't imagine a more complicated, knotted mass than her life at that moment. "You're a liar," she said simply.

Gwen's arms hung at her sides. She hunched over at the waist. "This isn't how we wanted you to find out. I'm sorry, Maddie. Time passed so much more quickly than I ever imagined—please, you can't see him—you don't know what he's capable of."

Maddie wanted Gwen to say something real, for once. She wanted her to explain all the random accidents that had made her who she was. She was real, Maddie was certain of it; her body was real. It had felt everything. She had been alive for eighteen years. It was the how of it that she never really understood.

Maddie watched her mother open her jaw, then slowly shut it. Then open, then shut, fishily.

Tell me, Maddie willed it. *Tell me*. But Gwen did not say anything.

Maddie turned and trudged upstairs, arms wrapped around her torso, holding herself in.

She stopped at Eli's room, because the door was wide open. Maddie flipped on the light. His sleepwalking mat had been shoved to the foot of his bed, useless. His sheets were balled. He was gone.

GWEN

There it was, then. It had happened. She had thought that she would feel relieved when instead, she felt ablaze. She had burned down the world.

Did he rape you? That was Maddie's question. She had to tell

Maddie that there was violence, but not only, and that seemed an impossible task. She couldn't understand it herself, the swirling duality of that time, the love and brutality conjoined.

A sudden breeze entered the house. The front door was open. Gwen didn't know what scared her more: someone coming in, or someone going out. She went to shut it.

Maddie appeared at the top of the stairs. "Eli's not here," she said.

Gwen looked up at Maddie, letting the fact sink in, then shot out through the open door. Barefoot, she moved on instinct, tripping her way down the landing to the driveway. There was no moon. The sidewalk seemed far away and dark.

"Eli!" called Gwen, her eyes searching the lawn and the garden. "Eli!" She ran around the side of the house to the back, to the pool. The gate was open. Automatic light flooded the pool's empty walls. No Eli. Now she ran, barefoot, back to the front of the house, her thin pyjama top flapping. Yonge Street, with its speeding cars and night buses, was only a few blocks away. Gwen tripped on the cobblestone, braced herself on the fence and looked left, then right. Nothing, and no one. The only light was on a single porch far away. Windows were black next to their manicured hedges and lawns.

Gwen ran the most dangerous route she could imagine, toward Yonge, calling "Eli! Eli!" When she was a block from the traffic, she stood in the middle of the road and spun in a full circle. A car went by slowly. Gwen stepped toward it, frantic. The windows were tinted. It slowed to a crawl and she lunged at the driver, screaming, "My son! Please!" The car swerved and sped up, passing her.

Gwen caught movement back where she had come from: a figure in the distance. She sprinted.

"Mom!" There was Maddie, directly across the street from her, on the sidewalk. She was barefoot, too, but she was young and faster. "I see him!"

Gwen couldn't believe how fast her daughter could move, her legs kicking as if swimming, chopping water. Ahead, cars flew past on Yonge Street. By the traffic light, at the intersection, Gwen could see Eli's small back. He was on the sidewalk, standing and rocking side to side. Then he stopped suddenly— Maddie was closing in now—and moved forward, as if to take a step. It would be a step into traffic, between cars. Gwen ran— she couldn't tell if he had stepped off the curb—what was she seeing? Two cars came hurtling out of the dark; one leaned on the horn. Gwen knew that loud sounds did nothing. Shaking him didn't work either. He needed a quiet voice, at a distance, a slow rousing. But there was no time.

He stood rigid, and then Gwen saw it: the slight lean, the intention—he was going to try to cross, toward the flower store, the organic butcher, the gourmet grocer, all closed and dimmed for night. Gwen panted, clutching her heart.

Maddie got there first, tackling Eli, knocking them both to the ground. She heard him wail, letting loose the strange high-pitched sound of the night terrors of his childhood. Gwen reached them, breathless, and fell onto their bodies, their two bodies, trying to tangle her own arms with theirs. But they were impenetrable, braided together.

Maddie looked up at her mother angrily. "Why didn't you lock up?" she hissed. Eli was silent now, limp in Maddie's arms.

She was hopeless against them. Gwen stood, pulled Eli from the ground, and he leaned into her, groggy. Gwen buried her face in his hair.

"You ran away," Gwen murmured.

Eli didn't say anything.

Then Maddie took his hand, severed him from Gwen, and they walked ahead of her in the streetlight, toward the big house.

Gwen straggled behind, her head bowed in shame, the endless, years-long shame a shroud that, at last, all the neighbourhood, all the world, could see, if it weren't asleep.

× × ×

Pulse racing, Gwen sat in the kitchen all night, waiting. The doors and windows had been secured, and the alarm punched. She couldn't talk to Seth about this on the phone. He kept texting: "Another hour" and "Big developments. Don't wait up." Gwen imagined Julia sitting across from Seth at a boardroom table, muscular arms typing away on her tablet, solving the company's problems, while Seth gazed at her admiringly.

The hours went by hazily until the birds began to sing in the dark, and a moment later, faint sun revealed the backyard. Dew gathered on the plants and deck furniture, beading. Summer was coming.

Gwen glanced at the clock on her phone: 5:45 a.m. The kids would be up in an hour and fifteen minutes. Or would they? Gwen tried to imagine Maddie coming down the stairs, Maddie eating breakfast. That these small occurrences would ever happen again seemed impossible now. Normal had ended.

Finally, just before 6 a.m., a car pulled up, and the front door slammed. Seth. Gwen smacked open her sour mouth.

He threw his keys down on the island, kissed her on the cheek. He didn't seem surprised to see her sitting there. "Oh good, you're up." His shirt was untucked, bunchy with perspiration. He began making coffee, a wild energy in his movements.

Something had happened, and Seth's excitement wedged itself to the front of the line, ahead of Gwen's heartbreak.

"Guess what?" he said.

Gwen thought how much he must sound like the eager magician he'd been when he was a kid. Young Seth standing before an audience of neighbours in his cape. "Guess what's in this hat? Guess what card I have?"

As he talked, he ground the coffee in the new grinder and blasted the espresso machine, which made jarring whale noises. In between sounds, he told her about his night. It was, in a way, a confession. Gwen, dazed with fatigue and the lingering fear of the night before, tried to make sense of what he was telling her. The company had been on the brink. The house, in fact, had been put up as surety.

Gwen blinked. "The house . . ."

But they pulled it together at the last minute, Seth said, as if announcing the surprise outcome of a football game. Julia figured it out. Julia pulled the rabbit out of the hat.

"Julia . . ." said Gwen.

Julia had brought in a buyer. A bully offer for the payroll software had been accepted, papers signed at 5 a.m., which would allow them to fund BuzzSwitch for its next phase. Seth was giddy, curls flying.

"Why didn't you tell me things were so bad?" Gwen asked.

"I didn't want to stress you out," he said. "There wasn't any reason to lay it on you, until we'd solved it. I mean, Gwen . . ." He took one of his long pauses, drank his coffee, leaning on the counter. "You never really want to know."

"Want to know what?"

"What's going on."

She looked at him searchingly. He attempted an explanation.

"I'm Canute, commanding the tides for you." He drank again. "I keep the world away. That's the arrangement."

Gwen understood. Withholding had passed for love in their marriage, and in their family. He was wrong, though: she, not he, was the one who held back the waters, kept everything in place. He made the money, but she fed and wiped and built and tended. She made them whole, and protected them from the cold real world that only she, of all of them, really understood at all. And she was bone tired of the effort, the corralling and containing. Gwen closed her eyes.

Finally, she said, "I need to tell you something."

So she did. She told Seth of Daniel's return. The money she'd paid him. The email to Maddie. The looming threat against them all. And then she told him about the crime, and how she had stood there as a man's blood pooled beneath the industrial refrigerator, and done nothing. How she had, in fact, grabbed the money, as ordered, and run.

Seth listened. He put his coffee down and slid his hands into his pockets. He moved from the counter and stood alone in the middle of the huge kitchen, silent. But he didn't gasp or buckle at the knees. He was silent. Outside the French doors, chickadees swarmed the maple tree.

Gwen felt at once a twin certainty: that she had never loved her husband more, and that she was losing him. They had arrived at the end of his constancy, his faithfulness. It had finally been spent.

She asked, "Are we still married?"

Seth didn't answer for a moment, and Gwen couldn't look at him. When he spoke at last, he said, "But I know this story, Gwen." She straightened.

"You told me all of this when we met, and you've been telling me again and again for years, in different ways."

"I never told you about the store—the manager . . ."

He shook his head. "About being a messed-up kid. You forget that I met you not long afterwards. You forget that you flinched when I touched you. You forget that it took months for you to let me in."

Gwen was unsure now. That wasn't the story. He came into the dentist's office, and they fell in love.

"You saw this weird guy who was too close to his mother, and was probably never going to get married. You were smart and fierce, protecting your daughter. You were . . ." He searched for a word, and said finally, "Unsung."

Gwen was crying.

"Oh, Gwen. I know you. I know you." And he took her in his arms, and she laid her head on his creased shoulder and felt the brush of his unshaven chin.

For sixteen years, their bodies had been together. They had imprinted on one another, but also, they had been apart—lost to that awful, inevitable apartness that drifted, unremarked upon, through all marriages. Gwen had always believed that they were so different from everybody else. She had hung her identity on that difference. But it was ordinary, really, the great distance between two people that came and went like daylight.

× × ×

Maddie and Eli did come downstairs after all, as they did every day. Seth had led Gwen to the couch, pulled a blanket over her, and she was still there, half asleep, adjacent to the start of the day but not its driver.

"Weird," Eli declared when he saw her.

"Shh," said Seth, launching the routine.

Gwen listened to their morning noises. Dishes clattered. "Can you sign this form?" Eli asked Seth. Gwen realized that she had never missed a morning exit before; even when she'd been feverish with the flu, she would haul herself up to pack lunches, empty the dishwasher. Such martyrdom seemed like madness to her now.

When the door slammed and they were gone, Gwen propped herself up and looked out through the picture window. She saw Seth and Maddie standing by the van, Seth with his hands on Maddie's shoulders. Her head hung, chin on chest. He was talking. Maddie nodded. Then he hugged her close, kissed the top of her head. Oh, Seth, she thought, before falling into sleep. Oh, my husband.

16

The Canada geese had taken over, swarming and screeching, leaving cigarette-butt–shaped feces all over the boardwalk. Maddie tried to shoo one away with her hand. It honked back angrily, so okay, they'd share the patch of beachfront.

She'd chosen a public place on purpose: if he was crazy, like Gwen said, Maddie could yell, or run away. A jogger went by. If she screamed, Maddie was pretty sure someone would hear her.

As she waited, Maddie thought of Seth. She touched her earrings.

He had apologized in the driveway that morning. It wasn't his fault, she told him. It was Gwen, her relentless tight grip. Did he ever notice that Gwen was always the first mom at pickup at school and playdates, always rushing to get them away from others, back home? She was always on Maddie, had he noticed? But Seth wouldn't hear it. There were things she didn't know, he told her. Yes, yes, Maddie muttered, all those things she didn't know.

But she felt better when Seth hugged her. Even though he'd been away so much since they moved to the city, and even though he had this crazy new lined face when he showed up late from his new company, he was the same dad. He was her dad, right? That didn't seem even a tiny bit diluted to her. *You are my daughter. I love you. Nothing changes.* He dropped her off at the back of the school. *Give your mom and me some time to make this right.*

But Maddie didn't enter the school. She was missing a practice test in Functions. She'd already failed a pop quiz the week before. But would universities really take back their acceptance letters? Did any of it matter? She wasn't sure.

Maddie waited until Seth's car was gone, then walked to the subway. After a transfer to a streetcar, she wandered the east end until noon when she made her way to the beach.

She looked up. That was him; she could tell. He was holding two coffee cups and wearing a black leather jacket, like it was still the '90s. She had expected to see herself, but he didn't look like her, really, except for the dark eyes. Taller, and older than she'd imagined. Maybe he had been handsome once. Maddie couldn't tell, with old people, who had been what.

"Maddie?"

"Yes."

Were they supposed to hug now? She didn't want to touch him. He held out the coffee, and she took it, even though she only drank coffee when it seemed uncool to order hot chocolate.

He sat down next to her. Maddie tried to sneak glances, but they were caught in a weird sideways formation. She could see his hands most clearly. In those hands was something familiar: she recognized her own tapered fingers and red knuckles.

"Tell me about yourself," he said, like a teacher from the U. He sounded like he'd just woken up.

Maddie wanted to tell him that—topical question!—there was no self to describe. Her self had been shattered a couple of times lately, first by Joshua, and now by her mom. But instead, she told him that she liked school, especially History. He didn't say anything in response—he didn't do the adult "mms" and "aahs"—and in that absence, she kept listing things nervously, waiting for them to add up. She couldn't have a dog, because her brother was allergic. She liked stand-up comedy (watching, not doing). She thought that by now she'd be a better artist than she is.

To that, he finally spoke. "I bet you're a good artist. Your mom was always a creative type."

"Yeah?"

"Oh yeah. She would make things nicer. Get a little bouquet of flowers from God knows where, put them in a cleaned out jar."

"What else did she do?"

"Apples. She was always trying to make me eat apples."

This was something Maddie could imagine.

He pulled a pack of cigarettes out of his jacket and lit one without asking. The package had a picture of a woman sticking out her tongue, black and half-rotted: SMOKING CAUSES MOUTH CANCER.

Sideways, Daniel said, "I'm sorry I wasn't around. I didn't know about you."

Today is the day of dads apologizing, Maddie thought.

"I was a secret."

"Just to me. The guy who raised you—you were pretty real to him, I'm guessing."

"Seth. My dad." She said the last word loudly. Maddie couldn't tell if it hurt this man to hear her talk about her dad, but she hoped it did, a little.

He asked, "Why didn't your mom tell you about me?"

"I don't know. Maybe it didn't fit her picture of this perfect family."

He frowned, tilting his head back and blowing upwards in a stream. The smoke immediately drifted back down over both of them. "I was in prison for a while."

"Oh."

"Yeah—you should, uh, stay out of trouble." He tacked on that piece of advice like he'd been coached to do so.

Maddie almost smiled. Then she had a thought about who goes to prison (murderers and rapists), and asked, "Why? What'd you do?"

He looked away, expelling smoke. "Stupid stuff. Drug stuff."

Maddie had no idea what that stuff could be. She wondered if she would get in trouble for smelling like smoke, and this made her think of her mother, alone and asleep on the couch.

"What else do you want to know?" he asked.

It was better that they were sideways, because if she'd been able to see him, then maybe she wouldn't have been bold enough to ask him about his medical history, checking imaginary boxes. Overall health? Not bad, he said, and he was lucky, considering. Family history of cancer? He didn't know. Heart disease? Blood disease? Kidney? He didn't know. He was from the north, he explained, lighting a new cigarette off the butt of the old one. He never knew his parents. There was an aunt, but she died, so he was in foster care most of his life. Maddie noticed that one of his front teeth was split and yellow at the seam, like he'd fallen, or been hit.

He kept circling back to Gwen, maybe because it was the one common thing between them. Maddie learned that he loved music, like Gwen. Maddie was slack-jawed: her mother listening to a band in a bar; her mother sleeping in a park. It was confusing. The more he told her about himself, the less she knew about Gwen.

"I had a temper," he said. "But only when I was drunk. Or high. I don't do that now." "Temper" was a wide-open word. Maddie suddenly feared for this hypothetical Gwen, this young Goth Gwen who might have been in peril. But her head really swivelled at "high." "Stupid stuff. Drug stuff." She might have the same predilections, she thought; she was partly this man. She did have an appetite, a voracious appetite that had been sated in the past year with Joshua. She knew what it was like to want to slip out of your own body. Sex was like that—screaming, fleeing, vanishing—and these leanings seemed to suggest something unhinged inside her, something inherited, inborn. This link between them didn't trouble her, though; it was just a curiosity, specimen-like.

In the morning that she'd spent walking around the east end of the city alone, going through a basket of hats in a vintage shop and flipping through graphic novels at a used book store, Maddie had wondered if she would love him instantly, simply because he was her father. After a half hour in his presence, she realized that this was a stupid thing to have even considered. She didn't love this man instantly, or at all. He was a series of mildly interesting facts in a leather jacket. He was a stranger who had never known her. On TV, there's weeping, and the dad holds the girl's face and says, *I'd recognize you anywhere.*

"My plan now is to get away, to go west," he said. "But I don't have any money."

He got quiet then, and the air hung heavy, while Maddie figured it out: money. He wanted her money, not her.

She let it bite, then shoved back: So what? They were both ruthless, then. She had come for one reason. He had information she needed that only he could give her, and now she had it.

Maddie stood up. "I should go." She hadn't drunk any coffee. The cup sat at her feet.

"Okay. I'll drive you." He stood up, too, grinding his cigarette butt with the heel of his work boot.

"No. That's okay."

"Just come on," he said firmly. She hesitated, but he said it like a command, and one more time. "Let's go."

Maddie nodded.

She followed him to the parking lot, past a flock of loud Canada geese on the grass, away from the people on the beach. Maddie tiptoed to avoid shit.

His car was banged up—a loaner, he told her. As he fumbled with the lock on the door, a goose approached. Suddenly, the goose charged, screaming its strangled cry.

"The fuck . . ." said Daniel, and then, in a split second, he leaned down and grabbed the beast by its neck. It thrust and screamed, and Maddie was sure it would peck out his eyes, but Daniel heaved and flung the feathered thing. It went sailing through the parking lot, smash landing on the concrete in front of a minivan, a gnarled heap of unmoving feathers.

Maddie gasped, and when she looked at Daniel, he looked back at her with still black eyes.

"Those things will attack," he said. "Get in."

Maddie looked across the parking lot at the bird, lying still on the ground. She searched for other people, anyone to bear witness, but there was no one else. She got in the car, heart racing.

Daniel flicked at a piece of lint on the dashboard before

driving. Maddie did up her seatbelt nervously as they drove past the limp bird.

Maddie stared out the window at the city, repeating the names of the streets in her head to stay calm. He didn't say much. She had the feeling that it was her job to keep him level, to get herself home. *Take the safest route*, she thought, like her mom would, giving him directions, performing normal.

"You should come with me," he said. "Have you ever seen the Rockies?" She hadn't. "You're almost done school, right? Think about it." She would.

At their driveway, he said, "Nice house," craning to look. As he did, his jacket fell open, and Maddie saw the black handle of a knife in a sheath, strapped across his chest.

Eli had once been given a toy plastic combat knife with a serrated edge from a neighbour. After a few days of Eli waving the knife around, popping up behind furniture and out of corners with it in his hand, Gwen took it away. This knife looked the same, carbon black and heavy, strapped to his chest, at the ready.

Maddie pretended not to see it. Her throat went dry.

"Well, bye."

"Think about it," he said.

And as Maddie walked away—fast, without looking behind her—she wondered if he knew she'd see the knife. She wondered what was intentional and what was an accident. She headed toward the house, and her heart sank: *He knows where we live.*

GWEN

A delivery van brought elephant ears and begonias. The plants stood in the front garden in attentive little pots, waiting for the gardener to come the next morning. But in the afternoon, after a day of unsuccessfully trying to reach Maddie on the phone, Gwen decided to plant them herself. A distraction. She had new gardening gloves and tools, and she dug down deep in the soil, turning and sniffing the sweetness. This was good work; she had forgotten how much she liked it. The sun rested on the exposed back of her neck, and she could almost forget the chaos, and her daughter, unmoored in the world today.

Eli came on the front porch, carrying a bowl of cereal.

"I like the orange one," he said.

"Me too. Sunburst," said Gwen, wiping her face with the back of her glove.

"Isn't there a dude who does this for us now?" said Eli, shovelling Cheerios.

"Yes, but it's nice to do things for yourself sometimes, isn't it?"

Eli nodded lightly, unconvinced, then said, "Who's that?"

Gwen looked over at a grey sedan sitting on the road. In the land of driveways, nobody ever parked on the road. Gwen stood up. The car idled.

The passenger door opened, and Maddie appeared. Gwen dropped her spade and began walking to the car, leaning to see who was in the driver's seat. She caught a glimpse of black leather jacket and drew closer. Maddie slammed the door.

"Mom—"

Before Gwen could get there, the car revved and sped away.

Gwen spun toward Maddie, who was walking toward the house quickly. "Was that Daniel?"

"Yes," said Maddie.

Gwen walked fast to keep up with her.

"Who's the guy?" asked Eli, when the three of them were on the porch.

Maddie pushed past him into the house. Gwen followed her

to the kitchen, dropping her gardening gloves as she walked, tracking dirt.

"Why would you bring him here? I told you—it's not safe." She was trying very hard not to scream. Screaming might set Maddie off, send her back out there.

Maddie didn't answer. She took a glass from a cupboard and filled it with water, still without answering.

Gwen asked, "What did he tell you?"

"Nothing you don't know, presumably," said Maddie, drinking. "He's some kind of addict, huh?"

Gwen winced. He's more than that, she wanted to say. She scrambled to handle the situation. Why hadn't she prepared for this? "Maybe. I don't know. Maddie . . . I . . ." Gwen didn't know what would keep her tethered, so she went back to the beginning. "I love you. I don't say it enough—"

"You let me know that all the time."

"But not the words."

"It doesn't matter. I know I'm lucky."

Gwen was confused by Maddie's leap from love to luck.

Maddie went on, suddenly spilling over: "There are all these people out there—so many places where no one gets what they want." She had a faraway look on her face.

"Well, we can do more," said Gwen. She remembered how little Maddie had counted her UNICEF pennies at Halloween before she counted her candy. "We'll find an organization, something we can donate to or—"

Maddie snorted. "You know it's all bullshit, right? The system is rigged. We can cut as many cheques as we want, but none of it matters. You get your place on the ladder, and you just hang on there."

"You sound very teen right now."

Maddie shrugged. "Those are my people."

"What are you fighting about?" Eli appeared, looking back and forth between the two of them.

"Nothing," said Gwen. "Eli, why don't you give us a few minutes?"

He nodded, backing out of the kitchen.

"You don't have to worry. He doesn't care about me. He just needs money," Maddie said, and her voice faltered.

"Oh, Maddie . . ." said Gwen, moving closer. "He doesn't know you."

Maddie put her hand out to keep Gwen at bay. Gwen felt the cord between them unravelling, faster and faster.

"He told me you guys were homeless one summer. Why didn't you ever tell me that?"

Her voice was thick with disbelief, suspicion. Gwen grasped for the words to pull her back.

"Mom . . ." said Maddie, her voice ravaged, pleading.

The way forward was simple, and dreadful.

"Sit down," Gwen said. "I'll tell you."

Gwen told Maddie as much as she could remember about those years, her version at least. After, she promised that she would go to the police and inform them about the attack in the shop.

Maddie stared. "Oh, Mom," she said.

Gwen cringed at the compassion in her voice. She wondered how altered she was in Maddie's eyes. She felt unfamiliar to herself, too.

She couldn't dwell on this shift between them. Urgently, she asked Maddie to wait to see Daniel again, wait until everything had been sorted out.

"I don't need to see him. He's leaving anyway," said Maddie. "He asked me to go with him."

Gwen started at the revelation. "What did you say?"

"Nothing," said Maddie. "He's kind of scary. He wears this knife—"

"What?" Gwen gasped.

"And anyway . . ." Maddie said, shoulders still stooped, looking up at her mother, speaking shyly, "I have a family already."

× × ×

Gwen stood in front of the tower, next to the parking lot, and counted the floors, up to the third, where Daniel was staying. The tower was at least twenty floors higher than that, on the edge of Cabbagetown, across from a cemetery and the entrance to the freeway. Next to the parking lot, a group of tenants had set up lawn chairs on a patch of grass, gathering around a bubble-shaped barbecue in the semi-shade of a thatch of skinny trees. The smell of barbecue smoke met up with the smell of cut grass and the sound of people laughing, making a happy early-summer afternoon scene. A young man, muscular in a tank top, a decade younger, offered Gwen a plastic cup of beer. She said no, no, she couldn't—

"You sure?" He smiled at her, a big gappy smile, jiggling the cup flirtatiously. "Beautiful day for a drink."

She declined again, looking up, counting the floors a second time. On a balcony, a woman leaned against a rusty railing. Others sat, fanning themselves. Music spilled out of apartments, overlapping.

Ran into some problems, his text had said. *Can't leave until I pay off this place. $1,000.* And instantly, Gwen had come as summoned. She drove numbly, trying to construct a plan, the final one.

One elevator was broken, and the other crowded. They packed in together, hot, stopping at every floor, the doors wheezing with effort. Gwen got off on the third floor to a muffled TV blaring. A mother held the hand of her toddler and unlocked a nearby door, giving Gwen a neighbourly nod as she disappeared inside.

Daniel opened the door in bare feet, his forehead damp. The guy who rented the place was a slob, Daniel explained as Gwen entered. Even with the balcony doors open, the small space was stifling. Clothes were strewn across beige wall-to-wall carpet. Gwen stepped around plastic toys and video game equipment. The couch had been made up into a tidy bed, with the edge of a sheet pulled back in a perfect rectangle, and a neatly folded stack of clothes at the foot. Daniel had built a corner of order for himself, but still, the room smelled oily. Gwen breathed shallowly, catching grease and heat in her lungs.

He led her outside to the small balcony. She stood next to a webbed lawn chair, as far from him as possible.

"Out west there's warm winds in winter," said Daniel, closing the sliding doors behind them and lighting a cigarette, leaning against the railing. "Covered in snow and a warm wind comes in, warms you right up. Sounds pretty good to me. I've had enough winters."

Below, the man in the tank top was talking animatedly to a woman who was laughing and swaying, almost dancing, her loose Afro shaking. Cars slid by on the freeway beyond, through the valley that snaked through the city. Gwen looked at Daniel from the corner of her eye, taking in his pretty lashes and concave cheeks, his languid chatter about weather. Then she noticed a sudden bend in his knee—a flutter. He blinked slowly, wobbling.

His human timing was just a fraction off. Gwen snapped to attention: he was on something. He wasn't drunk, which she would have recognized. This was a different kind of high. He stood soft and still, with half-mast eyelids, lips slightly apart. Gwen's shoulders folded in protectively. She was an idiot to have come.

"Did you ever go there, Gwennie? Alberta?" Daniel swung his cigarette outward, as if pointing west, though he wasn't. "You used to go to the library and look at those big picture books of places, like you were always going to leave." She was surprised he remembered those books. He was the only person on the planet who knew her when she was young. He held her memories, and when he was gone, those memories would be gone, too. Her heart began beating faster, but she willed herself to stay calm, to keep talking and contain him.

"I've been raising kids for eighteen years."

"Mmm. You got it all right at home." A jab, Gwen thought. "Maddie might come with me, to Alberta," Daniel said, eyes unfocused. "She's a good kid. I'd like having her around. I could show her things. Adventures." He slowly rotated his wrist on "things," cigarette circling. "My turn with her."

Gwen swelled with panic. "She's not going with you." Daniel rubbed his lips together. She said, "I already told her everything about you, about us."

His eyes drifted to a space behind her. "But you don't know everything about her, do you? You don't know what she wants."

Gwen realized then that he would never leave them alone. He would come back, again and again, for her money, for her time, for Maddie. He had never left, really. She carried traces of him on her body, and in the way she had lived her life. Maddie bore those traces most of all.

Gwen spoke slowly, words she had prepared, lines she had

rehearsed on the drive over, unsure if she would have the strength to say them. "I need you to go away. I don't want you to contact Maddie again, or come to my house. I've hired people. They're watching you. I have the money to do it."

"Do what?" He was teasing her, forcing her to say it.

She placed her right hand on her bag, feeling the outline of the gun. This time she had left it resting on top of her wallet, the first object at the mouth of her open bag.

"If you come near her, I'll have you killed," she said thinly. "Or I'll kill you myself. I have a gun."

Daniel smiled. "Come on, Gwen. You're going to shoot me? The father of your daughter?"

"She has a father."

He flinched, then his eyes seemed to draw back into his head. His lips disappeared again. Whatever he had taken was kicking in, Gwen thought.

He spoke slowly. "I was going to make amends, you know. I looked for you. You changed your name. Why'd you do that? Was it all so bad?" He let out a low moaning sound and pawed at his face.

Gwen was alarmed. Was he about to cry?

Then his hands dropped and he said, sadly, "You never looked for me."

He was asking for her pity, she realized. This request gave her power. She stood taller. "No," said Gwen. "I never looked for you. Not once."

Something awoke in Daniel, an old instinct pushing through his haze. She watched it happen: he uncoiled, his neck straightened. She had forgotten how suddenly the violence would arrive. He was upon her, striking her with a fist on the chin. Her purse dropped to the ground. His arms enfolded her and shoved her body, face first, to the glass doors. She made a sound she couldn't hear, and his hand was over her mouth, salty and hot, muffling her nose, too, cutting off her breath. Blood trickled from her forehead, warming the glass, and her face was immoveable as he held her head to the door, pressing against her backside, pinning her. Gwen tried to yell through his hand, kicking the air, her view forced to the cigarette burning near her foot, and nearby, the open purse.

In those seconds, as she writhed, she thought that all of it had long ago been decided. From the moment he was born, unwanted, he was moving toward this moment, just as she had been loosed into the world from her cold childhood at seventeen, and arrived, as expected, at this paint-peeled balcony that repeated itself for twenty floors.

And then—he let go. Gwen sputtered, taking a long gasping breath before turning to see him, standing with the gun in his hand, raised. She took it in: a gun pointed directly at her from a few feet away—a man holding a gun. She knew that in such moments, people fought to live; instinct took over, and women howled, tore the air, punched back. But finally, after all the struggle of a moment ago, she didn't feel ferocious. Her body settled. Warmth wrapped around her: acceptance, or resignation. She had done her best, really, with what she had been given, and what she had been given was an abundance, an embarrassment of riches. Seth. Maddie. Eli. This sun-soaked day, and the one before, and the one before. Her great, good fortune. She closed her eyes and waited.

At the crack of the bullet, her heartbeat accelerated and her eyes snapped open. But she couldn't feel the bullet, couldn't locate any new injury in her body. Daniel was standing strangely, with his arm extended overhead and the gun in his hand, pointed at the sky. His chin rested on his chest, and his other arm dangled, boneless. Gwen's ears rang, but she could hear him, fuzzily: "Get out." Then he moved fast, putting one boot on the railing, then both hands, still gripping the gun. He hoisted his other leg. He pulled himself up to his full height, spine and neck straight, eyes forward, then balanced on the very top of the railing, as if he had been walking and decided to stop at this spot to take a rest. For a fraction of a second, they stayed in their places, sharing the balcony, Daniel standing and Gwen cowering. Then, without any movement, without jumping, he dropped away; no bend in the knee, no exertion, just a sudden absence.

Gwen fell to the railing, gripping to hold herself up, tasting blood in her mouth. She looked for him, but her vision was smudged, and she could only make out the block shapes of the green hedges below, and farther away, the blur of the picnickers, scrambling and screaming. She felt her way around the edge of the patio to the latch on the door, fumbling until it opened, pushing through, into the apartment. Lurching, she made it to the living room, tripping on toys, toward the sound of the front door, where people were now banging, yelling from the hallway. *What's going on in there?*

Gwen looked back at the empty balcony. She shook the lock. The door opened—she had opened the door—and people charged in. "Are you okay?" The man in the tank top went past her, striding to the balcony. She fell on the woman who had been dancing, and this stranger put her arms out and held up Gwen in her collapse.

SUMMER

17

Maddie barely studied for exams. To her surprise, though, it didn't really matter. It turned out that she knew things, most things, in fact. She had been absorbing information for years, training herself to think. When she didn't know a question on a test, she examined it carefully, and then found a crack, and inside the crack, an answer, some kind of answer, even if not the exact right one. There were lots of answers inside her: strange ones, produced by this other brain that had somehow replaced her old one. No—it was her own mind, unsealed. She had been working so hard for so long that she hadn't noticed it forming, the way a tree in spring is bare one day and thick with leaves the next.

On the last day of her exams, Maddie was cleaning out her locker when she saw Joshua at a distance. She had imagined this moment so often that it almost seemed predictable, although it had been many weeks: Joshua in a black T-shirt, checking his phone. He looked up and saw her, and turned away. She followed him to the end of the corridor, leaving her backpack and books strewn next to her open locker.

"Hey," she said.

He faced her. She wanted to tell him about Daniel, and all the insanity at home; her mom's bruised face, and her dad's uneasy voice when he sat her down and explained what had happened. Daniel died. He had jumped off a balcony. Maybe he thought he would survive it, just three floors, or maybe he had redirected his body mid-air, meaning to hit the concrete, not the grass. Seth had scanned Maddie's face with such concern—"I'm so sorry, Mads"—that she'd tried to summon grief for him. But her sadness was general, not specific to Daniel, or to herself. She didn't feel any different, now that she was a girl whose orbit had been invaded by violence, by death. She didn't feel bad for Daniel, exactly, but for any person like him. Her sadness reached past him, to all the damaged people. And still, she was angry on Gwen's behalf, because Daniel had been something to her, a long time ago, and look what he had done. But Maddie wasn't wounded. She hadn't lost someone; she had never been looking.

The bruises on Gwen's face helped Maddie see her more clearly. So that's what her mother had endured. Her lies made a little more sense anyway, and let the air out of Maddie's frustrations. She wanted to forget about all of it, and get on with finishing high school and becoming someone else.

"Hey," Joshua said. "I have an exam in five."

"How's your mom?" This was a fake question, because, of course, Maddie knew. She had just seen his mom the night before, while Joshua was at work and Alexis at a friend's. Mrs. Andrada was at home on bedrest, buried under blankets. They drank tea together and watched a mystery show on TV before Maddie slipped out.

The bell rang. The hall began to empty out.

"I know what you're trying to do. I told my mom it's crazy," said Joshua.

Maddie jutted out her chin. She shrugged.

"Maddie, you can't do it. You can't do it for me."

"It's for your mom."

Joshua, exasperated, lay it before her. "I don't love you anymore. I just stopped, okay?"

But it didn't work. She thrilled at the "anymore," even in the negative: they had never said they loved each other, but it turned out that he had loved her once.

"I hate this white saviour part of you. I always wondered if it was the reason you went out with me."

"No—what?" Maddie reeled. "I . . . I went out with you because you're amazing—you're . . . Joshua, you don't need saving—"

"Maddie. Stop. It isn't up to you. Just enjoy your good luck. Stop torturing yourself."

They were the only two people left in the hall. That high school smell of industrial cleaner drifted past.

"My exam's starting," Joshua said.

"It's safe," Maddie blurted. "I swear. We're being careful." He nodded and began to walk away. "Joshua—" He turned back. "Please don't tell my parents."

He shook his head and turned down the hall to his exam.

When Joshua was out of sight, Maddie walked slowly back to her locker and emptied it out. She dumped all her binders in the garbage bin by the front doors without recycling the paper. She would skip graduation, and prom, and the adjacent house parties and yearbook signings. When Sophie and Clara were getting their nails done the afternoon before walking across the stage to get their diplomas, Maddie would be halfway around the world. She let the school doors slam behind her.

18

GWEN

Gwen and Seth sat side by side at the kitchen island, drinking coffee and reading the morning news on their tablets. He kissed the top of her head as he brought her toast, which she ate in tiny bites, her bruised jaw burning. Seth watched her chew, a stricken look on his face. She waved him off.

Later, Seth and Tom would be meeting with lawyers to examine the papers and complete the sale. A steadiness had returned to the family that hadn't been felt since Shadow Pines. Maddie was in the last days of high school. Eli had made the select soccer team, and refused to take off his new uniform. At night, Gwen slept soundly.

Moving on would take time, Seth kept saying, bringing her tea, rubbing her feet. In the fall, Maddie would be away at school (Gwen's stomach constricted at the thought), but not yet. They had these last months together as a family, free of threat, with the sale of the company promising future comfort. This was the agreement: to enjoy these gains, to be whole.

But Maddie broke the pact. Eli alerted them. He bounded into the kitchen, his rumpled blazer in one hand.

"Where's Maddie? I need her headphones."

Gwen looked up. "What do you mean?"

"She's not in her room."

"Maybe she had a club meeting this morning," said Seth.

But Gwen knew her schedule. She shook her head, no, and hopped off the kitchen stool.

Maddie's bed was made, the room tidy as ever. The blinds were up, and sun streaked in. On her desk, next to her computer, was a piece of paper.

Dear Mom and Dad,
Please don't worry. I have gone away for a little while,
NOT with Joshua. I will be back in a week or so, but if it's
more, please don't be concerned. What I'm doing is a good
thing and I'm going to be fine. You will see. I love you. M.

"Seth," called Gwen, floating down the hall, her head ringing. "Seth, Seth, Seth . . ."

MADDIE

On her eighteenth birthday, a few hours before her parents took her on a helicopter ride, Maddie had made her pitch to the hospital ethics board. The next day, she got a call that she had been rejected as an altruistic donor, despite being of age.

As the family flew over the city that night, Maddie saw the mall below, and her determination grew. She would not be put off by the hospital's ridiculous ruling, she decided.

"Joshua works there," she'd said to Gwen.

Maddie began to visit Mrs. Andrada during her dialysis treatments at the hospital. Mrs. Andrada reclined in her astronaut chair, two red tubes poking out of the white gauze patch on her forearm that covered the fistula but not the bruises. The tubes rested in her open left hand, then trailed to a refrigerator of a machine, humming.

"Madeline," she said, and turned her smile to Maddie.

From the beginning, Maddie timed her visits according to Joshua's work schedule and Alexis's activities, so they would never cross paths. When Maddie first came, Mrs. Andrada was suspicious. "You will call Children's Aid?" She pinned her with yellowy eyes. Mrs. Andrada saw her as another stranger who might upset the delicate balance that kept the family safe. Maddie might alert authorities who would snatch the children, put Joshua on a plane back to the Philippines. But Maddie kept visiting. Mrs. Andrada said her hands were always cold, so Maddie brought her warm pink mittens. The next time she came, Mrs. Andrada was wearing the mittens, holding the tubes in her bright pink hand. She looked happy to see Maddie.

Maddie liked sitting in the small chair pulled up next to the big one, listening to Mrs. Andrada's stories about being a teenager growing up on a lake in the Philippines. She could run faster than all of her brothers by the time she was eight. "Alexis is almost as fast," she said. She looked Maddie up and down. "You should run!" she told her. "You look like a strong girl. Long distance, maybe, not sprints."

The other patients in the clinic didn't have visitors. One girl attached to a machine was younger even than Maddie. She sat playing on her phone with her free hand, flicking her retainer in and out of her mouth with her tongue.

When, at last, Maddie brought up altruistic donation, Mrs.

Andrada laughed. "You are a silly girl. Hush." Maddie had never been called silly before, and she kind of liked it.

When the hospital turned her down, Maddie became relentless. She did the research, like the good student she was. And soon, she had a different plan. With each return visit to the clinic, Maddie kept bringing it up, bearing emails and broker information for Mrs. Andrada. It wasn't that crazy after all. It happened all the time, in fact, and it was the best way—the only way—to make sure that Joshua could go to university, and get his citizenship, to make sure that Alexis wasn't taken into foster care. But it had to happen quickly. It had to happen now.

Finally, Maddie wore her down. Mrs. Andrada said, "I must speak to your parents."

"They're fine with it," she lied.

"They agree to this?"

Mrs. Andrada had made a few references to the permissive ways of white parents—her job as a nanny was, essentially, to compensate for their lack of involvement—so perhaps she really did believe that this plan of taking an organ from a teenager in a hospital in Manila would sit well with a white family. But Maddie sensed something else at play: Mrs. Andrada didn't have the luxury of worrying about Maddie's parents. A switch had been hit. She didn't ask for Gwen's number. She had dropped the performance of reluctance.

"Don't tell Joshua yet," said Maddie.

Their eyes met, each of them knowing that Joshua opposed the plan, but there was no way forward other than to deceive him. He might be angry for a while, but his mother would be alive. Or they could acquiesce and abandon the plan, and she would die. Either way, he was done with Maddie, so what did it matter? But as the days passed, and Maddie's mind filled with the task at hand, her ache for him subsided a little. Whenever the yearning returned (late at night, or walking through the city's ravines), she reminded herself that she was now a person who had endured a broken heart, and that felt like an achievement.

Once the decision was made, Mrs. Andrada was ruthless in her quest to live. She and Maddie set to the labour of it (Maddie demonstrating Gwen's propensity for organization): communicating with the hospital in Manila; finding a hotel for Maddie to stay in, after. Mrs. Andrada had decided, above all, to survive. Maddie admired it, really. If a rich person made an offer that propelled that survival, she was not so stupid as to turn it down. Maddie knew that Mrs. Andrada had faith in God, and God had delivered her, Maddie, a girl with a superfluous kidney. Now medicine would do the rest.

Maddie used Seth's credit card to buy the tickets, the same numbers she'd plugged in to pay for her college applications. She had $24,000 American in her bank account, from her college fund. Ten thousand went right away, via wire transfer, and the other ten would be sent when they arrived. It was so easy. Maddie had worried that they would ask for cash, and she didn't know how to obtain paper money. But Maddie was a legal adult in a digital world where money was just an idea, bytes zooming, bouncing off towers, moving through cables beneath the sea.

Susan would come to help pack, and move in with Joshua and Alexis while they were gone. Susan owed them, Mrs. Andrada implied. Thanks to Joshua, Susan's children would arrive from Manila in a month.

GWEN

Gwen tried Maddie's phone and the tracking device beeped: the phone was at their house. It was, in fact, in the drawer of Maddie's bedside table.

There was nothing the police could do. Maddie was eighteen, and she had left them a note. She wasn't a missing person to anyone but her parents.

Frantically, Gwen told Seth to try Tom, to see if Tom could call someone in the RCMP, because he seemed like the most powerful person they knew. Seth seemed baffled by the request, but he called.

Gwen called the school. "Joshua," Gwen said to the principal, her voice both lower and louder than usual. "Get Joshua."

Gwen had never met Clara and Sophie, the sole social evidence of Maddie's year at the U. Half friends. But she asked the principal to call them in. She had no phone numbers for any of these kids; they were all locked away on her daughter's cell phone. She didn't know their parents, their addresses, their last names.

Gwen tore up the bedroom and found nothing surprising except a box of condoms and a notebook with one unfinished line in it: "What about the girls who . . ." But in the bottom drawer of a dresser, she found the laptop, not even hidden.

"Eli . . ." Gwen called. He appeared, pale, chewing his fingernail.

"Do you know Maddie's passwords?"

He looked sheepish, and then nodded.

Seth, clutching his phone, stood over Eli at Maddie's desk. "Check her history," he said.

Organ brokers. Philippines. Recent Google questions: *Are transplant hospitals in the Philippines safe?*

"My God, my God," said Gwen.

"What's in Manila?" asked Eli.

Gwen was standing, but moving side to side: one foot, the other foot.

"Can you get into her email?"

Again, Eli had the little brother codes. In the Sent file were forms to the hospital with check-marked boxes: "Any history of family cancer?" One column was headed "Mother": "No," Maddie had ticked. Under "Father," she'd ticked "No." She had answers to all of the "Father" questions from just that one meeting with Daniel, Gwen realized with awe.

And then, near the top of the Inbox: plane tickets.

Gwen grabbed Seth's arm with one hand, curled her fingers and dug in. Then she pried herself away from him and went to find her purse and her passport.

MADDIE

The taxi sped along the expressway, cutting through suburban sprawl, past the giant inflatable gorilla advertising tiles, past IKEA and the multiplex. Maddie pulled the mohair throw, taken from Gwen's bed, tight over Mrs. Andrada's knees. Out of the hospital and in the back seat of the taxi, Mrs. Andrada looked even more ragged, a tiny old woman with an inflated face.

"I know that this is dangerous, but also, it is very safe," Mrs. Andrada said, and Maddie nodded. She had said exactly that to Mrs. Andrada several times. "I must thank you."

"No, no . . ." Maddie waved her off.

"What you are doing, it is difficult. I did the same thing once, for Joshua. You knew that, didn't you?"

Maddie nodded.

"So we are the same," she said. Then Mrs. Andrada scanned

Maddie, searchingly. "You will be a good adult. You did what only God can do. You will be rewarded."

Maddie didn't want a reward. Less. She felt the pull of less. Less body would be the first step, and then maybe something else. She would try university, at least for a year, to put off her parents, because she loved them, and they needed that from her. But after that—she might veer. She could imagine vanishing for a while. There were other ways of being, she was certain of it. Other places. Other people. Places where she was the other person. She would see all of it.

The taxi went by a cluster of apartment buildings. She thought of her mother, bloodied on a balcony. Suddenly, she wanted her mother as urgently as she had wanted her when she'd woken up from a nightmare as a child. She wanted Gwen to appear, but only for a moment, just long enough that she could say, "Look at this kind thing I'm doing. And I'm not afraid." Her mother would be proud, maybe. Gwen must have been bold herself, to leave her parents, to sleep in a park, to have a baby all alone. It occurred to her for the first time that Gwen wasn't actually scared of the world, as Maddie had always assumed. Her mother was, in fact, fearless, and that's how she had survived.

GWEN

At every step, the credit card acted like a prison guard's key in a jailhouse, opening door after door. In the cab to the airport, Gwen used it on her phone to buy a plane ticket. She paid for a hotel room. When she went through security, the credit card was in her pocket, not her wallet, like a talisman, and she dumped it in the plastic bin, watched it go through the machine, leaving an X-ray trace.

Once through security, Gwen rushed to the gate, checking clocks, checking boards, almost sprinting. She was dizzy and breathless, the lace on her right running shoe clacking on the gleaming airport floor.

MADDIE

In the lounge, Mrs. Andrada was asleep in her wheelchair, her mouth slightly open. Maddie sat next to her at the end of the row of seating, watching the rushing people, considering the stirring inside her. Night had arrived at the window, wrapping the big white airplane.

She saw her mother before her mother saw her. Gwen's foot was trailing a shoelace. She was turning this way and that, frantically searching.

"Mom . . ." Maddie rose and moved toward her. Gwen's embrace was so familiar that Maddie's defiance fell away. She was suddenly glassy with fatigue. The presence of her mother released her from her courage, and relief took over. She could never fall off into the precipice, not entirely, while her mother was in the world, fixing Maddie in place with her watchful eye.

"You're too young, Maddie," said Gwen, into Maddie's ear.

"I'm not so young," said Maddie, still holding her mother.

She disentangled from the hug. Mrs. Andrada opened her eyes sleepily.

"She'll be okay. I promise," said Gwen to Maddie.

Maddie tried to remember a promise her mother had broken, but there wasn't one, in all those years—not one.

FALL

19

GWEN

When Gwen pulled in, Eli's bicycle was lying on the grass, as it had been the day before. She should get him to lock it up as soon as he gets home, she thought, but then again— did it matter?

She sat in the car for an extra moment and took in the house, because it pleased her. It was white-sided and plain, like a house in a children's book, with a triangle roof and twin squared eyes for windows. But it was messier in the back, bordered by an untended row of balsam firs that went on and on, and through them, only more trees. To see another house, Gwen would have to get in her car and drive straight down the gravel road for ten minutes.

She had taken the afternoon off work and driven into the city. The detective who had recorded her statement hadn't seemed interested in talking to her the first time, but she went to the station again, demanding to see him. When he finally ushered her

inside, she sat on the other side of his desk, and he explained—
again, as he had on the phone—that there was no record of a
violent crime at the donut shop, which was now an espresso
bar. And certainly no record of a murder (Gwen had him repeat
that certainty twice). There was no record of a manager named
Steve, either. Maybe he was an illegal, working under a false
name. Perhaps he had survived whatever violence she had wit-
nessed, and vanished into the city. The file would stay open, he
told her.

Gwen tried to feel unburdened, but she wasn't used to it yet.
She would never fully believe in her own innocence. Even with
this exoneration, she wasn't inclined toward self-forgiveness. *I
could have done more*, she believed, as some mothers do. For-
giving herself seemed like another form of denial, or erasure,
and she didn't want to forget her story, after the agonizing effort
to do so all those years. Instead of soothing herself with forgive-
ness, she would take comfort in the fact of goodness, remind-
ing herself of other people's goodness, which was all around
her, again and again, and had been throughout her life, if she
remembered it right.

She stepped out of the car and inhaled. Autumn had begun.

Tonight, she and Eli would make dinner together. This was a
new evening ritual, because it was usually just the two of them
until Seth arrived on the train from the city. Some nights, he slept
in the apartment they kept downtown, purchased with money
not from the lottery, but from BuzzSwitch. Against all odds, the
company had become a success. The money had begot more
money. But Seth still tried to get back to his family before dark,
a change he had committed to after Enid died. She had passed
suddenly in July. Gwen noted that mothers died suddenly, dra-
matically; a blood clot to the brain, like Enid, or a car crash, like

her own mother. Isaac wanted to stay in Florida for now, but they had made sure there was room for him in the new house, when the time came.

In the wake of his mother's death, Seth was frequently solemn, holding Gwen tight at night. She would drive over to the train station and pick him up at 6:35 p.m., while Eli finished cooking.

There was a bedroom for Maddie, though she had only seen it once, the week before she left for university. She had gone west, to a school by the ocean. Gwen suspected that she wouldn't stay long. A new restlessness had taken over her daughter. She was growing into someone a little shambolic, and it suited her. She was in process, privately becoming, out of Gwen's view. She texted sometimes but called only once a week, on Sunday nights, telling Gwen and Seth about the big ideas banging in her head, and sighing at the beer-pong–playing students down the hall, and the general dumbness of collegiate life. It was fun, she agreed, but only for now.

On a FaceTime call, Maddie told Gwen that, one day in the future, she might do a DNA test, and try to figure out who Daniel's people were. Maybe that aunt he mentioned, the one who took care of him, had some kids? Maybe someone up there would want to know that he had died. She was thinking about going north, she said, a question mark in her voice, but defiant. Even on the tiny cracked screen of her phone, Gwen could see that Maddie's shoulders were back, face tilted up. Gwen took a deep breath and said: Go.

Daniel was Maddie's now. Gwen had no say in what his daughter would make of him, no ability to train the story in one direction or another. This felt like liberation.

Gwen found herself surprised to have survived Maddie's leaving. The job at the doctor's office helped. She liked the charts, filled with personal, sometimes grotesque details. The potty-mouthed doctor, a young woman barely older than Maddie, relied on Gwen, and respected her. Gwen appreciated a climate of gratitude.

She needed a bath before dinner. She would strip down and look at herself in the mirror, examining the shark-bite scar around her right side. She looked forward to this daily reveal. When Seth saw her admiring the scar in the mirror, he would say, "Your stigmata," coming up behind her, kissing her neck.

He was wrong, though. The mark didn't stand for sacrifice. She was glad that Mrs. Andrada was doing well, and grateful for Joshua's emails, which arrived every few months. They were coolly written medical updates, as if Gwen had sponsored a child in a village in a developing country. Perhaps he was as shocked by what had transpired as Gwen, as all of them. The greatest good fortune had turned out to be that these two families were linked, mirroring one another in deepest, invisible flesh. Gwen had passed the same tests as Maddie, astonished at each step of a long process that scrutinized her blood, antibodies, genetic markers—and the verdicts came, one after another: compatible. Two women, strangers, in an accidental moment, in an accidental place, had matched and were now coiled together forever.

Joshua was studying at the university next to the U, living with his mother and his sister. There would be no dorm life for him, no beer pong. But he had a mother who was alive. Gwen savoured it, she had to admit. She revelled in the very fact of another human's life, just as she had when Maddie and Eli were born.

The scar looked cool, she thought. She had it because Maddie didn't, which was the right order of things.

Gwen wrapped her bathrobe, expensive and soft, around her.

She played a song on her phone, a loud song by angry women, a band she'd seen years ago, when she was young.

She brushed her hair, which was growing out, roots revealed, while walking into the bedroom. On the dresser sat the Lawren Harris study of the sagging house in the ice blue evening. Gwen didn't yet know where she wanted to hang it.

Julia had come by for a visit the week before. The two were forging a friendship. Gwen liked her, and realized that what she had mistaken for pretentiousness was actually a kind of eccentricity. Julia knew Gwen's whole true story now, and sat with it, unfazed.

In the yard at the new house one cool evening, wine in hand, Julia asked Gwen why she had bought the lottery ticket. No one except that long-ago reporter had asked Gwen that question. She had never bought a lottery ticket in her life.

She told Julia that she had filled the car at 7-Eleven, and gone inside to buy the newspaper. She was the only one in the family who read the paper on paper anymore, and it was her small indulgence a few times a week to purchase one after dropping off the kids, in anticipation of an hour at the kitchen table, reading the news and feeling sorry and safe.

In front of her, a man was slowly examining the lottery tickets under glass. The woman behind the counter pulled out a scratch ticket, and the man shook his head, rejecting it, pointing at another. The clerk grew impatient. The customer grunted. His shoes were untied and thick-soled—prescription shoes, for a damaged limb. He filled in the circles, scrawling outside the lines, and bought three more tickets from the machine, which the woman rang through with irritation. Bells beeped. Waxy pepperoni pizza warmed in its glass case. Gwen tried to smile to put the woman behind the counter at ease. She wanted to convey that she was in no rush. After her newspaper, she would have to get groceries, and take Eli to swimming class after school. But that was all she had planned for her day. Nothing to hurry toward. Gwen was not bothered.

When the man finally shuffled out the door, Gwen turned to the woman behind the counter, who seemed shaken, and said, "I'll take a Quick Pick," an expression he'd used. She added the cost (two dollars) to her gas and paper debt, paying with cash to avoid bankcard fees. There was no science or poetry in the numbers. A machine had plucked them from its digital brain and seared them onto paper, and the paper became Gwen's because of the lottery-ticket–buying man in front of her in line, and the morning, and Gwen's melancholy about the end of print newspapers.

A week later, she sat at the kitchen table, considering the crumbed breakfast dishes her kids had left behind. This was the time of day when a coolness crept over her, and she fell into her past memories, and would slip sometimes into a trance that could last an hour, even two. There was too much nothing on either side of her mornings now that the kids were older. Soon she would not be their mother like she was their mother now. The days of constant touch and endless need, of Gwen as the centre of everything—those days were gone. This was her incantation then, in the morning, before lunch.

But not that day. She would, instead of mourning, sit and read the paper.

The lottery numbers were on the front page. She remembered what she'd done, and went to her wallet, where the ticket was folded, tucked between two five-dollar bills, untouched. The first number matched. Then, the second, the third, and so on. Then she was laughing, laughing until she was crying. She called Seth with rubbery fingers. He answered her gibberish squeal with fear. "My God! What's wrong? Gwen? Gwen? Is it the kids?"

× × ×

Gwen was dressed now, and sitting on the edge of her bed. The steam of the drained tub drifted in through the bathroom door. The song had ended, and in the quiet, she heard the screen door bang open downstairs. Eli. There would be only so many comings and goings before the final one.

"Mom!" he called joyfully, his feet running up the stairs, closer and closer. "Where are you?" he called, and the question rang out through the big house, a voice on the edge of cracking.

ACKNOWLEDGEMENTS

I want to thank Canada Council for the Arts, and the Toronto Arts Council for their support of this book.

Many people generously gave their time and wisdom along the way through reading, listening and research. Thank you sincerely to Stephanie Hodnett, Lisa Gabriele, Andrea Curtis, Maryam Sanati, Kate Robson, Robyn Matuto, and Gary and Cindy Onstad.

I was inspired by a decade of excellent reporting in the *Toronto Star* on the stark realities of caregiving. I also want to thank the caregivers who shared their stories with me, but I can't reveal their names, for privacy reasons.

I was grateful to have encountered the excellent documentary *Tales from the Organ Trade*, by Ric Esther Bienstock, while writing this book. I encourage anyone who hasn't already signed up to be an organ donor to do so (www.beadonor.ca).

Thank you to the wonderful team at HarperCollins Canada: publisher Iris Tupholme; my extraordinarily talented editor, Jennifer Lambert; and copy editor Angelika Glover. And I am so lucky to have Fletcher and Company in my corner, especially Christy Fletcher and Sarah Fuentes—thank you for your intelligence and support.

Much gratitude to the Toronto Writers Collective for the afternoons among bold, brave writers who helped shape this story.

And to Judah and Mia, and Julian, for everything, always.